A FIGHTING CHANCE

CLAUDIA MELÉNDEZ SALINAS

PIÑATA
BOOKS

PIÑATA BOOKS
ARTE PÚBLICO PRESS
HOUSTON, TEXAS

A Fighting Chance is funded in part by a grant from the City of Houston through the Houston Arts Alliance. We are grateful for their support.

Piñata Books are full of surprises!

Arte Público Press
University of Houston
4902 Gulf Fwy, Bldg 19, Rm 100
Houston, Texas 77204-2004

Cover design by John-Michael Perkins

Printed in the United States of America
September 2015–October 2015
United Graphics, Inc., Matoon, IL

10 9 8 7 6 5 4 3 2 1

To my parents:

Fernando Meléndez†
Yolanda Salinas
Their love has made it all possible.

Years before it happened, Miguel Ángel replayed this moment over and over again: the cold touch of a gun barrel to the back of his head, drops of sweat running down his forehead. It could happen to anyone anywhere. It happened dozens of times each year to guys like him across Salinas, and his greatest fear was it would also happen to him.

He would be ready: he would swivel around, like he'd seen Kung-Fu masters do in the movies, kick the gun off the *cholo*'s hand, pin him to the ground and beat the crap out of him. That's not what you're supposed to do if you learned how to fight honorably, but a fool that points a gun to your head can't have honorable intentions, right?

The Kung-Fu kick was frozen somewhere in Miguel Ángel's gut. Instead, he felt his legs glued to the ground, heavy as sacks of beans. He slowly raised his hands, and before he could feel his mouth work, he heard himself mutter.

"Don't do it, man. Please don't."

CHAPTER 1

Television vans were never a good omen for the Alisal. Like vultures, they only arrived in Salinas' poorest neighborhood when they smelled blood. Miguel Ángel saw the gleaming white vans parked outside his boxing club, their antennas disappearing into the evening fog, and he shivered. No way. He looked around for other tell-tales; sweat beginning to dampen his hands. No cop cars. No yellow tape. Why the hell were TWO news vans outside HIS boxing club?

"Brother, you're hurting me," Mary Carmen whimpered.

Dang, he was so nervous he didn't even realize he was squeezing his little sister's hand so hard.

"I'm so sorry, Pan con Mantequilla," he said, calling her by the special nickname he had for her: Bread 'n Butter. His favorite treat. "I just get nervous about all these TV cameras."

"Why are they here, Miguel Ángel?"

"Not sure. Let's go inside."

Were they going to cover the boxing match? It was just a friendly bout. TV didn't even show up for the Golden Gloves championship.

The idea of running into dumb television reporters turned his stomach. All these guys ever reported on were car chases and murders, and Miguel Ángel always changed the channel when their blonde horse-faces appeared on the screen. Maybe it was nothing. Still, he pulled Mary Carmen around the back entrance of the Packing Shed. Maybe they'd be able to get through the bouts, and the vans would be gone by the time he went home.

Fat chance. Inside the Packing Shed, the scene was even worse. Besides the TV cameras, there were dozens of strangers walking around the huge warehouse, dismantling the boxing ring, arranging chairs and tables in a semi-circle, as if some sort of meeting was going to take place. Miguel Ángel stood frozen for a few minutes, watching his boxing pals and complete strangers scurrying around like ants after a storm.

Dismantling the boxing ring? What the hell?

"What's happening, Miguel Ángel?" Mary Carmen asked, as if sensing something was wrong.

"Let's find out," he said, pulling on his little sister's arm.

The curiosity was stronger than his revulsion for the TV reporter, so Miguel Ángel approached him as he was getting ready for his live six o'clock shot. A tan make-up line wrapped around his jaw, in front of his ears, by his hairline. That's why he looks like a clown, Miguel Ángel thought.

"Nice of you to join us." He heard the squeaky and unmistakable voice of Coach, lowering himself to Mary Carmen's level. "And who's this little boxer joining us?"

"Coach!" she screamed, throwing her arms around the bearded, round man.

"How are you, *preciosa*?" Coach asked Mary Carmen as he gave her a peck on her cheek. Then he turned to Miguel Ángel, "You think you can give us a hand here?"

"What's going on, Coach?" Miguel Ángel dropped his gym bag to the ground with a loud thud and let go of Mary Carmen. "Aren't we supposed to spar tonight with the Watsonville guys?"

"Man, you really are in love, aren't you? That's not the kind of fight we're having tonight. We're having a council hearing, remember? To decide whether or not we can stay here?"

"Oh, man. You're right. I forgot. My bad."

"*Ándale*, help me set up these chairs. I don't like *flojos* standing around, you know that."

"And I don't like it when you call me lazy, *you* know that," Miguel Ángel responded, raising his fists and bouncing on the balls of his feet.

"Mary Carmen, you can sit here or you can help pull chairs out," Coach told the little girl.

"I'll help," she said eagerly.

A month ago, when Coach found out the city was going to evict the boxing club from the Packing Shed, he hauled all the fighters down to the Salinas City Hall to speak to the mayor and city council. The council's response: a subcommittee hearing at the frigid gym. Three council members would come down to see for themselves what was going on at the Packing Shed before deciding the boxing club's fate.

For Miguel Ángel, it was better to be at the Packing Shed than at city hall, though. Coach had wanted him to say something, but when they visited all those bright offices smelling of cleaning chemicals, Miguel Ángel froze. All those ladies wearing suits and high heels and smelling of perfume were too much. Not even the high school principal dressed like that.

Miguel Ángel promised Coach he'd prepare next time. When they had their hearing, he'd have a speech all ready.

And he totally forgot about it. Three weeks with his stomach in a knot about the fate of his beloved gym, and he completely forgot about the hearing. Was he dumb or what? Fool, fool, fool. Maybe Coach was right: it was Britney's fault. Now, as he walked to the far end of the gym, where the chairs were stacked, he barely began to think about what to say. If it weren't for the Packing Shed and for Coach, he'd still be in the streets beating up punks and gangster-wanna-bes. Maybe he'd be selling dope and stuff, just like Beto. Maybe he would have joined the gang, like Beto. Hell, maybe he'd be dead.

"What time are you going to fight, Miguel Ángel?" Mary Carmen broke his spell.

"Oh, man. I'm not going to fight, Pan con Mantequilla. Not like that. We're going to talk to these people. It's a hearing, you know?"

"What's a hearing?" she asked, trying to lift a chair over her head.

"Wait, no, you're going to hurt yourself," Miguel Ángel stopped her. "These people are going to come talk to us. Then they're going to tell us if we can stay here or not."

"Where are you going to go?"

"I don't know." He felt like he was going to fight but completely forgot to train. Like he'd been eating potato chips before the weigh-in and he'd gained all these pounds.

It was as if chairs were attracting people: the more chairs they put out, the more quickly they filled up. The only time he'd seen such a crowd was two years ago, when he gave a lesson on fighting to the L.A. punk who ran out of gas by the second round. He didn't really like seeing that fool all messed up. He didn't like fighting. It was just that when he climbed into the ring, he could finally let loose. When the bell rang, it was his signal to become somebody else, somebody who could leave his shyness, his crowded apartment and his ghosts behind. Somebody who was somebody.

Mary Carmen's question echoed in his head. Where am I going to train if they close the Packing Shed?

"So, what are you going to say, bro?" asked Ricky, one of the scrawniest boxers.

"I'm not sure," Miguel Ángel said. "What about you?"

Ricky just shrugged his shoulders, as if that were an answer.

"I feel like just going over to city hall and throwing a bomb in there or something," said Raúl, the tiniest boxer at the Packing Shed.

"Tst, don't let them hear you say that," Ricky whispered. "They already treat us like terrorists. If you give them any excuse, they'll haul your butt to juvie."

"Yeah, you're right," Raúl said. "I'm just so mad."

"Remember what Coach says, right?" Miguel Ángel said. "Channel your anger."

"I know, I know. I just want to channel my anger at those idiots."

"He said 'idiots,' Miguel Ángel." Mary Carmen turned to her big brother in disbelief.

Miguel Ángel just glared at Raúl.

Truth was, Miguel Ángel wasn't really prepared for this kind of battle either. He knew about punches and footwork, but of speaking in public and trying to convince a bunch of politicians to keep his gym open, he knew nothing. The thought made him sweat even more. But he didn't want to talk smack in front of Mary Carmen.

"We should find a place to sit, or we're going to have to stand the whole time," he told his buddies, pushing them all along, including his little sister.

No sooner had Miguel Ángel and his bunch found a seat, than the council people began to talk.

"Good evening, ladies and gentlemen," a gray-haired old Mexican spoke into the microphone. "We're here tonight because we need to decide what to do with the Packing Shed. As some of you may already know, Salinas is having some financial problems, and we need to find ways to save money and, at the same time, still provide services to our residents. Some of us think Alisal residents would be better served if we opened the Packing Shed for other uses. But we want to hear what you have to say."

Miguel Ángel buried his head between his hands. It was the exact same speech this guy gave last time, give or take a few words, and Miguel Ángel hadn't even thought about what to say today.

"Please fill out a form if you want to talk," the councilman continued. "Form a line right in front of the mic, and don't go over the two-minute time limit. We have a lot of people, and we don't want to stay here all night."

Miguel Ángel surveyed the room one more time. There were dozens of people he'd never seen before. Some occupied the metal chairs, others rambled around the warehouse-turned-gymnasium. Everyone began to line up before the microphone, and Miguel Ángel decided to get it over with.

"Brother, when are we going to go home? I'm getting hungry," Mary Carmen said.

"We'll go home like in twenty minutes, okay? But first I have to go and talk to these people. Wait for me here. I'll buy you a taco from the truck, okay?"

"Okay," the girl said, crossing her arms and settling into her chair.

Miguel Ángel surveyed the room once again, looking for his guardian angel. But no sign of Ita. Where was his chain-smoking great-grandmother when he needed her? She never disappeared for more than a week at a time, but he hadn't seen her in what felt like forever. And Miguel Ángel could use her grouchy advice right now.

As he got up to join the line, he drew the sign of the cross across his face. He began bouncing lightly on the balls of his feet. It was partially out of habit but also—and this, he'd never admit to anybody—he was cold. Yes, even with all these people around, the soaring warehouse still felt frigid to him. He had never felt this cold at the Packing Shed.

"Miguel Ángel, what's up with that girl?" Ricky asked, stretching his neck to point out a blonde teenager who'd just taken a seat in the back. "Is she the one? She's mighty fine."

"Shut up, man, I'm trying to concentrate here," Miguel Ángel said, trying hard to be serious but was betrayed by a half grin. He ignored the high-fives his friends were slapping behind his back.

"Man, what do you give 'em girls?" Raúl egged him on. "Did you steal the recipe from a *curandero*?" Another round of high-fives.

Miguel Ángel shook his head and turned his back to them.

Three more speakers and it would be his turn, but he wasn't listening. He was trying to tune it all out. He needed to ignore them—and Britney, and Mary Carmen. He was beginning to float.

These guys wanted to have a "public hearing" in the Packing Shed because it was election year, and they wanted the publicity, Coach told him. They had to make budget cuts, and the only cuts ever made are to programs for the poor. So here they were, these clueless fools trying to turn the Packing Shed into city hall.

It always seemed funny to Miguel Ángel how all the politicians said they wanted to get elected in Salinas so they could fight gangs, but once they became mayor, city councilman or school trustee, they voted to cut all the programs that helped fight gangs. Some gang busters!

Coach, he's for reals. He doesn't go around making pretty speeches, or even get money. But he looks at you with those small, beady eyes, and scares the bejesus out of you. You never wanna join no gangs.

Miguel Ángel turned his eyes to Mary Carmen—then he stole a brief glance at Britney. He didn't want her to catch him looking at her. It could go to her head. He stared at the buzzing fluorescent lights instead and at the hand-painted sign suspended above the pool tables: "This is a place of peace: no colors, no bullying." Yeah, right. He turned his head to the cage at the far end of the building, home of the gloves, helmets and training shoes piled on a mountain of plastic and leather. The loud ringing of the two-minute buzzer rose above the hum of the crowd and made him want to jump in the ring and start throwing punches. He slowly lifted himself on his toes, like a cat pulling its weight on its hind legs before pouncing on prey.

One more speaker.

He briefly thought about going back to his seat, but he couldn't do that now. Britney was there, shivering, her green eyes fixed on him. His sweet angel had actually come down from Pebble Beach heaven to see him fight, and instead, she had found this stupid hearing. Sucked.

Still, he was happy to see her. Finally, somebody would see him perform. Not the performance he was hoping for, but still . . .

It was his turn. He stepped up to the microphone, took a deep breath and threw his best jab.

CHAPTER 2

Britney hovered in the back of the gym for a few minutes, taking in the entire scene and trying to avoid the nasty stares from Tiffany. Miguel Ángel had described his hideaway many times; still, she'd pictured it differently. She hadn't imagined the washed out, ragged sweatshirts the kids were wearing, the smell of the locker room, the tall, dark ceiling where all dreams seemed to evaporate. She'd never been in a place like this, so bare and so cold. The tall, stocky girl looked around the cavernous warehouse building, imagining how much colder it would feel if there were no people inside it. When she heard the sound of the boxing bell for the first time, she jumped, startled.

The gym in her high school was very different. Probably three times as many fluorescent lights hung from the tall ceiling, so no darkness lurked in the corners. There was no boxing ring, and unlike the sole, freestanding basketball hoop leaning against the wall, her schools' basketball hoops hung from the ceiling and could be folded when volleyball tournaments took place. The walls of her gym were adorned with pictures of past winning teams. Go Pioneers: Champions of the 2004 Central Coast Section. Lewis and Clark Pioneers: California 2005 Lacrosse Champions. Apparently, there were no winners in this gym. Either that or they could not afford framed pictures.

Britney felt a bit disconcerted. Miguel Ángel told her there would be a fight, but this looked more like a lecture. All these metallic chairs lined up as if it were an auditorium, all those men and women sitting at a table as if dispensing information at a college fair.

"I thought this was going to be a fight," Tiffany said.

"Oh, shush," Britney answered. She scanned the crowded chairs and decided the second row from the front would do. She sat down with a clanking noise, and the cold metal chair made her tense.

"How long are we staying in this fridge?" Tiffany asked after taking the chair next to her, without raising her eyes from the cell phone. Texting her boyfriend, of course.

"Not sure, sis. Maybe an hour? I want to see what Miguel Ángel's up to."

"What are you, his mother now?" Tiffany asked, her eyes glued to the tiny screen. "Sporting events are for family, not for deranged girlfriends."

"I'm not deranged or his girlfriend," Britney replied, shoving Tiffany away. "It won't hurt you to be supportive, Tiffany."

"Whatever." Tiffany shrugged her shoulders. "The sooner we leave this dump, the better."

"Shhhhhhhh, I want to hear what they say." But Britney couldn't really hear anything. She was lost in her doubts, in the fascination and the unyielding attraction she felt for the willowy Miguel Ángel. Even from the back, as she watched him bounce on the balls of his feet, she melted, thinking about those full lips and crooked nose. The anger in his eyes that made Britney admire and fear him at the same time. And the way he kissed her. Britney forgot about the cold and stench of this place.

Her friends told her she was nuts. Why was a Pebble Beach girl, wealthy and gorgeous, sneaking away to the Alisal, the poorest barrio of California's central coast, to see a guy? Weren't there enough good-looking guys at her high school? Even Cleopatra, her best friend, often shook in disbelief.

Britney didn't feel gorgeous, though. She had long, blonde hair and dark green eyes, but her face was round, and the long training hours she'd put into cross-country and swimming had given her broad shoulders, thick arms and bulky legs. Not exactly what guys considered sexy. And it was not like she went out with him the first time he asked her. He courted her for months, casually dropping airplanes with poems written on them every time he walked by her at cross-country meets. Britney had actually started to believe Miguel Ángel would never ask her out. When he finally did, almost six months ago, she hadn't even flirted with a guy for almost a year—and she was more than enamored of Miguel Ángel and his romantic ways. She hadn't been this unpopular with other guys since the eighth grade, when Angelo Domenici gave her a surprise kiss on their last day of school. So when her friends told her she could have any guy she wanted, she just smiled dryly and looked away. If they only knew.

It's not like she was settling for just any guy, either. Miguel Ángel was attentive and fearless. One moment he'd be reading her a love poem and the next he'd be competing for the 100-meter race like his life depended on it. Most importantly, he told her she was beautiful, and Britney knew he meant it.

And the way he kissed her neck, touched her bare shoulders, embraced her. It was as if a black hole opened in the ground, swallowing them both and taking them to another galaxy. The world, her disparaging friends and critical sister all disappeared and became a meaningless blob that couldn't overshadow her bliss.

Yet such a torrid love affair couldn't go on without its consequences, and Britney was beginning to fear what would lie ahead if she continued seeing Miguel Ángel. She was old enough to drive, but her domineering father would not let her behind the wheel until she turned seventeen—still almost a year away. She could not continue relying on Tiffany or Cleopatra to drive her to Salinas. And riding the bus—forget it. Miguel Ángel often borrowed his friend's SUV, but that ride wasn't a given. Plus, Britney didn't even want to think what her father would do if he ever found out about Miguel Ángel.

And her missing period. She tried to push that out of her mind too, but the anxiety just kept creeping back.

At that moment, Miguel Ángel approached the microphone, interrupting Britney's thoughts.

CHAPTER 3

"I'm here to tell you that I don't want you to kick the Alisal Boxing Club out of this place . . . "

"I'm sorry," interrupted the loud councilman. "Before you start talking, you need to state your name for the record."

Miguel Ángel felt as if he'd been jabbed. As if talking in front of these people wasn't hard enough, he also had to remember to say his name? Damn!

"My name is Miguel Ángel Moreda. I'm here because I don't want you to kick the Alisal Boxing Club out into the streets. This is the only place I have where I can come and release stress, you know? Before I joined the club here, I was getting in trouble all the time, but my coach made me learn discipline, you know? Nobody had ever showed me what discipline was, and now I use it all the time. I don't get in trouble like before. Before, if somebody wanted to punch me, because I was chubby and stuff, I punched him back and the principal was calling me into his office all the time. Now I'm not fat, and the other kids at school and in my block don't tease me no more. It's all because of the exercise. I know you guys have to save money and stuff, but think about all the money you'll save on cops. If we're out there, the cops have to be chasing us all the time, and I wanna save you guys some money and stuff. No, serious. If you close the gym, you're seriously gonna mess me up. Please don't close the Packing Shed."

The show over, Miguel Ángel turned around without waiting for a response and darted back to his seat, his back hunched, his hands never leaving the front pockets of his sweatshirt. He let his weight fall into the chair right next to Coach, making a loud clanking noise that spoke the obscenities he didn't dare say.

Coach looked at him in silence and punched him playfully on the arm. Another young boxer had already stepped up to the microphone to tell the Salinas city officials why they shouldn't evict the boxing program from its home of twenty years.

Sometime in the last few weeks, somebody had decided that the heavy-set retired mechanic everyone knew as Coach was *persona non grata* and that his program was not serving enough children in the Alisal. Instead of having a boxing ring for only two dozen kids, the former packing shed could be split into classrooms, or transformed into a small theater, or sold to help the city pay its debts. Somewhere along the line, without anybody taking credit for it, a decision had been made. Like lettuce on a spring morning, the plan bloomed, a seed planted by an anonymous fieldworker. The council members blamed the city manager, and the city manager said he had drawn up reports at the request of the council. Everyone wanted to take credit for popular ideas, but the bad ones ended up like tainted produce, all piled up in the municipal dump.

The news arrived by mail, a brusque "You have thirty days to vacate the premises" that felt like a Mike Tyson punch to the solar plexus.

But if there was anything Coach never ran from, it was a good fight, and he was going to give city officials one. So he rounded up his boxers and prepped them on how to combat their elected officials, just as he would before a Silver Gloves tournament. Not until tonight, when he saw the council members following their "Robert Rules of Order," banging the gavel and cutting off the kids when they'd spoken their two minutes, had he realized how unprepared he was for the bout.

"I am Gloria Gonzales," another of his boxers spoke into the mic. "I've been training on this ring right here for nine years, since I was like nine or ten. I've gone to many state championships and Coach never asks for any money, you know? Sometimes, we have to wash cars or sell candy to get some money for the gear and stuff, but Coach gives us the money and pays for gas to drive us to the fights. Nobody else does that for me, you know. I don't want you to take it away from me."

Gloria dragged herself back to her seat, and the older man standing behind him took the microphone. He was shorter than the fighters, wrinkled and with more scars, the creased witnesses of many battles. Coach recognized the pretentious old fart and braced himself for his bile.

"My name is Romualdo Bautista and I used to work with Coach in this gym, until he kicked me out. We had our personal differences, but that's not why I'm here. I'm here because this man is using public facilities, paid for with my taxes, but he doesn't have an open operation. He keeps no records, he only agrees to train some boys, but others he just pushes aside. He berates the boxers, calls them stupid and other names. Sorry, I didn't mean to use this language here. All I'm saying is that he's using public facilities, paid for with taxpayers' money, but he operates it like a private club."

Coach squirmed in his seat and then buried his head in his hands. He turned to Miguel Ángel, his best boxer, trying to find a reassuring gaze.

Miguel Ángel wasn't there anymore. After coming back to his seat, he let his mind wander back again to the girl in the second row. Her long, blonde hair falling past her shoulders and the back of the metal chair where she squirmed. He closed his eyes and imagined her thin, pointy nose; her delicate, pink lips covered with gloss; her blue big eyes and the small, brown mole above her mouth.

There was always a time when it was more pleasant to escape, to close his eyes and imagine what it would be like if he were somebody else, somewhere else. What if he was just watching a movie of his life and could get up any time and leave? That's how he began floating. He floated when classes were boring, when his stepfathers beat his mom, when the rainy weather kept him indoors.

He had become a master of the technique: he'd close his eyes and imagine what it would be like to see everything from above. There he was, sitting with his arms folded and his head bowed, ignoring everybody around him. There was Coach sitting next to him, tapping his fingers on his cheek, rubbing his belly and ordering everybody around, and then there was Britney, sitting next to that other blonde girl he'd never seen. Could it be Tiffany? Britney spoke often of her older sister, and she sounded scary: so smart, so straight.

He watched his boxing buddies as one by one they went to the microphone and pleaded with those strangers to let them stay in their club. He saw them line up behind the microphone, walking back and forth like caged lions, climbing on top of the ring and jumping back down.

Then he saw Britney and the other girl get up and move toward the exit. Miguel Ángel shook his head and shot up from his seat, but before he darted to the door, he stopped himself. Rushing is not cool.

"You leaving?" he asked, brushing his hand across the small of her back.

"Yeah. Our parents are waiting for us," Britney said. "Oh, sorry. This is my sister." She leaned back to feel the pressure of his touch, her hand looking for his, finding it, squeezing it.

"Hi," he said, his eyes zeroing in on Tiffany's red lips and pale skin. "What'd you think?" he said without looking at Britney.

"You sounded good," Britney complemented him, turning around to meet his gaze. "I hope you guys don't get evicted."

"Yeah, me too. I need a place to train, you know?"

"Well, maybe you can join a gym if they close this one. I know a guy who trains at a club in north Salinas. It can't be that expensive."

Miguel Ángel felt as if his gut had just gotten kicked. His head began spinning. The thought of not having the Packing Shed made him miserable, and it hadn't occurred to him that there were other places he could box. Join another gym? What about Coach? And the other guys? Most importantly, where would he get the money?

❧❧❧

Tiffany stampeded toward her car without uttering a word. She aimed the remote at the BMW parked behind the Packing Shed, sandwiched between a VW bus and a rusty Lincoln Town car. After getting in and pulling out of the parking lot, Tiffany turned on her iPod. Good, Britney thought, she'd listen to her music and forget where she'd been. "Get your stinky feet off the dashboard!" Tiffany snapped. "You know how much I hate looking at your stupid toes!"

Tiffany and her foot phobia. It was the weirdest thing. Britney quietly pulled her legs under her seat and turned to look out the window.

"I can't believe you dragged me to this dump," Tiffany went on. "It's the filthiest place I've ever been to."

"I didn't drag you here!" Britney yelled. "Cleopatra was perfectly willing to bring me. You're the one who insisted on driving me."

And after a few seconds, she added, "And it's not a dump."

"Do I have to remind you what happened the last time you used Cleo as your chauffer?"

Britney pulled her long, stocky legs to her chest and sank into the bucket seat without responding.

Last year, on Labor Day weekend, Britney had been invited to a party at Lake San Antonio. But Tiffany had other plans: she wanted to spend the holiday at her boyfriend's family cabin in Arroyo Seco. Cleopatra had offered to drive Britney, but her dad didn't approve of the girl: everyone knew she had a drinking problem. Her car was off-limits to Britney, whether her friend had consumed alcohol or not. Britney pleaded with Tiffany for weeks to cover up for the Lake San Antonio escapade. She had the perfect plan: the sisters would tell their parents they were both going to Arroyo Seco, but Britney would drive with Cleopatra to the lake. On the way back, the sisters would reunite so they could arrive home together. On the way back from the lake, after Cleopatra had been drinking for hours straight from a bottle of whiskey, she pushed a bit too much on the gas pedal and lost control. She slammed her sports car into a tree. Both girls were taken to the hospital with bruises and a few broken ribs. Everyone at the hospital kept repeating how lucky they were.

Her parents were relieved to see Britney alive, but they were also furious. The sisters were grounded for a month, and punished with no shopping trip to New York for the holidays. No, Britney did not want to think about what happened the last time Cleopatra was her chauffer.

Tiffany drove south on Sanborn Road, a four-lane thoroughfare sprinkled with bright shopping centers and long stretches of darkness in between. A few men in hooded sweatshirts shuffled along the sidewalks, their feet heavy with the day's work in the fields. The girls had come to this part of town a couple of times during the day, mostly when their school took them on community service trips. Never at night. Alisal was not an area where strangers ventured lightly. In East Salinas, the poorest neighborhood in Monterey County, the presence of gangs loomed large. They controlled the drug trafficking, asked strangers which gang they claimed—*Norteños* or *Sureños*—and shot those who got in their way. It was a world away from their home in tony Pebble Beach, even if the street lighting in the golf club haven wasn't any better than that of East Salinas.

Her friends had warned them not to go, but Britney didn't care. How scary could it be? She wasn't a gang member. She was a tall blonde girl from the other side of the Lettuce Curtain. Nobody knew who she was. Nobody could push her to pick a side, nobody could tell her she should belong to a Northside or a Southside gang. Surely nobody would even notice she was there.

Besides, she'd come plenty of times and had seen nothing that could scare her. What's so frightening about a bunch of mothers pushing their babies in their strollers? What's so alien about the farm worker women getting off the buses—even if their handkerchiefs covered their faces, like Saudi women shielding themselves from the sun? What's so menacing about lowriders blasting music through car windows?

But she knew better than to try to dissuade Tiffany from her ideas. Britney pulled out her cell phone and was going to text Cleopatra when her sister lowered the music.

"I still don't understand what you see in this guy," she said. "I mean, he's cute, but there's plenty of cute boys in our school."

Oh, God, not again. Still hugging her legs close to her chest, Britney rocked herself back and forth without responding. She looked at the folding mountains, their profile barely visible in the darkness of the moonless night. She thought about Miguel Ángel's lips and the amazing things he did with them: he would look at her intently, slowly pulling closer to her. He first brushed his lips against hers, like a butterfly landing on a rose and lightly moving around its petals. He moved about the end of her lips, her nose, her forehead, and when she felt she couldn't take it anymore, Miguel Ángel came back for her mouth and pressed his lips against hers, hard and soft, cold and hot. It was like being under the ocean and surrounded by a wall of fire at the same time. It was like traveling to the moon and back in an instant, as if gravity didn't exist.

Britney didn't care if Tiffany never understood.

"I mean, Tony Valentini is crazy about you. He's been bugging Brian about the four of us going out together. He's not bad looking at all."

"Yeah, I know. And it would make Dad *sooooo* happy if I went out with him," Britney mumbled.

She wasn't interested in Tony Valentini, Ralph Gervais or Manuel Vallejo. She craved Miguel Ángel Moreda, the beautiful guy who pretended to write love poems just for her.

> And I pace around hungry, sniffing the twilight,
> Hunting for you, for your hot heart,
> Like a mountain lion in the solitude of the Gabi-
> lan Mountains.

It was the sweetest gesture she had ever received from a guy. Yes, she recognized it as a Neruda poem, but pretending to have written it for her just made Miguel Ángel more endearing. Instead of scolding him, she gave him a long, passionate kiss.

"He's just a friend, okay? And I wanted to see him fight."

"Well, he didn't fight. It was just a boring meeting."

"Oh, shush. You're so thick, you don't get anything."

Britney stared at the mountains and the sparse lights coming out of the mansions. Her mind flew back to the chilly Packing Shed, to Miguel Ángel's hazel eyes, pleading for mercy. Her thoughts, however, were suddenly snatched away by a strong stomach cramp.

"I think I need to throw up," she screamed. "Pull over, quick."

Right on Highway 68, before the hills Steinbeck had described as the "pastures of heaven," Britney lost her lunch.

CHAPTER 4

One by one, all of the boys who trained with Coach—and seemingly all those he ever crossed—pleaded with the council members about the future of the boxing club. The boxers begged for its life, Coach's enemies clamored for its eviction. The members of the council listened to all of them without interrupting—as long as they didn't take more than their two minutes. The tension hung in the warehouse like the heavy bags at the end of the gym.

The overweight councilman surveyed the room. Nobody else appeared to be waiting for a turn to speak. He rearranged himself in his chair. Droplets of sweat that seemed to freeze in the cold air hung on his temples. After a few seconds, he took the microphone again.

"Mr. Ramos, everyone calls you Coach, so I might as well do the same. A lot of people seem to have questions about your operation of the Packing Shed, and I want to get more information about it as well. Let me ask you: Do you have a contract with the city? How much is your lease and for how long? Who are the members of your board of directors? Have you filed income taxes in the last five years? How many children have you served in the last fifteen years? What's your annual budget? What's the requirement for children to join the boxing club?"

There was no pause in his speech, almost no room for air to enter his lungs. He threw the questions one after the other, bang, bang, bang, as if being fired by an automatic gun. Coach felt his knees weakening.

"Excuse me," he interrupted, "you're going too fast, let me write that down."

Coach patted his pants and jacket pockets. Miguel Ángel, slightly awake from his Britney trance, fished in his gym bag and found an old envelope and a "Ricos Tacos" pen. He handed them to his coach.

The councilman gave him a long, harsh look, and after a few uncomfortable moments, he repeated the first set of questions, then continued. "I want to know how much you're insured for, and if it covers the city. I want to know how much the students have to pay for joining. Do you provide them with equipment or do they have to buy their own? When you travel, how do you pay for your expenses? Let me see . . . I think that's it."

If at the beginning of the meeting Coach felt as if he were tied to a stake, the interrogation had the smell of burning logs at his feet. It was a witch hunt, and he didn't like the role he was playing. Coach saw his life flash before his eyes, a reel of neglected children reaching out to him.

He saw the night he visited the one-bedroom apartment of the family of one of his boxers. The parents were heavy drinkers, and their fights and late night parties were getting to their five kids. He gave them a scolding, and after a three-hour heated conversation, the Coach convinced them to join AA.

He saw a private tutor sitting at a hamburger joint, going over some lessons with two boys. "Can you teach that stuff to this kid?" Coach asked her, pointing to thirteen-year-old Luis, a rising boxing star. The boy had trouble reading and writing, and his failing grades were embarrassing him. The kid didn't want to go to school anymore. The tutor said she would do it for thirty dollars an hour. He paid and drove Luis to and from the lessons the entire summer. After thirteen sessions, the embarrassment stopped.

He saw ten boys piled up in his van, looking out the windows like curious gophers poking through their holes. During their frequent trips, he would ask them simple questions to test their knowledge. Who's the vice president of the United States? How many quarts are there in a gallon? Who discovered America? Simple as they were, many times the quiz questions went unanswered.

This was what it boiled down to: thousands of volunteer hours with the boys, the advice, the constant presence, the boxing lessons. They would all come to an end because somewhere, somehow, he had rubbed the wrong person the wrong way. Somebody in a position of power, maybe even the councilman who was questioning him right now, did not approve of his program, of the way he treated the children. They were going to take it out on him. Who hated him this much? Or did they simply not care about poor kids?

For nearly twenty years, he had run his boxing club at the Packing Shed with no contract, no signatures, no promises. It was just a handshake with Mayor Albert Stevens, who back then let him have the defunct produce packing plant the city had purchased for one dollar.

Before the Packing Shed came into the picture, Coach had installed a few exercise machines in the garage of his house. Every afternoon, after his son Junior was done with his homework, he would make him jump rope for half an hour, run around the elementary school, then hit the speed bag, the heavy bag, the double standing bag. Coach lavished Junior with all the attention the aging man never had. His son would be a champ.

"Coach, could you help me train?" Rudy, one of Junior's classmates, asked one day.

Coach thought about it for a few seconds. The scraggy runt was a troublemaker, always picking a fight with other kids in school. Like so many others, no dad to speak of, mother too busy working to pay attention beyond making ends meet. But Coach already had a child and didn't need more responsibilities. He had his hands full, but . . .

"I'll train you, but you have to promise me you're going to take this seriously," Coach said. "We train three hours a day, five days a week, rain or shine. And you have to stop those stupid fights at school, or I stop helping you."

Then came Alfredo. Then Agustín. Later Sebastián. The garage became too small for all the teenagers who congregated there after school.

He was driving home from his job one day when he saw that a tiny door to the vacant warehouse was open. He drove around the parking lot to investigate. Inside the humid building of concrete floors and metal curtains, Coach Ramos saw a maintenance man wearing the uniform of city employees.

"Can I help you?"

"You think I can rent this place?" Ramos asked.

"Don't know. You have to call the city manager. I'm here just to check on a busted pipe."

"You mind if I look around?"

"Be my guest."

He wasn't heavy then, when he strolled slowly around the building. The paint on the walls was peeling, the insulation spilling out from holes in the ceiling, puddles on the cement floor from the rain leaking in. Coach could picture the locker rooms, the walls papered with championship posters, the boxing rings. He could see Junior pounding at the speed bag, Sebastián on a heavy bag, Alfredo jumping rope.

"Who did you say I have to call?" he asked the plumber.

"Here, call this number and ask for the city manager. He'll tell you what to do."

A week later, almost twenty years ago, he was sitting in the mayor's office, talking to Mr. Stevens himself.

And now, he was facing the executioners.

"I've never had a contract, no, so I have no lease and I pay nothing to the city. The city should pay me for keeping these kids off the street when there's nothing for them to do out there. I don't know how many children I've had, one hundred and fifty? Three hundred? I don't know what's my annual budget, whatever the kids need and my own children don't. And all I ask of the kids is that they come every day ready to train. No colors, no drugs, no disobeying. That's all I ask."

"Thank you, Mr. Ramos," the councilman said, staring at him. "We're going to need a report in writing with all these answers."

Coach went back to his chair, making a loud plop when he dropped his full weight onto the metal seat. His light skin was red, his forehead scrunched up, and he felt a persistent ringing in his ears, the kind they say appears when you're losing your hearing. He was out of air, and that was only the first round.

CHAPTER 5

Tiffany and Britney drove up the driveway that mean-
dered through dozens of towering pine trees and
darting deer. Coming home from the Alisal was like
entering another galaxy, Britney thought. Parked at the
main entrance of their French Mediterranean mansion
they saw their dad's Jaguar. It wasn't even eight, and he
was usually never home that early, not even on family
dinner nights. The sisters exchanged a silent glance.

While Tiffany dashed upstairs to the small dining
room, Britney ran to her bedroom to brush her teeth and
put on a fresh blouse. When she finally made it to the
dining room, everyone's eyes betrayed their impatience.

"Well, well, well, look who decided to show up," Mr.
Scozzari said.

"Sorry, Dad," Britney said, running to peck him on the
cheek. "I was working on a school project." His breath
smelled of alcohol.

"Girls, you know you have to save Wednesdays for
family dinner. Dad and I have an event to attend tomorrow," said their mother.

"Sorry, Mom," Tiffany said.

Mrs. Scozzari rang a crystal bell, and a short, dark-
skinned woman entered the room, holding a silver serving bowl. She placed it in the center of the table and

poured a generous portion of a milky stew into Mrs. Scozzari's bowl. The four members of the Scozzari family watched as the plump woman went around the table repeating the process until all bowls were filled. Britney's stomach began protesting again.

"How was school today, girls?" their mother asked as soon as Alice disappeared behind the kitchen doors.

"I got an A plus on my essay about Shakespeare and his influence on modern theater, but I don't think that's fair because Sandra Alvarado also got an A plus and her ideas were not as polished as mine," Tiffany moaned and then she tasted her soup. "Her vocabulary is so limited."

"You just don't like Sandra because she flirts with your boyfriend, but she's smarter than you," Britney said, stirring her soup.

"Why'd you say that?" Tiffany fired at her sister. "Next time you want to see your boyfriend, don't ask me to drive you."

Mr. Scozzari raised his eyes from the bowl and stared at both girls. Britney bit her lip and lowered her head. Now she was downright nauseous. What possessed her to pick a fight with Tiffany? All eating stopped. Only the surf crashing on the beach and the faraway sound of the barking sea lions broke the silence.

"A boyfriend, Britney?" her father eventually questioned, using his best courtroom voice.

"No, Dad, it's not true," Britney rushed to answer. "Tiffany is being a brat."

"Does Britney have a boyfriend, Tiffany?" he interrogated his oldest daughter.

"No, Dad," she answered, casting a complicit sideglance to her sister. "I was just trying to get back at her."

"Your better not be lying to me," he hissed while glaring at his daughters.

Scozzari had lots of rules for his girls: no makeup until they turned fifteen, no driving until they were seventeen, and he had to approve of the boys they went out with. And they broke the rules on a regular basis, but they were very careful and always covered for each other. He had an extremely stressful job and a red hot temper. Although they'd seen the sweetest of his sides—the roses he brought for their mother, the expensive trips and flashy surprises—they'd also witnessed his wrath. The slapping, the dish-breaking, the bruises. They went out of their way to keep from pushing his buttons.

Britney remembered when Tiffany briefly dated Manolo Martínez a couple of years ago. A tall, black haired, well-mannered, straight-A student who'd been accepted to Harvard and Stanford, but hadn't decided where he would go.

"Where they give me the most money," he told Tiffany.

"You're not going out with a Mexican kid, are you?" her father asked.

"He's not Mexican, Dad!" she groaned. "He was born in the United States, he's an American!"

"But he eats beans and tortillas, right? His father speaks Spanish, right? He must be Mexican."

"Dad, his dad was born here too! I don't know, maybe his grandma was born in Mexico, but so what? Nanna was born in Sicily. And he's going to Harvard!"

"I don't want to see you with him," her father ordered, using the cold, calculating tone he reserved for multi-million dollar lawsuits.

Manolo drove Tiffany home one night, and they were chatting inside his beat-up truck when her father drove up. The man stormed out of his Jaguar, holding a black object in his hand. When Manolo rolled down the window to say hello, Scozzari propped the gun in the teenager's face.

"I don't want any dirty Mexican going out with my daughter," he said with a calm, steely voice. "Get out of my house. I don't ever want to see you here."

Manolo never returned her phone calls again.

Britney shuddered at the thought of what her father would do if he found out about Miguel Ángel.

CHAPTER 6

"**G**ood night, Coach," Miguel Ángel yelled as he left the building. The hearing had finished more than an hour earlier, but he had stayed behind to punch heavy bags.

"Are you staying long?"

"Nah, I'm taking off," Coach said. "Want a ride?"

"No, *gracias*, I wanna walk a little."

Miguel Ángel zipped up his jacket and pulled the hood over his head before stepping into the misty night. He needed to clear his head. The hearing and Britney had drained him, but thankfully, Blanca Rosa came over to pick up their sister; otherwise, he wouldn't have been able to stay and punch some bags.

He stood at the threshold of the gym's main entrance on North Sanborn and turned his head to the right, where the road was barely lit by the light of passing cars. No matter what anybody said, he loved the Alisal, he thought as he drew in a deep breath. Standing under the light by the Packing Shed, where he could see the quiet, dark streets, he marveled at how much the neighborhood changed between day and night. In a few hours, even before the sun came up, hundreds of men and women would crawl out from their houses to go pick lettuce and broccoli in the surrounding fields. Like his mom. The streets would be a cacophony of sounds, a well-orches-trated chaos of cars and people.

At night, hardly anybody ventured out. Some would think it was the fear gang members instilled in the neigh-bors, but the reality was, everyone needed to be in bed early so they could get up before the sun rose.

Miguel Ángel was not afraid. This was his barrio, his turf. He was safe. Maybe Ita would finally show up. Where was she?

He turned to the left and saw across the street the dark silhouette of a short man. Was that Beto? The per-son was leaning against a light pole, smoking a cigarette, as if waiting for somebody. It certainly looked like his friend. Ah, not now. He turned around and went back inside the gym.

"Coach, when did you say you're leaving?"

"Right now. Did you change your mind?"

"Yeah, it's cold out there. Don't want to get sick."

They exited through the back door that opened to the unpaved parking lot. Coach turned off the gym's lights and locked the door behind them. They climbed into his truck and drove north on Sanborn.

For a few blocks, all they could hear was the revved-up motor of the battered pick-up. The smell of oil com-ing from the engine blended with the whiff of *carne asada* emanating from the parked taco trucks.

"So, what'd you learn in school today, hey?" Coach asked Miguel Ángel.

"I finished reading the book you gave me. It's cool, man."

How typical. Coach was worried, Miguel Ángel could tell by the way the old man rapidly scratched his beard under his chin, the way a dog takes care of fleas. But

Coach wouldn't say anything. Miguel Ángel stole a glance toward the old man and saw his tightly pursed lips, his small eyes, and the red stain of salsa on his grayish T-shirt. Miguel Ángel suddenly felt like laughing.

"What you laughing at, punk?" Coach said, a faint smile on his face.

"You're funny, man."

"Yeah, funny how?"

"I don't know. They almost ate you alive in that place, and you ask me how my day was. It's funny."

Coach shook his head. "So tell me about that book," he said. "What'd you like about it?"

"I don't know. I mean, there are things that are cool, like when the kid starts to work to help his mom. I liked that."

It took some getting used to, but Miguel Ángel had developed a taste for reading. Coach was always lending books to his boxers, quizzing them about their contents afterwards. It was part of their training. Their bodies would function better if they also exercised their brains. Miguel Ángel was careful not to read around other boys, though: he was a fighter, not a brainiac.

"I liked that book, too. Villaseñor is a good writer. Maybe you should read this other one he wrote, what's it called? I think it's *Wild Steps to Heaven*.

"Do you have that one?"

"I don't know, I'll look for it at home. If not, we can always find it in the library."

"Yeah, when they open again."

Whenever he thought about the libraries, Miguel Ángel got the urge to punch somebody, anybody. The city had no money: no money for libraries, no money for the Packing Shed, no money for the children of farm workers who toiled endlessly to feed the country. Salinas was poor even though it rubbed elbows with Monterey, Carmel and all those fancy areas, because its residents were poor. Poor, exhausted and desperate farm workers, like his mother coming home every evening after an entire day bent over the lettuce fields. The harvesters were all like her: dark-skinned, hard-working, resilient and exploited. They worked from sunup to sundown, leaving their children at home to their fate, hoping *la Virgen de Guadalupe* would look after them. Tons of tourists came to Monterey County, but they looked past the hordes of immigrants picking artichokes and strawberries: they'd rather gawk at the great white shark at the Monterey Bay Aquarium or at multi-million-dollar mansions on 17 Mile Drive.

And with no money, Salinas was forced to close its three libraries. It angered Miguel Ángel not to have his libraries open on weekends anymore, and now, more than ever, he had to rely on the books Coach lent him.

No wonder boys like Beto become gang bangers. No libraries, no rec centers, no hope. What was a teenager to do?

"Thanks, Coach," the young boxer said when they reached his apartment building. "See you tomorrow."

"Hey," Coach stopped him, "you seem worried. Are you okay?" Coach had noticed the blonde girl eyeing his boy earlier.

Where to start? Miguel Ángel thought about the libraries, Britney, what he'd learned about love being with her. He thought about Beto and his inability to stay away from the gang. But he just chuckled and waved the old man off.

"I'm good, Coach, don't worry. Thanks."

"All right. See you tomorrow."

Miguel Ángel stayed by the curb to watch Coach leave. After the lights of his truck were gone, he headed to his apartment. From under the stairs, Beto leaped out.

"Are you hiding from me, *carnal?*"

Miguel Ángel jumped back, startled. "Man, why you do that? You scared the shit out of me!"

"I was waiting for you outside the gym, and you went inside. I didn't want you to sneak into your house and escape from me."

"I didn't see you. Where were you?"

"Don't try to play me, man."

Okay, time to stop pretending. It's not like he could hide from Beto. His best friend could read him like the graffiti tags on his apartment building.

"What you want? I gotta go in, my mom's gonna worry," Miguel Ángel said in hushed tones.

"Yeah, like you care what your mom thinks. I need a big favor. Come, let's take a walk."

Beto grabbed him by the elbow and pulled him away from the stairs, looking around. Miguel Ángel didn't resist. Ever since they were little, Beto held a strange power over him.

On their first day in first grade, almost a decade ago, Miguel Ángel got into a fight with a third-grader who snatched his lunch burrito. After classes were over, the third-grader and two of his friends followed Miguel Ángel without him noticing. But Beto noticed. He followed close behind, and when the three boys tried to jump Miguel Ángel, Beto came to the rescue. The fight was eventually stopped by a group of mothers walking by, but not before Beto and Miguel Ángel gave the three boys a memorable beating.

They became inseparable.

When they were little, it was hard to tell the chubby boys apart. But they had changed. Once Miguel Ángel had started training, he followed Coach's advice and changed his diet to one of fruits and veggies. Beto kept with the potato chips and soft drinks. Miguel Ángel shot up like a cornstalk, Beto bloomed to the sides like an iceberg lettuce.

These days, Beto's looks were changing every day. First, it was those wrap-around sunglasses that had become permanently embedded on his face. Next, it was the big old 49ers shirt. Today, it was the shaved-down head. And the now inseparable, yellow stress ball. The one with a happy face that scrunched up every time Beto squeezed it.

"Fool, you're looking more and more like Eddie Olmos in *American Me*. You working at McDonalds now?" Miguel Ángel said.

Beto ignored him.

"Remember that gas station robbery two nights ago? The one Pato was arrested for?" Beto finally spoke, throwing his yellow ball up in the air.

"Yeah."

"Remember *la chota* said there were two suspects? Well, the guy they didn't catch, that's me. And if they find I have the gun, they gonna put me away for breaking probation." As he spoke, he pulled a black Beretta from the back of his pants and tried to put it in his friend's hands.

"Shit, man, I'm not hiding your piece," said Miguel Ángel, jumping back toward a wall.

"*Carnal*, you're my homeboy, man. If the pigs find me with this, I'm screwed."

"I've told you, I don't want any part of your shit," Miguel Ángel yelled.

"Shhhhhh," said Beto, turning to see if somebody had heard them. "What shit are you talking about, man? What I do for a living brings in more money a week than you could make the whole year at a grocery store."

"You idiot, I'm not getting into your stupid game, and you know it. And you're gonna wake up my brothers," Miguel Ángel hissed.

Beto blew hard and softened his tone. "It's just for a couple of days, man. C'mon, you owe me. Besides, you know I'm right. You could make money fast if you wanted to."

Ah, shit. There he went again with the you-owe-me crap. Before Miguel Ángel's fighting skills became the stuff of legend in the Alisal, Beto had always been ready to jump to his defense. He was stronger, more fearless, and always ready to beat the crap out of anyone who dared touch his friend. Beto had saved his beautiful nose many times.

That was long ago. Now, no one dared touch Miguel Ángel unless they were prepared to leave blood and teeth on the sidewalk. And his nose was no longer beautiful.

So how many times do you repay a debt?

And to make matters more confusing, Beto loved to touch that sore spot. Was Miguel Ángel just fooling himself thinking he could become a prize fighter? Was he ever going to make enough money to move away from the Alisal?

"This is messed up, fool. Don't do this. Why are you so loyal to the gang, anyway?"

But Miguel Ángel knew why. Beto had to prove his "worth" to the gang, to a bunch of tough homies in the barrio who demanded respect. It was as if the old bangers had become his parents. They demanded loyalty, commitment, and hard work. They became the parents, the role models, especially when real parents were not around. And after his mother passed away, nobody else would give Beto the time of day. Not even Coach.

Worst of all, they demanded money for "La Causa," a bunch of old dudes in maximum security prison living off what guys like Beto could make on the streets.

Beto lowered his gaze, like old people do when scolding their children. His eyes narrowed, barely letting out a fiery spark. He turned away, his hands reaching for the gun.

"Listen, just for a couple of days, okay?" Miguel Ángel agreed. "And I don't want you comin' round, I don't want the cops to follow you here."

"No problem, man, I swear," Beto said, handing the gun to his friend. "I'll come get it soon, okay? Shit, I was close this time."

"Stop. I don't want to get involved. If you don't tell me things, I have nothing to tell the cops."

"What? You wouldn't rat on me, would you, man?" he snapped, a menacing finger poking his friend's chest.

"Don't mess with me man, I ain't no rat," he said, pushing away Beto's threatening finger.

"Okay, okay, I'm sorry. I'm nervous, all right? I didn't mean no disrespect."

"Don't be a fool, Beto. If you turn on me, you have nobody else."

Beto's real name was Alberto, but Beto was the nickname his mother used. Miguel Ángel was the only one who used it.

Miguel Ángel was the only one who never got on Beto's case about banging. Maybe that's why they remained friends for so long. Secretly, Miguel Ángel even admired Beto: he had the guts to be in a gang, even if everyone said he was gonna end up crippled, dead or in jail. Everyone around Miguel Ángel said gangs were the worst, but Beto made it look so cool.

Besides, lectures had not worked on Beto. What could Miguel Ángel say that was different?

"I gotta go home man," Miguel Ángel told Beto. "Gotta get up early tomorrow."

"All right. Want a little toke before you go? We all need to get high sometimes . . . " Beto reached into his jacket pocket.

Miguel Ángel shook his head and stepped back. "I don't do that stuff, *carnal*. You know that."

CHAPTER 7

As soon as dinner was over, Britney ran upstairs to her bedroom, locked the door and dove onto her bed, burying her head into the pillows. Away from the prying eyes of parents and sister, her tears flowed like the waters of the Carmel River.

She cried out of anger. Tiffany had almost given away her secret, and she did not even want to imagine what would happen if her dad found out about Miguel Ángel. She cried out of longing. She'd imagined breaking away from the meeting at the Packing Shed and finding a secluded spot to make out with Miguel Ángel. She missed his lips and his touch. The last time they found a place to kiss and explore each other's bodies was more than a week ago, when Miguel Ángel borrowed his friend's car, their mobile love nest.

But another reason for her tears was completely unexpected and puzzling. She was sad about the boxers, the skinny brown kids in tattered clothes, their lips blue from the cold, who looked like they hadn't eaten in a week. True, not all the kids were skinny, but the scrawny ones, the ones with their tennis shoes caked in mud and falling apart, those were the ones that broke Britney's heart.

In school, Britney learned about the developing world, of places like Haiti and Ethiopia, where kids sat in a daze with no shoes and no clothing and ate only once a day—if they were lucky. They lived in drafty huts that could not keep the rain out and they did not attend school because there was no school to speak of. But that was far away, in a world distant enough to put it out of your mind once you went shopping.

Britney could not imagine the boxers of the Alisal going to bed hungry and sleeping in huts. After all, even though East Salinas struck her as a poor neighborhood, she never saw anyone walking barefoot or begging for food. Still, there was something about those boys, something in their eyes and their appearance that revealed their need. These kids were not like her classmates, heirs to movie stars, stockbrokers and financiers who drove late model cars and jet-setted between Pebble Beach, New York and Paris. There was real hunger in the boxers' eyes, an emptiness she hadn't expected to find so close to home, across the "Lettuce Curtain," the imagined division between her home on the Monterey Peninsula and the poor Salinas Valley.

It wasn't like she'd never seen it, either. A couple of years back, on a service trip to fix a school in the Alisal, she had a chance to observe these kids. The differences didn't strike her as much at first: their clothes seemed baggier, their white T-shirts a bit gray, their tennis shoes not as trendy as those her own friends wore. The students were either rail skinny or butterballs, their hair was not shiny and their complexion was not rosy. They were so . . . brown.

But then Roland, her least favorite classmate, pointed out something else she hadn't noticed. Roland and Britney had been paired up—much to Britney's chagrin—to plant a tree at the school. As Britney huffed and puffed, trying to dig up the compact dirt, Roland looked around the drab looking playground, spruced up only by the energetic kids running around it. Instead of helping, Roland kept tripping about the way the children "looked at him," as if they could strip him of all his wealth just by staring at his expensive watch.

"They'd just as soon raid my room if the gates didn't keep them out."

What an odd comment, Britney thought. She hadn't noticed anything extraordinary about their eyes, about the way the boys looked at all the strangers visiting their school.

Until today.

Britney had been crying so much that she hadn't noticed her phone, frantically lighting up every time it received a text message. She had totally forgotten about Cleopatra.

"Where r u?" "Hey I have ur stuff" "Can I come over?" "Can I come up? I'm parked by ur door."

The last one was more than fifteen minutes old. Without taking the time to reply, Britney put on her shoes and squirreled downstairs, hoping her parents had gone to bed or at least were away from the door. After turning off the alarm, she opened to let her best friend in.

"Ask me again for a favor!" Cleopatra yelled. "Ask me."

"Shhhhh. My parents are asleep. Let's go upstairs."

While Britney glided, Cleopatra stomped. Once inside her bedroom, Britney leaned against her door. "I'm so sorry. It's been crazy. Did you bring the stuff?"

"Of course, I brought it. I AM a good friend, unlike somebody . . . "

"C'mon, Cleo. I said I'm sorry. Where is it?"

"Right here, in my bag," Cleopatra said, clutching a fuchsia handbag the size of a pillow. "Ah, ah, ah, ah. I want something in return."

First, Britney threw her arms in the air and looked at the ceiling, then brought her hands down to her hair and began pulling it. "What do you want, my good friend?" Britney mocked Cleopatra's voice.

"Dude, you have to invite me to tomorrow's dinner. Sean Schrattenthaler is going to be there, and I'm sure he's going to sit at your dad's table. I soooo want to be there," Cleopatra pleaded, stopping for barely a second to catch her breath. "Did you get another Danika poster? And who's this old chick? Girl, I feel like I just stepped into the History Channel or something."

"The packet, Cleopatra."

"Oh, yeah, sorry. Here it is." Cleopatra pulled a plastic pharmacy bag from the fuchsia handbag that Britney quickly snatched from her hands.

"Mmm, you're supposed to do this early in the morning for best results. I can't wait that long," Britney said as she read the label. "Remove test kit from its foil wrap. Dip the stick into urine sample and wait three to five minutes. How do I get a urine sample?"

"Duhhhhhh. You just pee into the thing. Let me show you," Cleopatra said, seizing the pregnancy test stick from Britney's hands and thrusting it between her legs.

"Gross. Give me that." Britney grabbed the stick back and walked into her bathroom.

"Who's this Gertrude Ederle chick? Is she your grandma?" Cleopatra yelled at Britney.

"Not my grandma, silly," Britney yelled back, holding her pregnancy test under a stream of pee. "She swam across the English Channel when she was twenty-one."

"Boy, she could have used a fashion consultant, look at that bikini. She musta saved a lot of money on waxes, though," Cleopatra said.

Britney almost felt like laughing, but she was more worried than amused.

"You gotta stop collecting chicks, dude," Cleopatra continued yelling. "What you need is photos of Chace Crawford. God, he's such a hunk! Really, Brit, why would you surround yourself with all these tomboys when there are so many beautiful boys in the world? Mmmmmm, eye candy of the highest order."

Britney was in the bathroom washing her hands, but still could see her friend, wriggling like a worm. That's exactly what Cleopatra did every time she talked about boys: she squirmed, licked her lips, rubbed her belly and shoulders, as if embracing an imaginary boy tightly wrapped around her body. Provocative. Hilarious. A bit uncomfortable.

The stick was lying on the black marble counter, staring at Britney, making fun of her. Faint lines began to appear in the test area. How could she have been so stupid?

"Chace Crawford, mmmmhhhhh mmmm." Cleopatra was lying on Britney's bed, her eyes closed and conjuring up a silhouette with her hands. "I could bite those lips all day and every day."

"It's positive, Cleo," Britney said, standing under the doorframe, her right hand holding the offending stick.

"You're joking, right?" Cleopatra cried, bolting up from the bed. "Let me see. Where's the instructions?"

"Shush, Cleo." Britney put her left index finger to her lips, then stretched her right arm and pointed to the bed with her head. Cleopatra took the stick, stared at it, then at Britney, then looked for the instructions.

"Shiiii, dude. You're preggers. Dang!"

All Britney could manage to do was hang her head and cry. Again.

"Dude, you have to stop all this crying. You're starting to look like a toad. C'mon, give me a smile."

"Don't you get it, Cleo? I'm pregnant. My life's absolutely ruined. What am I gonna do?"

"Heck if I know. Oh man, I wouldn't want to be in your shoes."

"You jerk," Britney said, throwing an eyeliner at her friend, the easiest object to grab from her vanity.

"Hey, don't take it out on me!" Cleopatra yelled after dodging the projectile. "I'm not the one who made you a woman, sister."

Those words were heavier on Britney than any eyeliner. She collapsed on the floor, sobbing uncontrollably.

"C'mon, don't cry, Britney. Miguel Ángel won't abandon you, he'll marry you and you'll be together for the rest of your lives."

Her cries grew even louder.

"Isn't that what you want? To be with Miguel Ángel day and night? Jesus, I don't get it, Britney!"

"I'm so tired of nobody getting it," Britney spat out, getting up from the floor and stomping to the bathroom to get some tissue. "You should go home now, I want to be alone."

"Okay, fine, I'll go. But can you invite me to your dad's event tomorrow? I so need to hook up with Sean. Would you ask your dad, Britgirl, pretty please with a cherry on top?"

Britney folded her arms and stared at her friend for a few moments, then closed her eyes. Her parents would wake up any minute now, if not from Cleopatra's loud voice, from the sound of her beating heart that was beginning to resemble out-of-control drumming.

"I'm in no mood for parties, Cleopatra."

"I'll drive you to see your boyfriend anytime you'd like," her friend pleaded.

Going back to Salinas was the farthest thing from Britney's mind. But at some point, Miguel Ángel would have to find out he was going to be a father.

CHAPTER 8

There was one time when Miguel Ángel did "that stuff."

Beto had been pestering him for weeks to try the weed he'd scored from his homeboys. "It's the real thing, man, it just makes you soft and you forget about your mom, your brothers. Their troubles don't bother you no more, it's just like you're floating down the Salinas River, with nothing but the sky and the tall grasses to watch you. I'm telling you, it's da bomb."

Miguel Ángel had been training for two years with Coach and had already been subjected to his lectures: no drugs, no alcohol, or you don't come into the gym. For the first time in his life, Miguel Ángel found a refuge and didn't want to mess it up. Besides, he had an important fight coming, and he didn't want to screw that up either.

But he was awfully curious. Everyone in school was smoking, everyone teasing him for being a "virgin."

"Just try a little . . . If you don't like it, I won't bother you no more. I promise," Beto insisted.

They were both twelve at the time, and Beto's mom was still alive. Back then, everyone still knew him as Beto, but he was already taking a different path. He was smoking the green plant that slowed him down, made him look goofy. He was hanging out with Bronco and

Jarocho, two mean-looking neighborhood thugs. Every time Beto was with them, he became cocky, belligerent. He was coming home late and skipping school often, but there was nobody to keep tabs on him. Unless his parents came home early from the fields, he had no reason to return to his tiny apartment.

Both boys had been training with Coach for a while now, and the old man knew by then their strengths and weaknesses. Miguel Ángel, you have talent, Coach used to tell him, "Beto, you have talent, drive and a bad attitude. If you don't learn to control your bad temper, you're not gonna make it in this life."

Coach caught Beto one day trying to sell dope to the older boxers. It was his third offense. The first happened when he brought a gun to the gym in his equipment bag. Coach told him to leave and not come back for a week, and never to bring weapons into the gym. The second, he was in the back smoking weed with Bronco and Jarocho. That time, he was banned from the gym for a month. When the third offense came around, he was gone from the boxing program forever.

"I've given you too many chances, and I don't want you to take my boxers on the path you're going. I'm sorry, but I can't have you here anymore," the old man told him.

Beto was missing school a lot, but he would wait for Miguel Ángel after classes to walk back together.

"How's Miss Rodríguez?" he would ask.

"She's okay. She gave me a C on my test, I'm kind of mad at her. I re-wrote it three times, you know, and still she wasn't happy. I think it was because my stupid brother spilled his coffee on it and it made this big stain."

"Serious, man. If you try some *mota, todos tus pro - blemas se te olvidan*." Beto promised his friend all his problems would go away, as he kicked a pebble on the sidewalk.

Miguel Ángel had always found the strength to say no. He was scared of Coach. The boxers who didn't behave were gone from the gym, and he didn't want to leave.

But if he only smoked it once, maybe Coach wouldn't find out. He would never do it again. And what's the point of all that homework if your little brother is going to stain it anyway and you can't get anything better than a C?

"All right, I'll try it," Miguel Ángel had said, his voice resigned and excited at the same time.

The boys walked from the middle school to Closter Park, where they knew they could spot the cops if they were coming. When they reached the rec center, Beto pulled out a joint and matches from his pants pocket. He lit it and took a hit.

"Watch me do it," he said.

Miguel Ángel took a drag. "This is nasty, man," he said, half choking.

"It's always hard the first time, but you get used to it."

"I don't feel anything."

"Wait a few minutes, you will. Take another hit."

Miguel Ángel sucked in smoke once more, this time without coughing. He closed his eyes. Nothing.

Suddenly, it hit him. His eyes. They felt funny, as if they were growing. He had the eyes of a frog now.

"Are you feeling anything?" Beto asked him.

"I'm not sure. My eyes feel funny."

"Yeah, you're feeling it, all right. Want another?"

"Okay."

Miguel Ángel took another drag and then let himself fall backwards on the grass. Something was happening to him. It was as if time was slowing down, as if the world was going to pose for a picture and he could now appreciate its details. The green leaves of the oak trees were greener. The sky's blue darker, the black of the crows shinier. It was as if he was floating but inside of his own body. He pulled his left hand in front of his face to see if the skin was browner: Yep. With his right forefinger, he drew its contours: he had an "M" on his palm. That was a happy discovery, and soon Miguel Ángel found himself smiling, then giggling, then laughing. It was the most hilarious thing he had ever seen. Perhaps Beto had an "A" on his palm, for his real name, Alberto. Or a "B."

"Let me see your hand, Beto," the boy said, laughing.

"Ora sí ya estás moto, güey," his friend giggled.

"I'm not high, *güey*," Miguel Ángel giggled.

But Beto was right: the world became foggy under a cloud of pot. Your problems traveled far away to a place where they stopped hurting you. You could close your eyes, stop seeing them and never let them bother you again. It was better than floating.

He didn't know how many minutes went by before he realized he was supposed to be at the gym.

No worries, he'd get there. "What time is it, Beto?" the voice coming from his mouth said. "It's six o'clock."

"Man, Coach was waiting for me at five. He's gonna be mad."

Miguel Ángel slowly got up and lumbered toward home to change and get his equipment. When he finally managed to get to the gym, a cross-armed Coach was waiting for him. He eyed him intently, but didn't utter a word.

The stoned boxer had been attempting to punch the speed bag for barely five minutes when he realized he wasn't going to last an entire session. The little red ball was moving too fast for his tired arms and confused eyes.

"I'm going home, Coach," the boy told him. "I have lots of homework to do."

The old man unfolded one of his crossed arms to scratch his beard. He shook his head, clicked his tongue. "You've been here less than half an hour. You know the rules."

Run for an hour and train for two every day. Yeah, he knew. "Serious, Coach, I have lots of homework, plus a test I have to study for. And I don't feel good today."

"Get in the ring. You're gonna fight today," the man ordered him.

The fighters sparred three or four times a week, but Coach usually warned them at least a day in advance. The command gave Miguel Ángel a bad feeling.

"No, Coach, I have to go, really."

"The fight's not gonna take long. Either you fight or you leave the program right now and never come back."

Miguel Ángel looked at Coach half dazed, but even in his stupor he could see the old man was serious. Reluctantly, he made his way to the equipment cage, and fished for a pair of gloves and head gear. By the time he was suited up, all the boxers were around the ring, their eyes moving between Miguel Ángel and Coach, trying not to miss any moves.

Miguel Ángel got in the ring and pretty soon was joined by Alfredo Zamarripa. Ha, the Oaxacan dude. Miguel Ángel had kicked the little one's butt a dozen times at least. No sweat.

Alfredo began circling around Miguel Ángel slowly, his gloved fists close to his face, his head bobbing side to side. To Miguel Ángel, the boy looked as if his image was being projected, a movie he could see but not reach. Suddenly, Alfredo threw a power punch that landed square on Miguel Ángel's nose. The boxer began bleeding.

It was the first time Alfredo's gloves had reached him. Miguel Ángel turned around to look at Coach, his eyes now wide open. What was happening? He looked at his friends, his boxing mates witnessing his defeat. Were they smirking? He turned around to find Alfredo and teach him a lesson, but he was moving way too fast. By the time his gloves landed a punch, the motion picture was gone.

The bell signaled the end of the first round. Miguel Ángel went to his corner and pleaded with Ramos.

"I'm done, Coach. Let me go home."

"No, you're not. You're going to finish your three rounds. What's the matter with you? You're fighting like a girl," Coach said, a grin on his face as wide as a watermelon slice. He didn't even bother to check Miguel Ángel's nose.

"Shut up, man," the bloodied fighter replied. "Gimme that towel." He got cleaned up just in time for the second round.

Alfredo began circling him again, slowly at first and then faster. Miguel Ángel spun on his legs, but couldn't move as fast as his opponent. He threw a gentle jab that landed nowhere and almost made him lose his balance. Alfredo then threw a hook with his left arm that made him bite the canvas.

"Coach, I think we have to end this fight," Alfredo yelled at Coach.

"No, no, no, go back in there. Miguel Ángel, get up. You're not trying hard enough. Get up and throw some punches."

Miguel Ángel pulled himself up with the help of the ropes and turned to Alfredo. The bell rang, ending the second round.

"Serious, Coach, I can't do this no more. I'm tired."

"But why are you so tired? Didn't you sleep good last night?" the Coach asked him, his voice loaded with sarcasm.

"I did. I mean, no, my sister was up with the flu and didn't let me sleep well."

"Well, this will be good training for you anyway," he told him with a pat on the back. "Fighting is about conquering adversity. It'll make you a better fighter. Last round, go back in there. Give him hell, champ." Was his grin getting wider? Was coach mocking him?

This time, Alfredo didn't even try to circle him. He was just moving back and forth, taunting him, bobbing his head to evade his gloves. It was as if Alfredo were fighting in front of the mirror, analyzing his own posture and admiring his well-connected jabs. He threw a punch to Miguel Ángel's face that landed, and after that one he didn't try to reach him anymore. What's the fun in kicking a dead dog?

When the bell announced the end of the third round, Miguel Ángel dropped to the ground, spread-eagled. His stomach was gurgling.

"Get up," Coach thundered. "So you think you're so smart, huh?"

"You know, huh?" Miguel Ángel whispered.

"Of course, I know. You're high, you knucklehead. Your eyes are all red, you speak slowly, you move like a turtle. Who do you think you're gonna fool? Not me, man. *Más sabe el diablo por viejo que por diablo.* Remember?"

Coach loved those old Mexican sayings, and the one about the wise devil was his favorite.

"Listen, boy, you're not going to fool me. But here's something even more important than trying to see if you can." Coach grabbed him by the shoulders and looked into his eyes. "If you smoke pot, you don't affect me at all. Nothing happens to me. Nothing. I'm going to go home to my wife, my kids, have my dinner and watch Jet Li movies with not a worry in the world. I have my pension, I have my toys, and they're gonna be there even if you smoke yourself silly. You ain't affecting me.

"But look at you. You look like a sack of wet clothes. And you know why? Because of that crap you inhale. Those are chemicals that crawl into your brain like worms eating up a fruit. That stuff affects your mind and doesn't let you think. It's the same with alcohol, with meth, with any other stuff you put into your body. It's like a piggy bank, if you put dollar bills in there, you have savings, right? If you put caca in there, well, you are not getting any money out of that, are you? So you'll never come into my gym again when you're high, you hear me? And you're not doing me any favor. You'll be doing your-self a favor."

Miguel Ángel swore off "that stuff" forever.

CHAPTER 9

"**H**ey, are you up?" Tiffany asked Britney from the other side of the door.

Britney got up from her canopy bed and unlocked her room. She opened the door and gave Tiffany a long look before letting her in. The younger girl's face was red, her eyes puffy, her nose runny.

"You were crying," Tiffany said.

"Dad's never gonna approve of him. And that's the least of my problems," she muttered under her breath.

"Dump him. You have no choice," the matter-of-fact Tiffany said. "Besides, like Mom always says, we're too young to have serious relationships."

"If Manolo hadn't dumped you, you wouldn't have left him."

"That's different," Tiffany said. "Do you want to wait until Dad puts a bullet through your boyfriend's head?"

"He's not my boyfriend," Britney cried, diving into her bed, bursting into tears.

"Stop crying. They're going to hear you."

"They never hear anything. They're probably fighting."

Britney felt so small, so insignificant. She was not like Tiffany: slender, long dark hair and red lips. Tiffany could get any boy she wanted. After Manolo disappeared, and after two weeks of grieving, Tiffany went out with a class-mate their father approved of. His name was Roger Berlusconi, a distant relative of the Italian prime minister. She dumped him after a few dates and then she hooked up with the child of a famous movie star. He was more interested in his cars than in Tiffany, so she let him pass, too. The list grew long, but Tiffany had told her sister she would never be the one being dumped ever again.

And she would have never gotten pregnant.

Britney never felt pretty, and could never believe a boy liked her, even when Tiffany pointed out the guys that were obviously attracted to her. She was athletic and strong, but she was also on the heavy side. Surrounded by her skinny, athletic girlfriends, she felt like a whale. That was one of the attractions of hanging out with Cleopatra: she described herself as "bodaciously bodylicious" and never once seemed to mind her double-X figure. Britney, on the other hand, would break out into obnoxious pim-ples once in a while and that made her feel as if she were wearing a Frankenstein mask.

From the moment she met Miguel Ángel, she felt dif-ferently. She had just run a 400-meter race, and her face was flush. It was the Central Coast Section finals, and she was beating herself up for her second place finish, ahead of Saint Thomas but behind Salinas High.

"Hey, you're a strong runner," a voice from her back called out. "You beat that *creída* from Saint Thomas."

"What's *creída* mean?" Britney asked, suddenly more embarrassed by her lack of Spanish than intrigued by the confident athlete.

"Means that she's stuck-up, that she thinks she's all that. *Pesada*, you know?"

"Oh, yeah, *pesada*, of course," Britney said nodding, thinking that she had no idea what he was talking about. "You're a strong runner too." And a beautiful guy, in spite of the crooked nose, she thought.

From that day on, hardly a moment went by without Britney thinking of Miguel Ángel. There had been many times when she had been attracted to guys, but this was the first time she felt an immediate connection, almost like the chemical reactions she saw in her high school experiments. Was it the smile, the crooked nose or the short, spiky hair? More likely, it was his hazel eyes, a dark cave full of mysterious emotions that beckoned her inside.

As if he could read her attraction, Miguel Ángel kept pushing. "You have really pretty eyes. I hope you don't mind me saying it. I don't mean no disrespect."

"No, that's all right. You can't ever get enough compliments, I suppose."

"Well, you probably get tons, because you're beautiful."

No, I don't get as many compliments as my sister, she thought.

"Serious. You're the most beautiful girl I've ever met in my entire life."

Maybe it was the fact that she'd never heard anybody tell her that. Maybe it was the messenger: a tall, handsome young man, strong and self-assured, almost cocky. Maybe it was the intensity in his stare. He didn't take his eyes off her the entire time he was talking. He didn't flinch or look away, like many boys do. He stared into her eyes, and it was as if the entire world had disappeared. As if she were being sucked into a vortex.

"Wanna go to the movies or something?" he blurted out.

He was wearing an Alisal High jersey. Not the kind of boy her dad would approve of. Who cares? "Maybe sometime. Call me."

At first, Britney was hesitant about the whole affair, so she would just talk to him on the phone—the guy didn't even have a cell so they could text. There was a dreaminess about his voice that she found hard to resist. He was going to become a world boxing champion, earn lots of money and buy his mom a huge house right next to hers in Pebble Beach. Lots of important people would come see his fights, and millions would watch on TV. He spoke with conviction, and it was hard to resist such passion, such exuberance.

But resist she tried. He lived in the East Side, for crying out loud, home to all those wayward shopping carts, gang bangers and drive-by shootings. Still, he was so earnest, so sweet. He would read her poetry, bring her roses and look at her as if nothing else in the world existed. He would look into her eyes, draw the contours of her lips with his fingers, and she was trapped. She was like a moth inexorably attracted to the flickering flame—so comforted by the heat it doesn't realize it's about to get burned.

From the start, Tiffany frowned upon the entire affair. She had already survived the Manolo episode and wanted to save her little sister from embarrassment and pain. Britney didn't listen.

Once a week at least—behind Tiffany's back—Britney would ask Cleopatra to drive her to Salinas, where she would meet with Miguel Ángel at the movie theater or the shopping mall. She wanted to see him more often, but he was religious about training. Sometimes, Miguel Ángel borrowed a friend's car and he would drive to Pacific Grove. They would find a secluded spot behind some rocks to hug, kiss, make out.

On the sand, Miguel Ángel drew a heart with the initials M.A. & B "Por Vida." He'd seen those words tattooed on some of his friends' biceps.

"For life, right?" Britney asked.

"Yeah, for life," he said with conviction.

She got to see him once or twice a week. He would never meet her parents, go with them to their vacation house in Puerto Vallarta or visit their relatives in New Jersey. They would never go horseback riding or have Thanksgiving meals with their friends in the Carmel Highlands.

How was she going to raise a child on her own? Her dad was going to kill her.

"Tiffany, I'm pregnant," Britney blurted out, her words escaping like their dog running out of their house.

I'm pregnant. The words echoed in her head with a hollow sound, lonely metal balls bouncing inside a pinball machine. I'm pregnant. I'm pregnant. I'm pregnant.

CHAPTER 10

It was past eleven when Miguel Ángel finally returned to the apartment. He turned the knob slowly, trying not to make the noise that would wake his mother and siblings. Still, the lights came on as if activated by a motion sensor.

"*M'ijito, te estaba esperando,*" his mother told him, still wearing her inseparable wide-brimmed red hat. Even though she'd have to get up in less than five hours, she was waiting up to serve him dinner.

"Ma, I'm not hungry," he told the hunched, weathered woman. Food was the last thing on his mind.

Miguel Ángel loved coming home to the apartment he shared with his mother and five siblings—so cozy. He also despised it: one bedroom, one bathroom, a tiny kitchen with a cramped dining-living room area. The room was crowded with bunk beds, a refrigerator, a china cabinet full of stuffed animals and a dining table with four metal folding chairs around it. There wasn't even room for thinking. He tried to stay away as much as he could, but he had to sleep somewhere.

Juan Carlos was already on the top bunk and Victor Manuel on the bottom in the bed they shared. Ana Estela, Mari Carmen and Blanca Rosa were already in the bedroom they slept in with their mother. Once they stopped talking, the muffled sounds of the children's breathing was the only audible noise in the room.

There was no place for the smells of beans and fried *carnitas* to escape, and Miguel Ángel could not resist his mother's *frijoles con chorizo*. He walked near the stove, where she was making herself a taco.

"Okay, Mom. Make me one too."

The woman smiled, gave him a quick hug and grabbed a tortilla from the plastic bag near the range. Boy, she sure looked funny with that red hat on. Miguel Ángel had teased her to no end when she first began wearing it, saying, "It's the fields you're going to, not Sunday mass. There's no bullfights in California. Tío Chano's wedding was over a year ago." His mom had ignored him. She wore that hat as if she were María Félix, the famous Mexican movie star.

His mother placed a tortilla on the *comal* and waited until brown freckles appeared on its yellow face. She turned it over and waited until small air bubbles popped up. She pulled it off with her hand and tossed it into a basket. Then she took a spoonful of *frijoles con chorizo* and spread them on the tortilla.

"*¿No hay chile, Ma?*" Miguel Ángel asked.

"Yes, there's some in the fridge. *Ahí búscalo.*"

Miguel Ángel pulled out the chair slowly, trying not to make noise, and sat down to eat his tacos. Still standing, his mother watched him, her arms crossed in front of her ample bosom, her red hat casting a shadow over her eyes, giving her an air of mystery.

"*¿Cómo te fue hoy, m'ijito?*" the woman asked in a tired, hushed voice.

"My day was fine, Ma," he said, suddenly remembering the gun in his front pocket.

"*¿Cómo está tu* Coach?"

"Coach is fine," he said, chomping on the taco.

"*¿Y la escuela?*"

"School's all right, Ma," he responded curtly, wanting to change the subject. The last thing he wanted after his encounter with Beto was to be interrogated.

The tired woman dragged out a chair from under the table and sat facing her oldest son. Miguel Ángel could read her thoughts almost as if she were speaking out loud. Soon, he'd start working full-time and would help her pay the bills, and maybe they could afford a bigger apartment. She hung to that hope and looked at him the way a shipwrecked sailor looks at a floating beam coming her way.

"I'm going to sleep, Ma," Miguel Ángel said, suddenly getting up from his metal chair. "Gotta get up early tomorrow."

"Me too," the woman said, slowly pulling herself up and picking the plates up from the table.

In one of the cupboards Miguel Ángel found a brown paper bag and tucked it inside his front pocket. He then took off his sweats and carefully clambered over his sleeping brother, trying not to touch him. Before tucking himself in, he placed the gun inside the brown paper bag and looked for a spot under the mattress where he could hide it. He would find a better spot in the morning.

He tried to fall asleep, but the noise of his mother washing dishes and scrubbing pots was too loud to ignore. It surprised him that it didn't wake his brothers up.

He lay there, squished between his brother and the wall, staring at the wire mesh of the top bunk, thinking about his girlfriend, his coach and his best friend.

Britney was always beautiful, but tonight she looked extraordinary: her shiny hair, her glossy lips, her small, pointy ears. How did he ever get so lucky? He had been watching the blonde princess compete for weeks before he mustered the courage to ask her out. When she said "maybe," his heart began beating like an Aztec drum. Beto had warned him against going out with a rich girl. "They're so whiny, and they want to go out to fancy places and shit. You can't keep up, dude."

But so far, Britney had seemed fine with his gifts of poetry and flowers, their walks on the beach, the movies, their riding around in cars he borrowed. Boy, her body was so soft! Her lips so moist! Every time they were together, he felt as if his body would explode with happiness. It was getting harder and harder to leave her after their love encounters, but what was the alternative?

He wanted to tell Coach about his girl, but had not found the chance. They were always surrounded by other people, and he didn't want anyone else to know. It was his secret, something that belonged only to him and did not have to be shared with his five brothers and sisters.

Finding Coach and his boxing program had been almost a miracle to Miguel Ángel, one he didn't think could be replicated. So when Britney suggested looking for another program if they were kicked out of the Packing Shed, it almost felt like an insult. There was no way he could find another coach, another gym. Coach had become like a father. He drove him to his matches, he even raised money for last year's national championship in Minneapolis. Boy, it was the first time he got into an airplane, and he was so scared. Of course, he didn't tell Coach that, but the man figured it out anyway. "It'll be over soon, you'll see," Coach told him. As usual, he was right.

Coach had also been telling him he needed to stay away from Beto, but that was harder and harder to do. First of all, he was the only friend he had who owned a car, and he sure needed Beto's to see Britney, to be with her. Boy, he sure wished he'd never walked out of the front door tonight, when Beto saw him. If he had taken the back door with Coach, he wouldn't have to be dealing with a gun under his mattress.

Maybe his brothers wouldn't find it.

It was then that he heard the old, familiar voice. "What are you hiding under there?"

CHAPTER 11

Tiffany looked like a marble statue standing next to Britney's bed post, her white skin almost translucent.

"You're joking, right? There's no way you're pregnant, sis . . . "

"I wish I was joking, Tiff," Britney mumbled, her long hair a curtain that covered her face. "I wish this was a bad dream and I could just pinch myself and wake up."

"How could you be so stupid, so immature? Dad's going to kill you, that's what he's going to do when he finds out, you idiot." Gesturing wildly, like their own father when he was upset, she stomped to Britney's bed with a menacing look, as if she were ready to slap her little sister at any minute. To Britney's delicate stomach, Tiffany even began to smell like sulfur.

Britney couldn't hold on hard enough to stop the room from spinning. It was suddenly hotter, darker, and she would have fainted were it not from the bile that suddenly rose from her stomach and rushed into her mouth. She ran to her bathroom to empty the contents of the uncomfortable dinner she'd had with her family.

When she was done throwing up, she curled up in a ball and rested her cheek on the cold, white marble floor. She began bawling uncontrollably.

Tiffany stared at her for a few seconds, shook her head and knelt down to help her sister off the floor.

"Okay, that's enough. Come, let's get your face cleaned. Gosh, you stink."

In silence, Tiffany helped her sister wash her face, and as Britney felt the warm water on her face, her crying began to subside. By the time Tiffany took her back to her bed, Britney was exhausted, ready to fall sleep. Without even taking off her clothes, she crawled under the down covers ready to pass out.

She couldn't. Instead of drifting off, Britney opened her eyes, her fears and worries keeping her up. She looked at the stars on the ceiling, the ones her Dad made one of the gardeners glue for her. They usually comforted her before falling sleep, but there was no relief now: she was trapped in a labyrinth and could not find the way out.

Amelia could. She crossed the Pacific by herself, she wrote books, she would not take no for an answer. No doubt she would have known what to do in this situation. Better yet, she would have never gotten herself into this type of situation. Same thing for Danika; she was beautiful *and* bold. And Gertrude. What's the point of being a strong athlete if you can't even handle boys?

Now Tiffany was going to take charge, and Britney hated it. She hated her bossy big sister. That's why she ended up abandoning all her projects: she stopped tutoring at the library, she stopped coaching little league, she stopped volunteering at the pool. It was that or being with her sister nearly 24/7. Worst part, Tiffany was right about half of the time. She should have stayed away from Miguel Ángel, or get on the pill. Insist on a condom. It's not like she didn't know how babies are made. But Miguel Ángel said nothing would happen if they only did it once.

The problem was, it was more than once.

She pulled the covers over her head to shut off the light that was hurting her eyes. It was cold, even beneath the sheets. What on earth was she going to do?

"Get up, Britney, we have work to do," Tiffany's voice pierced the blankets. "C'mon, get up," she insisted, peeling the covers off her sister's head.

Tiffany had dropped her laptop on her bed and was holding a steaming cup of tea. Britney hadn't even noticed when her sister had left the room.

"Tiff, can't this wait till tomorrow? I'm exhausted. I need to sleep."

"Nah, nah, time's a-wasting. If you're going to have an abortion, you have to do it soon. How many weeks are you pregnant?"

"What?" Britney yelled, springing up like a jack-in-the-box. "An abortion? What makes you think I want to have an . . . " But as the words came out of her mouth, all sorts of scenarios began playing in her head, as if she were choosing from a movie menu she could play or skip. If she couldn't tell her dad about being pregnant, she couldn't have a baby. She could run away with Miguel Ángel and live with him. Or maybe she could move in with her relatives in New Jersey—on her father's side of the family—until the baby arrived and then give it up for adoption. Could she ask her mother for help?

An abortion. Britney rubbed her arms as if giving herself a hug, sunk her head and took a deep breath. The smell of chamomile soothed her nerves, and she took the cup Tiffany had placed in front of her.

"Isn't that supposed to be a sin?" she asked in a very low voice.

"Britney, please. We don't even go to church," Tiffany said, throwing her little sister an exasperated look, then getting on the bed and opening her laptop.

"Let's find out what we should do next."

As Tiffany began pounding on her keyboard, Britney began thinking about their Nonna and what a devout Catholic she had been. Nonna Bella had insisted the girls get baptized, in spite of their mother's objections—their mom was an avowed agnostic. Nonna Bella taught her how to pray at the chapel of St. Lucy in the Newark cathedral, a building so towering and so impressive it would always give young Britney the goose bumps.

Nonna Bella died way before the girls could receive their first communion, way before Britney was old enough to hear about boys, sex and how babies are made. But Nonna, the wrinkled, hunched, lovable Nonna, did insist on the sacredness of life and the duty to protect the needy and defenseless.

"Isn't all life sacred, Tiffany?" Britney said, sitting up to face her sister.

"Britney, think about it," Tiffany said, turning away from her keyboard and readying herself to deliver a lecture. "If you take it out right now, is it alive? Does it breathe and eat on its own? Then it's not a life. It's just bunched up tissue and blood, nothing else. It's like saying you killed a flower when you dug up a seed."

Tiffany returned to her laptop and continued with her typing. "Besides, that's what the birth control pill does: it prevents fertilized eggs from attaching to the uterus. It's like a mini-abortive. I've been on the pill for two years and I'm not going to hell." Britney sometimes wondered if she and her sister were even related. Tiffany was so self-assured, so intelligent, so entrepreneurial. And so annoying.

"How do you know you're pregnant? Did you take a test?" Tiffany asked without turning away from her computer.

"Of course, I took a test, sis, what do you take me for?"

"Let me see it. Mmm. Okay. How many weeks has it been since your last period?"

"Seven or eight," Britney said, her voice going back to the sound of a deflated balloon.

"Mmmmm. I've got it. I'll make you a potion. You'll be back to normal in no time."

No, please, not again. Not one of Tiffany's potions.

CHAPTER 12

Miguel Ángel lifted his head and saw her sitting at the foot of the bed, leaning against the post. She was smoking her favorite brand of cigarettes. The sweet smell of the burning rice paper reached him before the sound of her voice.

"Ita, you startled me again. I thought you were going to give up smoking."

"I'm too old to abandon this vice. Besides, what good would it do? I'm already dead."

"Well, yeah, but you're setting a bad example."

"Stop changing the subject and tell me what on earth you have under there," the skinny woman growled, slapping her whip on the bed covers.

"You can probably see for yourself. Why do you ask?"

"Because I want you to be honest with me. So tell me, what's that?"

"It's a gun, Ita. I'll give it back soon, okay?"

Miguel Ángel had seen Ita for the first time on his grandmother's altar many years back. Abuelita Leo kept a picture of her mother surrounded by flowers and candles on a small table by the stove. "This is your great-grandmother Ita," she'd told him. Every time he paid a visit, Abue Leo made him say hello to the young woman wearing two ammunition bands crossing her chest. Ita had fought in the Mexican Revolution along with the soldiers of Pancho Villa, and grandma told him she was one of the toughest women in the entire continent.

He was staring at the picture one time when he noticed the woman's lips began to move. "Hey, *muchacho*, bring me a *cigarrito*," he heard Ita whisper.

He shook his head. The picture was as still as ever, but he had clearly heard something. He turned around to discover his grandma in the bathroom, two rooms away from the kitchen.

"Hey, I'm talking to you," he heard the voice again, the lips of the *soldadera* moving once more. "There, Leo keeps the cigarettes in the first drawer to the right."

Miguel Ángel moved slowly toward the kitchen counter. He pulled the drawer open, found the pack of Faros and pulled one out. Hesitantly, he placed it on the altar in front of Ita's picture.

"*Ay, hijo*, please," the woman cried in exasperation.

Just then, Abue Leo was coming back to the kitchen.

"A cigarette for Mamá Ita? She shouldn't be smoking, you know? That's what killed her. At least light it up," Leo said, as she walked to the stove and placed the cigarette in the burner's flame.

Little by little, Ita became a permanent figure in Miguel Ángel's life. She would show up if he called her or when he least expected her, on his long runs by the mountains or before his bouts out of town. At some point, he stopped wondering whether she was real or a figment of his imagination. He'd gotten used to her antics, her sense of humor and her wild stories about the Mexican Revolution. And her outfits. Today, Ita was wearing pants and a riding whip.

Ita shook her head and mumbled something under her breath. She looked into the distance for a few seconds, took a drag off her cigarette and turned to Miguel Ángel again.

"How many times have I told you to be careful? Haven't I told you to stay away from Beto?"

"I know, I know, I know. But he looks for me. He doesn't have any friends."

"Yes, he has lots of friends. Those good for nothings who are nothing but trouble. I told you, you either help him get out or get away from him. Gang life brings nothing but grief."

"Gosh, you make it sound like gangs are these big monsters. They're not. They're just fools kicking it."

"If that was true, why do they end up in juvie or jail?"

Sometimes, Miguel Ángel just hated Ita. He couldn't argue with her. "Ita, he's a boy just like me. He don't mean no harm."

"Look at me, *muchacho*. If he don't mean no harm, why is he going around robbing stores? You think that those old ladies he assaults are not harmed? I know he's been your friend since you were little, but he's hurting a lot of people. And he'll end up hurting you if you don't watch out."

Ita reminded him a bit of Coach, but she was a much grouchier version. Sometimes she made him laugh, especially when she told stories of chasing the soldiers who spied on her when she took baths in the river. Lately, when she showed up unexpectedly, it was to give him a hard time about something he was already worried about.

He needed her, though. "Ita, have you seen Grandma Leo?"

"Yeah, she's still battling against being dead. It's taking her a lot longer than the average spirit. But I think she's coming around." She took another drag from her cigarette, which was getting smaller and smaller. "Speaking of having a hard time, your *mamá* here doesn't look so good. She's lost some weight."

Miguel Ángel tried to peek out of his bed to see his mother still banging pots in the kitchen.

"She looks okay to me," he said, shrugging his shoulders.

"Nah, she's very lonely. I overheard a conversation she had with Leo this morning."

"How can she be lonely with six children running around the house all day long?"

"You don't understand. It's different kind of company she needs. She needs a man."

"She has me. I'm a man."

"Ah, this *machito* thing starts so damned early. You're her son, not a man, man," she said with a playful snap of her whip to his head.

"Ita, can you tell Grandma I miss her?"

"Maybe you'll tell her yourself soon," Ita responded, turning her face away from him.

CHAPTER 13

Britney peeked at her sister from under the blankets and let her head plop back again on her pillow.

"It's late, sis. I want to get some sleep."

"In a minute. I gotta bring my book of potions, make you a tea, and then you'll sleep like a baby."

"No Tiffany, really, I need to sleep. Besides, what do you want to do with this tea of yours? What is it for?"

"Can you stop being such a moron? It's for you to get rid of the . . . the . . . the fetus. It's like the day-after pill, only after eight weeks."

"Tiffany, seriously," Britney said, now looking intently at her sister and getting up from under the covers. "I don't even know what I want to do."

"What? Do you want to have a baby at sixteen and tie your life forever to that loser? Better yet, want Dad to find out and put a bullet through his head? Get real, sis. I'm going to get the book."

Tiffany skipped out of the room, leaving her laptop and the cup of tea she'd made for Britney on the nightstand. Britney drew her hands to her face and rubbed her eyes until her face felt hot.

Truth was, Britney hadn't even had time to think about what to do. Tiffany was already taking charge without even consulting with her. What if she wanted to have the baby? Wouldn't it be great, like Anne Marie Palermo, to have a little one you could coo and cuddle at all hours of the day? Okay, Anne Marie didn't look that happy or motherly, but still.

Britney wasn't very sure she wanted to try one of Tiffany's potions again. Last time, her sister made her drink an awful concoction that was supposed to make Patrick Heinz fall in love with Emma White. How that was supposed to happen was a mystery to Britney, as the person who would drink the elixir was Emma, not Patrick. Emma was already in love with him. But there was no use in challenging Tiffany, so Britney had agreed to be the guinea pig. She drank the brew and spent two days hugging the toilet bowl, and she didn't fall in love with Patrick. Emma refused to drink the tea and decided to go after another boy instead.

Tiffany had been into magic potions and weird supernatural stuff ever since she walked in on her best friend's big sister making an incantation in the basement. Tiffany was nine and became fascinated. No, obsessed. The big girl showed Tiffany how to make incantations and potions and "to respect Mother Earth and Father Sky. To live in harmony with the universe." All those concepts sounded attractive to Britney but the truth was, her sister's occult experiments scared her.

Britney wanted to stay up, but her eyelids began to feel like lead. She tried to go to the bathroom to wash her face, but it was too cold outside the covers and she ran back under them. She propped herself up with her pillows, opened one of the books she kept on her nightstand and tried to concentrate on the words. But the letters began to jump out of the page and spin out of control, making no sense whatsoever. Slowly, she began to doze off.

"Try this," Tiffany told her, putting a steaming cup of tea under her nose.

"What is it?"

"It's just some herbs I found in the kitchen. Don't worry about it, it's the kind of stuff Nana uses to cook with. It won't kill you. C'mon, drink it."

Britney was pulling away from the cup her sister was offering, her red cheeks rapidly becoming pale. A love potion is one thing, but an eight-week-after tea . . . "I don't know, sis. I don't even know what I want to do," Britney said meekly.

"Drink this," her sister said, loud enough to give Britney a start but not so their parents could hear. The voice, the piercing green eyes and the determination of Tiffany's arm offering the tea, all conspired to push Britney to a road she did not want to take. People could die with these potions. What if she grew warts on her face, arms and legs? She could become paralyzed.

"Drink it," Tiffany insisted.

Britney stretched out her hand and grabbed the cup. Under her sister's stare, Britney drank the concoction that tasted of mint and garlic. She was sure the light brown brew, like weak coffee without milk, had a ton of other ingredients in it, but she was afraid to ask.

Her stomach rumbled once the liquid hit bottom, and Britney was beginning to feel as if she had to throw up again. The nausea passed quickly, and Tiffany gave her a satisfied nod.

"Everything will be all right in the morning," she said, her voice spilling contentment. "Have a good night's sleep, sis."

CHAPTER 14

Miguel Ángel didn't realize how late it was when he fell asleep. When he woke up a few hours later, he heard the clanging of the pots, the sounds of his mother preparing herself some lunch before leaving for the fields.

It was as though she never went to bed.

The crow of a rooster woke him up again, but this time he didn't close his eyes. It wasn't as dark outside as when his mother had left. Soon he would have to get ready for school.

It was his favorite time of the day. Everyone was still sleeping, so he could read for a few minutes in peace.

He reached under his bed for his backpack and pulled out the book he'd been reading for a while. The moments of silence in the apartment were so brief, it was hard to sneak a page or two here and there. He wasn't in any hurry to finish. Like the silences, he liked to make his books last.

Soon Cassius started coming to Martin's gym on South Fourth Street, and after six weeks of learning the rudiments of boxing, he fought his first bout. The opponent was another stripling, named Ronnie O'Keefe. Each boy weighed eighty-nine pounds. The bout lasted three rounds, each round a minute long. The boys wore big forty-ounce gloves and flailed away at each other until they both had headaches. Cassius got in a few more blows and was awarded a split decision. He greeted the announcement by shouting to all that he would soon be "the greatest of all time."

He stopped. Reading had never been easy, but after getting the hang of it, few things gave him more pleasure. That stopped when he met Britney. Now, he could barely concentrate, and as soon as he picked up a book—even if it was for homework—the first thing he did was start thinking about his Pebble Beach Princess: her lips, her hair, her breasts. Her skin felt like rose petals—not like the callous hands of his mother or the dry cheeks of his siblings. Her smell made him think of those movie stars in commercials, where the wind blows their hair and their white skirts. Just thinking of her made Miguel Ángel sweat.

Britney was different, and it was not just the color of her skin or hair. It was the way she walked, tossed her hair, smiled. None of the girls he'd met, none of the women that surrounded him—his mother, sisters, teachers—had that confidence, that presence.

He took a deep breath and picked up the book again.

At first, Cassius "didn't know a left hook from a kick in the ass," Martin said later, but as he grew bigger and stronger, as he gained a sense of the ring, he began to develop the style of the fighting that would infuriate purists. Much like Sugar Ray Robinson, Clay carried his hands low, snaked out his left jab, and circled the ring on his toes. His greatest defense was his quickness, his uncanny ability to gauge an opponent's punch and lean just far enough away from it to avoid getting hit—and then strike back. Clay had remarkable eyes. They seemed never to close, never to blink, never to tip off an opponent. They were eyes that took everything in. And the instant his eyes registered an opening, an opportunity for mayhem, his hands reacted in kind.

Once, Britney confessed to feeling insecure around her sister, her best friend, her mother. How can somebody so smart and so beautiful not be confident? And so compassionate. Britney had told him she wanted to be a physical education teacher, or open a gym for disadvantaged kids. He had seen her around the little kids who attended their meets, how she was always trying to play with them.

She loved sports. What more could a guy need from a girl?

All his friends at the Packing Shed wanted to grow up to be like Oscar de la Hoya and Julio César Chávez, and wave the Mexican flag when they were hoisted in victory at Cesar's Palace. They were also Miguel Ángel's heroes, until he found Muhammad Ali. Coach had lent him a copy of *The Greatest*, and since then, he'd devoured anything he could find about the boxing legend. Britney gave him a poster she found on the Internet of Ali's win against Liston, which he hung on the wall inside his bunk bed. It made it easier to write essays. When teachers allowed him to write about the champ, he could just draw on the books in the library and articles pulled from the

Internet. That was the type of assignment he enjoyed the most.

Ten minutes into his reading, Víctor Manuel turned around on the bed and asked half asleep, "What time is it?"

"It's seven fifteen. You need to get up, it's getting late."

The rickety sounds of the upper bunk announced another riser.

"Miguel Ángel, can you make me something to eat? I want to eat before I go to school."

"If you're gonna make something to eat for Juan Carlos, I wanna eat too," Blanca Rosa yelled out from the bedroom.

"*¿Me haces mi leche?*" María del Carmen, the youngest, wanted her milk.

"Wait guys, I can't do everything at once," Miguel Ángel yelled, the magic of his Ali moment evaporating like the morning fog. "I'm going, I'm going, I'm just waking up myself."

Miguel Ángel crawled out of the bed and returned the book to his backpack. He furtively glanced at the place where the gun was stashed before heading for the fridge. He opened the fridge door and surveyed its nearly empty shelves.

"I'm going to bring your milk," he told the little one. "But there's only two tortillas left and almost no frijoles. I can make you a taco, Juan Carlos, and leave the other one for Blanca Rosa."

"What about me?" asked Víctor Manuel, still under the covers.

"And you what? You didn't say you wanted breakfast."

"But I'm hungry. I'm always hungry. My stomach makes lots of noise all day long, and my friends just giggle and make fun of me."

"Just get to school early and you can have breakfast," Miguel Ángel said, exasperated.

Blanca Rosa walked into the room brushing her long hair.

"That's all right, Miguel Ángel. Give the taco to Víctor. I'll wait for lunch at school."

"We can all have coffee. I'll make a pot right now."

When Coach found out Miguel Ángel and his brothers and sisters drank coffee, he almost passed out. "Are you crazy? You can't be giving your brothers coffee. It's a drug."

"You drink what you have," Miguel Ángel told him.

Ana Estela, the only member of the family who took morning showers, walked into the kitchen all dressed up and ready to dress everybody else.

"Mari Carmen, hurry, it's getting late. Juan Carlos, Blanca, are you all ready?"

Miguel Ángel was the oldest, but Ana Estela was the bossiest. She was only sixteen, but she treated everyone like she was their mom.

Miguel Ángel and Ana Estela had the same dad, but he left them when they were little. Their mother remarried, and Blanca Rosa was born soon afterward. When Blanca Rosa was little, Ana Estela helped changing diapers and rocking her to sleep. She also helped with Juan Carlos, Víctor Manuel and Mari Carmen. Their fathers, too, had left.

While Miguel Ángel helped a little getting his brothers and sisters ready for school in the morning, when they all came back from school and were tired, hungry and had homework to do, Miguel Ángel couldn't stay far enough away.

Ana Estela would walk Juan Carlos, Víctor Manuel and Mari Carmen to the nearby elementary school, and then she would walk to her own high school. Miguel Ángel would walk Blanca Rosa and Juan Carlos to the middle school, which was a bit farther, and then he would head to school himself. They all walked home by themselves in the afternoon, except for Mari Carmen, who was delivered to the gym or the house by one of the after-school volunteers.

Ana Estela and Miguel Ángel would sometimes confide in each other how angry it made them that their mother had so many babies. If it'd only been the two of them, they'd say, we wouldn't need so many bunk beds. We wouldn't need to walk them all to school, feed them in the morning or bathe them in the evening. Ana Estela could join the soccer team and Miguel Ángel would have more time to read before starting his day.

Then they turned to Mari Carmen and her soft, pudgy arms, and they would feel horribly guilty.

Miguel Ángel usually tried to finish his homework at school before going to the gym, but one day, a particularly hectic one, he had to come home to finish an essay about the founding fathers. Reading he liked, but writing was a different animal. After two hours at the table, where his brothers were competing with him for a space and his mother was trying to chop some vegetables, he was almost done. Mari Carmen came near Miguel Ángel to ask for a hug. She tripped, spilling her chocolate milk on his essay.

"Mom, look what she did," he exploded. "She's ruined my essay."

"I'm sorry, *m'ijo*," said their mother, running from the stove with a rag in her hand, immediately tackling the catastrophe.

"What's the point of all this? I don't even have a place to do my homework," Miguel Ángel moaned. "Why in hell did you have to have so many children?"

The force of his mother's hand across his cheek almost made him lose his balance.

"Don't talk to me that way," she said. "Your brothers and sisters are children of God, just like you are. Have some respect."

But if God sent children, and God was supposed to be all-powerful, how come He never sent anything to feed them? Miguel Ángel thought as he placed his cool hand on his glowing cheek.

CHAPTER 15

"**M**iss Britney, it's time to get up," said Rosa, the girls' nanny, as she drew open the curtains. "You're going to be late for school."

The sun flooded Britney's bedroom, forcing the girl to find refuge under the darkness of her covers. Darned Indian summers. Where was the fog when she needed it? The concoction Tiffany gave her upset her stomach, so she couldn't really sleep. She didn't want to get up and face the world either. Maybe if she stayed under the down comforter long enough, it would all go away.

"Miss Britney, Miss Tiffany is going to be mad if you're not ready when she is," Rosa insisted, pulling the covers from the girl's head.

"Let me sleep, Rosa. I'm not feeling well," the girl replied, not entirely lying.

"*¿Qué tienes?*" the woman said, a frown of worry on her forehead. Every time she needed to baby her *niñas*, she reverted to her first language, her mother tongue. "Let me see, do you have a fever?"

"No, no. It's okay. I think I ate something bad last night. I have a stomach ache."

"Let me go downstairs to fix you a tea," the woman said, rushing out to the kitchen.

No, please, not another tea. Maybe she should tell Rosa of her dilemma. The gray-haired Mexican woman always seemed more attuned to her problems than her mother, who was always busy with charity fundraisers and tennis tournaments. But if she told Rosa and her mother found out, she would throw a fit.

Britney threw the comforter away from her face. The alarm clock on her nightstand read 6:17. Yeah, she felt a little funny in the stomach, but nothing that would warrant staying home. She should get dressed, she decided. As soon as Britney stood up, she felt a rush of vile run up her throat, the unmistakable sign something even more bitter was on its way.

When she was finally done spewing and convulsing, Britney sat by the toilet bowl again and began crying. Tiffany's potion better provoke more than just another round of vomiting.

Slowly, she wiped her tears and walked into the shower. What was she thinking, going all the way with Miguel Ángel with no protection, no birth control? She turned on the faucets and let the torrent of water wash away the fright in her. What was she going to do? If her father found out, he'd killed her. If she told her mother, she for sure would tell him. For some reason, she didn't have much faith in Tiffany's brew solving her dilemma.

The more Britney thought about it, the more she realized her sister was right. She had to end her pregnancy.

She shook her head, trying to think of something else. After she finished, she opened the shower door and reached for her towel in the usual place. Rosa was there, holding it for her.

"I brought you your tea, *m'ija*," the woman said.

"Thanks, Rosa," Britney said. "Leave it on my vanity. I'll drink it while I get dressed."

After getting dry, Britney walked into her closet to find what to wear, one towel wrapped around her body and another around her head.

"*M'ija*, are you okay?" asked Rosa. "You seem upset or something. What's wrong?"

"It's nothing, Rosa! Okay?" the girl yelled, immediately feeling bad about the outburst. She never screamed at anybody, much less at Rosa.

"I'm sorry, Nana. I didn't mean to yell."

She stood in the middle of her room, looking at the woman wearing a pink dress and white apron who often substituted for her own mother. She looked so small and frail standing at the foot of her canopy bed. The guilt almost made her say something. Maybe her old nanny had some Mexican potion she could give her, one of those teas that always fixed her ailments, one that would really work. But it was probably not a good idea to say anything just yet.

"It's nothing, Nana, really," the girl said softly. "I'm just worried about some exams coming up, and I still have this science project to finish. You know I don't like science very much."

"Are you still seeing that boy, Miguel Ángel?" the woman asked, trying to help Britney dry her hair.

"Yes, Nana, but that has nothing to do with this," she said, softly taking the woman's hands away from her. She put her right arm on Rosa's shoulder to lead her toward the bed. "You shouldn't be mentioning his name in the house. What if Mom hears you?"

The old woman lowered her head.

"I'm sorry, Miss Britney. I just want to help," Rosa said, biting her lip.

The girl looked at her maid's shaky hands. There had been many occasions in which she'd been mean to her and seldom did she feel remorse. Why did she feel bad for her this time? She didn't even do anything on purpose.

"It's okay, Nana. Is breakfast ready? Let me get dressed before Tiffany comes in here screaming."

Rosa left the room, and Britney walked into her closet, immediately forgetting about the old woman. Getting dressed was always the most stressful part of the day. She never felt like she had anything appropriate to wear. The red pants were too slutty, the black dress too heavy for a sunny day like today, she'd been using the gauchos too often—yeah, those were her favorite. Maybe if she wore them with a different blouse, nobody would notice she'd worn them already on Monday. She put them on, found a pink blouse with a V-neck and put on black sandals.

She walked out of the closet to admire her full-length figure. She turned around. This blouse always made her chest look too flat, but this time, her breasts looked bigger. Wow, they were already getting bigger. Her stomach looked as flat as ever, though. She wondered how long she'd be able to hide her sin.

God, if she'd only taken the frigging pill. Tiffany had given her a prescription she was using. But she didn't even have a boyfriend—pregnancy only happens to the most popular girls, to those who are not paying attention, right? She was paying attention, wasn't she?

Well, she had always wished her boobs were rounder, bigger, like Cleopatra's. But this wasn't what she had in mind.

In the closet, she fished for different clothes. She pulled out a paisley dress that made her breasts look small, but also narrowed her hips. She hated her hips. She took off that dress and looked for her favorite black cashmere slacks. Those would go well with a baby blue knit blouse and black pumps.

The ensemble made her look like she was going to work for her dad's law firm. She couldn't decide if she felt like a lawyer today or just a tramp that let her boyfriend go past first base and hit a homerun.

Tiffany peeked into her room. "How you feeling? Did the tea work?"

"I've been puking all morning, does that count?"

"Mmmmm, don't know. Gotta look it up. But let's go, we're gonna be late for school," she said, running out again.

Half an hour later, Britney rushed into the kitchen. She found her parents having breakfast and reading the newspaper. She surveyed the room in search of her sister.

"Where's Tiffany?" she said anxiously. Often, Tiffany would take off without her, leaving her at the mercy of their parents. Oh God, not today.

"She said she had an exam at eight that she didn't want to miss. I'll drive you," her mother said.

Britney sat down in her usual spot at the kitchen table. She had taken so long that her eggs got cold. The smell made her nauseous, so she just pushed them away.

Britney's mother noticed the gesture and looked at her quizzically. She lowered her copy of the local newspaper and looked at her daughter and her untouched mushroom and spinach omelet.

"That's your favorite breakfast. You're acting a bit odd lately," she probed. "Is everything okay?"

The question took Britney by surprise. Mrs. Scozzari was the type of woman who made heads turn entering a room: slender, poised, her shoulder-length blonde hair always perfectly styled, her manicure and make-up impeccable. She received so much attention that it was hard for Britney to tell if she ever paid any attention. Could she tell she was pregnant?

"It's nothing, Mom," she said, swallowing hard. "I have exams coming up and I'm a bit nervous."

Her mother fixed her gaze intently on Britney as if trying to decide whether she could trust the answer. After a few, long seconds, she returned to her reading.

"Britney, I want you to come with me to a reception I have to attend tonight," her dad told her, speaking from behind the sports section. "It's at the Inn at seven, so I'll pick you up at six-thirty."

The reception. Britney had forgotten all about the dinner Cleopatra wanted to attend. The last thing Britney wanted to do was be near her dad's business partners, but Cleopatra would not stop hounding her if she found out about the invitation. Like she needed another dilemma.

"But, Dad, I have lots of homework, and I'm really behind in my science project," she protested. Besides, I need to tell Miguel Ángel something important, she thought.

"Sweetie, please go with your dad," her mother said, lowering once again the newspaper. "I was going to, but I have a special board meeting I can't miss."

"Can I bring Cleopatra along, then?" Britney said, hiding her crossed fingers under the table."

Her father did not speak for about two minutes while concentrating on his newspaper. "Yet another shooting in Salinas. Those people are like animals over there. Somebody should bring the National Guard to set them straight," he said, folding the paper and getting up from his chair.

"Be home at six o'clock sharp," her dad said, finally addressing his daughter. "Wear something nice. And if Cleopatra starts chasing after one of my clients, I'll have her kicked out."

CHAPTER 16

Another one of Coach's rules: If you want to be a champion, you have to run every day. Make the foggy mornings and windy afternoons your homeboys.

When Miguel Ángel first started training at the Packing Shed, becoming a prizefighter was the farthest thing from his mind. He just liked punching the bag and having a place to go after school. He was still trying to get the hang of the speed bag when he overheard Coach giving a speech to a ten-year-old who had been jumping rope like a lunatic. Bobby would go up and down frantically like a loose piston on an engine for about a minute and then lie on the cold cement floor for ten minutes to catch his breath.

"I'm only going to train you if you become serious about this," Coach was telling pudgy Bobby. "This is a serious commitment, and you're only gonna be good if you put your mind to it. You have to do what I tell you to, even if you think it's dumb. You have to run every day, at least an hour, and then you have to train another two. You have to build your lung capacity, you know. There's not time for friends or fooling around."

Miguel Ángel replayed Coach's monologue so many times in his head it began to hurt. Eventually, he became convinced the speech was for him. Miguel Ángel would become a boxer. He started having dreams that he ran around his neighborhood, past the mothers with their strollers and the *paleteros* thrusting his fists in the air against an invisible contender. He floated in class and saw himself not doodling in his math notebook, but training to take on renowned adversaries. Miguel Ángel Moreda defeats the Russian champ.

The tall, blonde brute Miguel Ángel defeated over and over in his dreams was hanging from the ropes one day, just at the moment Miguel Ángel was walking into his apartment. But what he saw in the corner wasn't a boxer; it was his mother, cowering between the stove and the kitchen sink. Eduardo, the only father he'd ever known, was holding his belt in his right hand, the silver "Jalisco" buckle scratching the linoleum. Both turned to look at Miguel Ángel, and Eduardo almost immediately started spitting fire.

"What are you doing here? Don't you have homework to do at school or something? Aren't you supposed to go to the gym?"

"But, but, but . . . I'm hungry. I wanted to see if there was a snack, or something," Miguel Ángel managed to say.

"Go buy yourself a taco, or whatever, and leave me and your mother alone. Can't you see we're busy?" the rabid man ordered, throwing a bunch of coins in his direction.

Miguel Ángel stood silently, moving his gaze from the coins on the floor to his mother in the corner to his stepfather standing like a cowboy with a horsewhip in his hand, ready to make the cattle fall in line. His mother was looking at him with a plea in her eyes.

"*M'ijito*, go buy yourself some sweet bread, *corazón*," his mother urged him. "Dinner will be ready when you're done with training."

The boy bent down to pick up the six pennies, three dimes and two Mexican pesos. He put them in his pocket and shuffled toward the door. He had reached the first floor of the apartment building when he heard a thud, the clatter of pots and pans falling and his mother's plea.

"Please, Eduardo, leave me alone, *por Dios!*"

Miguel Ángel took off running and didn't stop until he'd reached the Packing Shed. Coach was showing one of the boxers how to punch the heavy bag.

"What's wrong with you? Why are you crying?" the old man asked him.

"I got something stuck in my eye," Miguel Ángel said, wiping his face with the bottom of his T-shirt. "Will you train me, Coach? Will you make me a champ?"

Coach seemed surprised at first, but soon he was just as convinced as Miguel Ángel that the boy would be the next big name on Las Vegas marquees.

So Miguel Ángel started jogging. At first, Coach would drive him at 5 a.m. to the Salinas municipal airport, where he would see the white contractors' buses drive out to the fields as he ran outside the chain-link fence for about an hour. Later he switched to running around the track of his middle school. When he joined the track team at his high school, he began running long distances.

That's how he discovered the Gabilan Mountains, the green and gold sentinels that guarded his neighborhood. Reaching them had never crossed his mind, even though they looked close and were even closer than he'd imagined. One day in mid-summer, as he peered at them from a distance, he felt the mountains reveal their secrets.

"You will be a champion," they whispered, and Miguel Ángel ran ten times faster.

They were his "jolly mountains," and just like Jody in Steinbeck's *The Red Pony,* he felt safe in them. Three days a week, after classes were done, Miguel Ángel would leave his books in his locker, his worries in his backpack and take off for the hills. Forget about the Packing Shed, he told himself. It will still be here when you come back from your run.

After stretching, he would begin a gentle jog along Williams Road, the most boring part of the three-mile stretch. Once the strawberry fields were behind him, there were no rows to count, no guessing how many pickers had just arrived from Río Colorado, Oaxaca or El Salvador. Now it was just a high stucco wall keeping the new mansions away from the reality of working-class Salinas.

He was past the improbable wall in a flash. What followed next was a stretch of unfriendly road, a one-lane thoroughfare flanked by a weed-covered ditch, and once again rows of strawberry and lettuce on his right side as far as the eye could see. It was the most perilous part of the journey. One time, he took a wrong step and twisted his ankle, a painful and humiliating experience he didn't want to repeat. Cars speeding by left behind columns of dust and fumes, and their pungent odor became indistinguishable from the sweet scent of strawberries.

From there until he reached Old Stage Road, he would be facing the mountains, his ultimate destination. From the corner of his eyes, he would look at the wire fence he was trotting by and the plastic sheets covering the greenhouses flapping in the wind. Depending on the time of day or season, he would see workers thinning the rows of lettuce or bent over picking strawberries, looking like busy ants carrying their load back and forth to their refuge. But it was the hills he wanted to take in: their round peaks, their gentle slopes, their stark beauty.

A little over a mile into his jog, he was at the edge of paradise. He crossed Old Stage Road and took a break at a red iron gate to contemplate the Gabilans. No wonder Jody named his pony after them, "They were the grandest and prettiest things he knew." Every time Miguel Ángel reached this point, he just stood there, fists on his hips, breathing deeply, looking at the titans covered in wilting grass.

There were thousands, perhaps millions of students who read Steinbeck and his descriptions of Monterey County, but only a few who could actually breath its air, touch its mountains. Miguel Ángel was one of them, and that made him feel special.

Many times, he felt tempted to jump the fence on Williams Road and continue running into those hills, get lost into their sinuous ups and downs. He'd feel the sweat running down his temples; he'd wipe it with the back of his hand, but he wouldn't be hot. The cool air of the mountains would keep him refreshed. He'd be near the carefree cows and their young calves, always at a safe distance from the generous brutes. He would then see a *ga - vilán*, a sparrow hawk, glide above its namesake mountains and dive in search of a prey. At the highest point of his jog, he would let himself fall flat on the grass and look up at the sky, contemplating the ocean fog coming into the valley. Then he would run back to the road, to the sound and fumes of the speeding cars.

Out on the lonely county road, Miguel Ángel would see the path he was to follow as clearly as he saw the clouds in the sky. He would use his powerful left punch to defeat all his rivals, tall and short, skinny and stocky, black and Mexican. He would enter the rings in the fancy Las Vegas hotels dressed as an Aztec emperor, wearing a headdress like the one the Europeans had stolen from this continent. The loudspeakers would be playing "*Soy el jefe de jefes*," a *corrido* ballad in honor of a mean, powerful guy. And when he stepped onto the stage, the crowd would go wild, chanting his boxing nickname: Chato, Chato, Chato, Chato, Chato, Chato. The chants would grow even wilder after the eighth round, when his rival fell to the ground for the third time and couldn't get up again. Nine, eight, seven, six, five, four, three, two, one. Miguel Ángel would jump up and down and Coach would come and embrace him. His cut men and the assistant coaches on his team would all jump up and down in excitement. He would turn around and wave at his mother and Britney sitting in the first row and would blow kisses at them.

Nah, maybe that wouldn't be cool.

With all the money he would earn, he would buy a house for his mother, a big one in the neighborhood where Britney lived, overlooking Monterey Bay and the green golf courses. His Mediterranean mansion would have seven rooms, one for each of his brothers and sisters and one for his mom. He would hire a maid to do all the work, a chauffeur to drive them to school and a gardener to trim the grass and prune the roses. He would take his mom to Mexico in a limousine, and everyone in the old *rancho* would know how successful the son of Lupita had become.

Under the lonely, watchful eyes of the Gabilans, Miguel Ángel became a champion boxer, the meanest fighter the world had ever known. The mountains, like

Coach and his mother and Britney, knew what he was capable of.

☙☙☙

The horn of a pick-up truck roaring past him brought him back to the reality of Old Stage Road. He cursed at the mad driver without gesturing. You never knew what these crazy people were into. They could be just as crazy as Beto.

"Yeah, you never know what these people are into," the voice by the fence said. Miguel Ángel turned around and saw Ita, this time smoking a thick, dark cigar.

"Ita, you sure are popping up everywhere these days," the boy said, a bit exasperated.

"*Caramba, muchacho.* First you complain I haven't been around enough. Now you say I'm popping up everywhere. What's the deal?"

"Sorry, Ita, I'm just worried."

"Don't mind me. Just go on back home, your mother's waiting for you," she said, puffing smoke in his face.

"Mom doesn't come home until late tonight, remember?"

"Oh, shush, just go home now, *ándale*."

"What's that over there? Let me see."

Miguel Ángel took a few steps and recognized the slumped body of a man. He got closer and saw a pool of blood trickling from the back of his head. He was wearing a red shirt and blue denim pants.

"*Mira*, I'm telling you to go now," Ita urged him. "Listen to me, *por Dios*. You're gonna get in trouble."

Miguel Ángel wasn't listening anymore. He stood frozen, spellbound. The only dead people he'd seen were already dressed up inside a casket. But maybe this guy wasn't dead, just wounded and needed help. He wondered what he should do. Call the police? An ambulance? Check his pulse, like they do in the movies? He knelt and put his hand on the guy's arm. It wasn't very cold. He looked at his pants and thought he probably had a driver's license or something that could tell him who he was. He patted the pockets and found a wallet. Raúl Versamin. He was twenty-seven. The name didn't ring a bell. Maybe he should turn him around to see his face. Maybe he would recognize him.

"Miguel Ángel, *por Dios*, get out of here," Ita begged.

But the boxer was stunned and couldn't even pay attention to his great-grandmother. This guy was a total goner. Deader than Tupac. This is what Miguel Ángel had been trying to tell Beto: It looked so cool to be in a gang, to be a Norteño or a Sureño and carry a red bandana and a gun and burst into a liquor store and scare the shit out of everybody. In reality, the best that bangers could hope for was to end up dead by the side of the road. Or in jail, facing life in prison for murder. That was no way to live life.

He left the wallet on the ground and pushed the body by the shoulder, using little force at first as if trying not to wake him. When the body resisted, Miguel Ángel pushed harder, managing to twist the man so the torso would face up while the lower body was still facing the ground.

When he saw the face, he took a step back.

Jarocho. Beto's homeboy, the guy who got him into gangs and guns.

Shit, Ita's right. I have to get out of here.

And just as he was getting up, he heard the sound of tires gnashing little pebbles on the unpaved shoulder, doors slamming open and triggers clicking into place.

"Put your hands up where we can see them," a loudspeaker blared behind Miguel Ángel's back.

CHAPTER 17

When Britney's father said "wear something nice," he usually meant "wear something black." That should have reduced Britney's options, but certainly didn't help. After half an hour of dressing and undressing, and several dresses spread across her bedroom floor, she still had not decided what to wear.

Tiffany was lying on Britney's bed, still typing madly on her computer.

"Sis, you're amazing. All you have to do is pick a black dress."

"But it has to be the right dress, and the fabric of that one's too thin," she moped. "That one is too short, and that one doesn't have a wide skirt. I want to wear something with a wide skirt. Do you have something I can borrow?"

"Yeah, you can borrow one of my three dresses right there," Tiffany said, pointing at the floor. "You can have the thin one, the tight one or the short one."

"I'm the one who should be mad at you for leaving me behind this morning. Mom was just staring at my breasts. What if the dress is too tight and I show a belly?"

Tiffany rolled her eyes. "I know what to do next. We need to go to a clinic where they'll make sure you're really pregnant, and then they'll schedule you for a 'procedure,'" Tiffany said, making air quotes. She could tell Britney was now thinking again about her pregnancy.

"Are you sure that's the way to go?" Britney asked, twisting her mouth, her shoulders drooping and her head tilting sideways.

"Of course, I'm sure, there's no other way."

"What about adoption?" Britney asked.

"What, you want Dad to see you inflate like a balloon? What d'ya think he's gonna do, give you a prize? C'mon, Britney."

Tiffany returned to her keyboard and didn't speak for a few minutes. Britney drew a big sigh while contemplating the sea of black fabric lying at her feet.

"Have you told Miguel Ángel yet?" Tiffany asked without lifting her head.

"No, I couldn't find him. He wasn't home when I called."

Actually, Britney had been calling Miguel Ángel at least every fifteen minutes since she couldn't locate him in the afternoon. He usually was there around four to get his gear, but he hadn't been home since he left for school in the morning, his sister said. She should have heard from him by now. If only he had a cell phone, like the rest of the world.

There was a knock on the door.

"Britney, are you ready yet? We're leaving in fifteen minutes."

"Yes, Dad. I'm coming."

The black dress Britney opted for had spaghetti straps, was fitted on the torso and had an A-line skirt. Not as ample as Britney wanted, but the only thing resembling her true wish. Luckily, there was no belly yet.

The drive between their home and the Inn at Spanish Bay took less than two minutes. In the daytime, it was a short walk on trails among the forest, but it was getting dark and neither Britney nor her dad wanted to risk getting their shoes muddy.

"You look nice, Britney. How's school?"

"Fine. I didn't finish my homework, though."

"Well, if you took less time changing dresses, maybe you could spend more time doing homework, don't you think?"

"I suppose so."

They didn't say anything else for the rest of the drive.

Britney's dad represented Hollywood stars, huge developers and corporations in their fights against environmentalists when they wanted to build hotels and homes on the coast overlooking the Monterey Bay sanctuary. Britney hated it. All her classes about the environment made her feel Mr. Scozzari was working for evil corporations who wanted to destroy the planet. Her father usually managed to win for his clients, much to the chagrin of the Sierra Club and Save Our Shores.

Tonight, she'd be dining with all of them.

Britney followed her father into the ballroom, a cavernous space of tall ceilings and forged-iron chandeliers. It made her feel claustrophobic. It wasn't like Tripoli, her favorite Italian restaurant, or Crabs, both overlooking the ocean. This was just a big, drab, grown-up room that was already getting crowded with guests. They were people her father's age, older couples of the area's social elite. They were the investment bankers, the judges, the businessmen and landowners, the wheels of the county's power machine, all dressed in impeccable suits and stylish dresses. They all knew her dad, admired him, maybe even feared him. They all greeted him and Britney warmly.

"Britney, you're here!" a cheerful voice reached her from behind.

"Cleo, I'm so glad you came! I never know what you're actually going to do."

"Girlfriend, I don't ever lie to you. Come, let's go sit outside. I have a little surprise for you."

To get to one of the outdoor lounges you had to go through the restaurants, which were located at the edge of the links, overlooking the ocean. They found an empty table, where they sat down and pulled their feet under their legs. Britney was never cold, but it was downright chilly. The summer fog was enveloping everything—even her arms felt wrapped with cold moisture. Britney wished she hadn't dropped her coat at the cloakroom.

From her pocket, Cleopatra pulled out a silver flask with a "C" engraved on it.

"Want some?" she said, giggling and throwing her head back.

"Cleopatra! My dad's going to come and see you!"

"Nah, don't worry about it," she said, leaning the bottle against her lips. "He's too busy with his clients."

Her father too seemed to have escaped from the stuffy ballroom. Britney could see him near the entrance to the restaurant, sharing a laugh with Carl Schrattenthaler, the movie star well known for his macho roles in popular movies. Her father had cleared the way for Schrattenthaler to build golf courses, restaurants, hotels and resorts—including the one hosting tonight's affair.

Her dad seemed relaxed, carefree. He was never like that at home. That was a smile she'd never seen on him.

"Wanna smoke?" Cleopatra asked, pulling a silver cigarette case and a matching lighter. "Oh, sorry, maybe you shouldn't."

"Just give me one," Britney said, trying to ignore the remark. Would that damage the baby? She shrugged her shoulders. She leaned toward her friend with the cigarette on her lips and took a drag as the tip touched the flame.

"So, what did you want to tell me?" Cleopatra giggled. This was clearly not the first swig of whiskey she'd had.

"Cleo, you can't tell anybody. Swear to me."

"I swear, I swear. Gosh, is this really serious? This can't be more secret than getting pregnant. You're scaring me," she said, giggling some more.

"I don't think I can trust you when you're drunk, Cleopatra. You're being silly."

"No, Brit, no, I swear, you can trust me. I swear, I'll be serious," she said, covering her mouth to keep a laugh from bursting out. "I haven't told anybody you're pregnant. Yet."

"Cleopatra, you can't be playing with this shit. I mean it."

"Okay, okay, I'll behave." Cleopatra straightened up and patted her cheeks. "What is it?"

"I'm going to end the pregnancy."

"You're gonna have an abortion? Dang, dude," Cleopatra's flask almost slipped from her hands. "Are you frigging serious?"

Britney didn't answer. She just stared at her friend, struggling to keep the tears from spoiling her make-up.

"Oh my God, you're serious," Cleopatra exploded. "How? When?"

Cleopatra took a deep breath, then looked around her as if looking for a purse, a coat or any other lifesaver. She took another drag off her cigarette and took her time before speaking again.

"Do you have some tissue?"

Cleopatra fished in her coat pockets and found a small packet of paper tissues. She tossed it Britney's way.

After she had dabbed her eyes and blew her nose, Britney started. "I'm scared, Cleo. I don't know what to do! I keep on thinking 'If I only had taken those stupid pills.' I'm only sixteen and my dad is going to kill me if he finds out!"

Cleopatra moved close to her friend and put her arms around her. Britney let out a few sobs before Cleo pushed her back, giving her instructions with alarm in her voice.

"Quick, put these sunglasses on! Your dad's coming this way!"

CHAPTER 18

Miguel Ángel was handcuffed and pushed into the back of a police car after he was frisked. Sitting in that uncomfortable position, he witnessed the full might of the cops.

Three more patrols arrived after he was arrested. With the yellow "crime scene" tape, they cordoned off the area where Jarocho lay twisted face up. The uniformed men, some wearing khaki and some dark blue, talked into their shoulder walkie-talkies, paced around examining the ground and looked intently at the few cars that crawled by trying to get a peek at the events. A news van had parked near the patrol, and a heavily made-up man was standing in front of the yellow tape, talking directly into a camera. From out of nowhere, the calm of the Gabilans had been replaced by a circus.

He was getting cold. The sun was going down, and he had left for his run with just a T-shirt and shorts. The sweat had dampened his T-shirt, and now in the car there was nothing to keep his temperature up. He began to shiver.

Miguel Ángel was supposed to come home to do some homework before going to the gym. His brothers and sisters would worry. It made him sick to think they'd be upset. It was his job to protect them at all cost, and worry wasn't in the plan. His mother wouldn't come home until six or seven. By then, he was usually not home anyway, so she wouldn't think anything of him not being there. He hoped they'd let him out in time for practice. He hoped he wouldn't have to spend the night in jail. Or juvie. He would punch himself if he could. Why didn't he listen to Ita? She was always giving him good advice, but he was always stubborn.

What would they do with Jarocho? He had been to the funerals of neighbors who had gotten involved in gangs—and of kids who'd been killed by gangs, even if they had nothing to do with them. His mother made him go to the funerals, it was a good way to show respect, she told him. He would walk up to the open caskets and become unsettled by the sight of the waxed remains of boys his age. Yes, they were all boys, a lot of them younger than him. After being to three funerals, he stopped counting.

The one he remembered the most was Federico's. He was thirteen years old when one day he was buying a popsicle from a push-cart *paletero*. As he bent down to choose a flavor from the icy pit, a group of gang members opened fire on their rivals, who happened to be buying popsicles next to Federico. He was hit in the back. The bullet shattered his ribs, pierced his right lung and lodged near his heart. The rivals fled unharmed, and Federico was flown to San Jose on a helicopter. His family took him off life support five days later.

At the funeral home, the day before the burial, Miguel Ángel spent the entire afternoon keeping the family company. Dressed in white, with his hands placed on his lap holding a rosary, Federico looked like an ashen angel. It was Federico the doll and not Federico the young boy who ran around climbing on trees and helping his mother carry grocery bags. This Federico had fake eyelashes curling up from his closed eyelids, not the deep brown eyes of the live Federico. This Federico would never wake up again to eat *chicharrones* with lemon and hot sauce. This Federico would never again give his mother a hug.

Miguel Ángel was watching Federico sleep in his casket when the boy's mother approached him. He hugged her and held her arm while she stood contemplating her youngest boy asleep in his white, satin bed.

She got near her boy and began to whisper, as if not wanting to wake him.

"Over there you're not going to suffer anymore, *m'ijito*. There, where you are, the streets are clean, there's lots of toys, and nobody is ever going to taunt you for wearing glasses. You're going to be so happy playing with the other angels, and God's going to be watching you, and nothing bad is ever going to happen to you again. Don't worry about me, *m'ijito*. I know you always did, but don't. I'm going to be okay. I swear to you, sweetheart, I'm going to be okay."

The calm whispers of Federico's mother slowly escalated into out-of-control sobs and desperate cries.

Miguel Ángel held on to her arm, keeping her from collapsing. By then, other family members had congregated around them and were trying to embrace her, attempting to pry her away from the casket. A discreet funeral employee waved at one of the mourners that it was time to close the casket. The mother was still weeping inconsolably when she was dragged out of the building.

Whenever Miguel Ángel evoked death, he would think of Federico surrounded by white satin and his crying mother. Now he had a new image of death: the face of Jarocho, staring blankly at the sky, the life gone from his eyes and a creek of blood snaking down from his mouth. His lean, beefed up chest contorted in an unnatural pose, forced to look up when Miguel Ángel pushed his body against the ground.

An ambulance was ushered past the yellow ribbons and the patrol cars. Two paramedics rushed out of the vehicle, as if Jarocho still could be saved. Miguel Ángel knew better.

The patrol car where he was sitting began moving.

There was little doubt in Miguel Ángel's mind that Jarocho had been killed for being in the gang. The story was the same everywhere: from Chicago to Los Angeles, in small towns and big cities, dudes like Jarocho were dying at the hands of other dudes, usually with a gunshot to the head, execution style. They were soldiers on a stupid battlefield; they had promised allegiance to their gang and swore to defend it with blood. Any transgression on the group, real or imaginary, demanded swift and lethal retaliation. It was about honor, about loyalty—the group that had become your family.

That was the part that Miguel Ángel understood. After all, if anybody ever hurt his mother, wouldn't he want to do something about it? Beto and Miguel Ángel became best friends because Beto defended him in a fight. When somebody showed you loyalty, you had to respect that. That's what family was all about. What he didn't get was why join the gang to begin with. Sure, selling dope was an easy way to make money, but who wants to spend life in prison for getting caught? Seemed a lot more trouble than it was worth. For his friends who had older relatives in the lifestyle—parents, uncles, cousins—there was almost no choice. But for someone like Beto, who had no direct connection to gangs, it was all so stupid. Miguel

Ángel knew better than try to steer his friend away from his homeboys. He had tried, but after the death of Beto's mother, the older gangbangers had become his family.

ဢ ဢ ဢ

Miguel Ángel was pushed into a small, dank room that reeked of fear. It had three walls painted dark blue and one covered with a mirror. Just like in the cop shows. The large, round faced deputy who brought him in pointed to a chair with his chin. He hadn't said a word in the eternity it took to drive from Old Stage Road to the sheriff's office by the county jail. Miguel Ángel felt the silence ringing in his ear, pressing on his chest.

"Why am I here? I didn't do anything. What do you want from me, man?"

The round deputy looked at him in silence. He turned around to respond to a knock on the door, took the sheaf of papers being offered to him and closed the door again. He looked at Miguel Ángel, sat down and began asking questions. The round deputy took all his information—his name, age, address, date of birth and social security number—without lifting his face from the report he was preparing. But before asking what Miguel Ángel was doing at the crime scene, he paused and looked at the shivering boxer intently.

"Are you a *Sureño* or *Norteño*?" he asked, his voice as cold as a supermarket freezer.

"I ain't no gangster," Miguel Ángel slurred through clenched teeth. "I'm an athlete. I'm a boxer."

"Young man, you're the prime suspect of a homicide investigation, and hits in this town don't happen unless they're gang-related. The man you killed was executed gang style. Are you a *Sureño* or *Norteño*?"

"I didn't kill anybody. I ain't *Sureño* or *Norteño*. I box, man, every day, at the Packing Shed. I have no time for cruising or nothing."

"The man was killed around two p.m. Where were you then? Why did you come back to the scene?" the interrogator asked, suddenly changing the course of the conversation.

"I was in class, man. It was last period, government and politics with Mr. Pulido. We were talking about Congress and stuff. Ask him, ask Mr. Pulido."

"You live on Kilbreth, that's *Sureño* territory. Are you a *sureño*?"

"I'm not *sureño*. I'm nothing, man, I'm telling you the truth," Miguel Ángel said, his voice rising ever so slightly. "I didn't do nothing. I was just running, that's my training route for cross-country. I didn't do anything."

"If you were training for cross-country, how come there was nobody else with you? You guys always run in groups."

"We're not in season right now, but I always run anyway for my boxing career, you know? I'm a boxer, I told you. I train with the coach at the Packing Shed. I'm not lying, man."

"We'll see about that. How come you were so close to the body? Did you want to steal his wallet?"

"No!" Miguel Ángel yelled. "I wanted to see who he was. Maybe I could tell the family or something. I don't know, I've never seen a body like that before."

"When you found him, was he facing up?"

"No, his face was down. I looked for his wallet to see if I could recognize his name. When I saw the name, it didn't sound familiar, so I pushed his shoulder to see his face."

"Did you recognize him? Who is he?"

"They call him Jarocho, but I really don't know him. I just see him around."

"Is he banging?"

"I don't know. He hangs out with his homeboys. Does that make him a gang member?"

"Don't try to be a wiseass with me, kid. Are you a gang banger?

"No, I'm not! I already told you! Don't I have any rights? I need a lawyer, man."

"A lawyer? You damned kids watch too much TV," the cop grunted.

"Yeah, man, a lawyer. I ain't no gang banger."

"Here," he said, getting up and moving toward the door, "let's make your phone call."

CHAPTER 19

Coach arrived at the gym a little later than usual. When he got there, a throng of kids ambushed him.

"Hi, Coach," a skinny boy ran to him, giving him the signature slap and fist bump.

"Mouse, you're sniffling. Are you still sick? Tomás, tomorrow you have a birthday, no? Are your parents buying you a cake? Don't eat too much, you have a fight coming up and you have to be in good shape. Paco, I saw your dad in the store this morning. He's walking better, *¿qué no?*"

Coach had a rough morning, hoping to get answers from city officials. He'd gone to city hall and managed to talk to some big honchos, but he got nowhere. He was so distraught, he couldn't even manage to unplug a drain at one of his rentals.

It was the best part of being at the Packing Shed. He could forget all about his troubles. As he greeted the boys, Coach opened the cage to let them come in and look for their gear. Mouse got the jumping rope. Luis got in to weigh himself as Paco watched. Outside, Kevin pounded the speed bag rhythmically while Jorge boxed with his own image in the mirror. Coach walked around studying the boys—and one or two girls—sometimes giving them advice as they worked. "Kevin, you're punching too slowly, gotta try to speed it up a little. Jorge, try to move your head a bit more, don't forget that's where your opponent is going to try to hit you. Yeah, that's it. Gema, keep your hands up when you punch the bag, don't drop them like that."

After five, when all the kids got restless at home and came to the Packing Shed to escape from boredom and their crowded apartments, his section of the gym wasn't the only one full of children. Toward the entrance, where the pool and foosball tables were—the ones the city eventually got around to installing—dozens of kids milled around with pool sticks in their hands, yelling at each other or concentrating behind the cue balls. A handful of teenagers ran behind a basketball toward the center of the building while a group of grown men lifted weights in the Nautilus section reserved for adults.

Coach was sitting by the heavy bags when he saw Bruno Hernández walk through the parking lot door. The anti-gang counselor had an office in the building, and he, too, had been served with eviction papers. He also would have to go through the song and dance of what his program did, how many children it served, how much money it raised. Maybe he could be a good ally in the battle against the city. Why didn't he think of this before? Coach followed him with his eyes into his office. A while later, he got up to see him.

"Hey Bruno, whazzup man?"

"Hey Coach, *¿qué onda?*" They shook and bumped fists. "Man, I just had the biggest dinner ever. Look at my belly, it's all swollen now," Bruno said, laughing at his own joke. That was Bruno, a jolly old timer with no time for worries or regrets. He couldn't afford that in his line of work.

"Bruno, what's going on? These guys tell us to leave, then they ask for a full-blown presentation that looks like the inquisition, and the moron city manager tells me we're not serving enough children. I don't get it."

Bruno's smile dimmed. He shook his head, as if trying to scare away unpleasant thoughts.

"Wanna hear the whole story? Well, make yourself comfortable. I'm not sure if it began six months ago, when Esteban decided to run for mayor, or when he worked for me as a counselor."

"Esteban? That cocky idiot? What does he have to do with this?"

"Well, the Latino intelligentsia is feeling it's time for a Latino to be in charge of the city. The city is seventy percent Latino, so they feel it's about time one of them gets the crown. Latino elected all over the county are putting their weight behind Esteban."

"I still don't get it," Coach told him, shaking his head, a puzzled look in his eyes.

"Esteban came to see me about three months ago, because he wanted me to help with his campaign. I tell you, sometimes being too political gets you in trouble."

Coach was scratching his head. "Didn't you help him?"

"Trouble was," Bruno said as he lined up paper clips on his desk, "I had already told Agnes I would help her."

Agnes was the active community member everyone loved. She served food to the homeless, coordinated efforts for neighborhood clean-ups and, most recently, had led efforts to save libraries when they were in danger of closing down. It made international news: "Salinas, birthplace of Nobel Prize winner John Steinbeck, will have no libraries." The shame was also of international proportions. So when Agnes whipped up local support to pass a new tax to keep the libraries open, she paved the way into everyone's heart in Salinas, brown and white.

Bruno took a deep breath and continued. "I have my eyes on the prize, man. If I ever smelled a winner, this is the one: Agnes is going to be our next mayor."

Coach looked at the César Chávez poster tacked to the wall. He could see the rest of the pieces fitting neatly into the holes. Esteban's father was on the city council, and he was the one who wrote the report spelling out their eviction, putting in motion his revenge machine.

"But why me? I can understand kicking you out, but what do I have to do with this?" Coach asked.

"That would be too obvious, man," Bruno said, his eyes downcast. "It's easier to say they want the entire space to give it to the theater arts group."

"The group they evicted from the armory building two years ago? Are you kidding me?" Coach shouted, getting up from his chair, running his fingers through his hair. "Is that why they're causing this mess, to get back at you?"

"People do it all the time, Coach. It's the game they're used to playing."

"I know people play games, but the kids? What about the kids? What about Luis? He has a fight in the next two weeks and now he can't sleep 'cause he's worried sick he may not have a place to train anymore? And what about Mouse? If he's on the streets, he's gonna get killed, man. What's got into these morons?"

"I hear you, man, but isn't that what everyone does? They have to get their way, no matter what. That's politics."

"That's politics my ass, man. I'm going to raise a stink. I ain't gonna let them kick me out. I have to do it for the kids."

"You have to start making more alliances, man, get more connected. That's how you save your ass in times of trouble."

"Oh, yeah? Look where it's got us. No thanks, I ain't playing no political game. I have plenty of work to do training those kids."

Coach's cell phone rang and he reached into his belt to turn the sound off. He didn't recognize the number, but a little voice inside his head told him to answer.

"Hello?"

"Coach, I didn't do anything, you have to come get me!"

"Miguel Ángel? Is that you?"

"Yes, Coach, it's me. They've got me in the Sheriff's Department, but I didn't do anything. Come get me, please!"

CHAPTER 20

"**B**ritney, sweetheart, I was looking for you," she heard her father say.

"Oh, hi, Dad. I'm keeping Cleopatra company."

"Hi, Cleo. Girls, I want you to meet my very good friends, Carl Schrattenthaler, and Carl's son, Sean. This is my daughter, Britney, and her troublemaker friend, Cleopatra."

"It's so good to see you, Mr. Scozzari. I had forgotten how charming you always are," Cleopatra said, shaking everybody's hand but looking only at Sean. "Sean, I didn't know you'd be here."

"We should all go inside," Mr. Scozzari said, pulling Sean away from Cleopatra. "Dinner's about to be served."

Britney sat between her dad and Sean Schrattenthaler, much to Cleopatra's displeasure. Although Britney had seen him at school, they'd never actually spoken to each other. He was too busy being captain of the football team, and she'd been too busy hanging out with Miguel Ángel. Plus, Sean was a senior, and she was a sophomore.

The first course was brought out among the clanking of dishes and murmur of a dozen conversations going on at the same time: a wild arugula salad with toasted walnuts and grapes. This place, unlike her favorite Mexican restaurant, served miniature portions of everything.

Lucky for her, since her stomach was a mess. She took a couple of bites of the arugula and then pushed the plate aside.

"What's the matter, sweetheart? Aren't you hungry?" her dad asked in a sweet, uncharacteristic tone of voice.

"I'm trying to save room for the main dish and dessert, Dad."

"Sean, did Britney tell you we're spending Labor Day weekend in our Vail home? You should come, it will be fun. Do you have any plans yet?"

"Actually, I don't think so, but let me check with my dad. He asked me to help him with a new project, but I don't know if he needs me for that weekend."

"Great, well, I'll be expecting you. No pressure, if you can't. I understand. You can make it next time."

"Do you go to Vail often, Britney?" Sean asked.

"We go twice or three times a year. We like to go in the summer for the rapids and in winter for the skiing. We also get some skiing done in Lake Tahoe, but Vail is more fun. There's more interesting people there."

"I bet. Last time I went skiing there, I crashed at the governor's vacation home, and everyone was there. It was a blast. Snowboarding's the best. I can teach you some-time, if you're interested."

Hmmmm. Sean could be trying to be nice to her dad, but the offer to teach her snowboarding was surprising. Could he actually be interested in her? Sean was not only the captain of the football team and the son of a famous Hollywood director, but the hottest guy in school. Buff, tanned, tall, with a sexy beauty spot on the right side of his mouth. "Schrattenlicious," Cleopatra called him.

Britney turned to face him. He was looking at her with a warm smile on his face. She had never noticed the heart shape of his lips, his thin, straight nose, or his long eyelashes. When their eyes met, it was as if Britney received an electric shock. Sean kept looking at her, his smile growing wider.

"I, I, I . . . like snowboarding," she mumbled. "But I'm not very good at it."

"Great, we can practice together. You'll see, it's very easy," he said, taking another bite of his salad.

"But there's no snow in Vail right now. We'll have to wait a few weeks."

"Well, if my dad doesn't need me around, we can go ride the rapids now. I'm pretty good at whitewater rafting, too."

"I bet you are," she said.

Sean's sudden attention made Britney suspicious. She wasn't used to this kind of treatment from boys around her. They were all either too insecure or too stuck up, and neither attitude led to good conversations. But there was something in Sean that felt different. He was relaxed and comfortable. He looked mature in his blue suit, but playful with his Dr. Seuss tie. He rested both arms on the table and leaned forward to eat his meal with appetite and gusto, but still kept an eye on her, as if she was the most interesting creature in the universe. No wonder all the girls were after him.

She certainly wasn't used to this much attention. It was either her sister or Cleopatra who got all the boys drooling over them.

As if on cue, the waiters fanned across the room, ready to serve the second course. Veal shank with wine and gremolata. Away from the watchful eyes of her friends, this would have been the perfect time to eat "baby cow," as her PC friends called it. Veal was one of her favorite dishes, but food was the last thing on her mind at the moment. Sean Schrattenlicious, the most eligible boy at Lewis and Clark, had looked directly into her eyes and told her he would teach her how to snowboard.

Britney lifted her gaze and found Cleopatra's dagger eyes aimed directly at her. That wasn't exactly a dream.

Britney slowly began cutting her veal, but she just couldn't eat. The food was making her queasy. She pretended to eat, though, because she didn't want to arouse her father's suspicion. Fortunately, neither her dad nor Sean seemed to notice what was on her plate.

After swallowing his food in two bites, Sean turned to Britney again and began chatting, as if they'd known each other forever. "My dad wants me to make movies just like him, but I'm not very interested. I'd rather play football. My game's getting better and better, and this year we've got an awesome defense, so I'll be able to connect more passes. I've heard there's some scouts out there who are interested. I have lots of options, but if I were to choose, I'd go with the Niners. Yeah, they're not doing very well lately, but that's what's good. If you start with a team that's not doing well, you come in, play good, and then the team improves, then you'll be the savior, right? The man who made things happen. I know I can do it: I can throw well, I have the charisma, I can bring them out of their doldrums and turn them around. Of course, I'd have to wait to get out of college, but it's not impossible. I'm hoping to end up playing at Stanford. Or USC at least."

It was just her luck. Nobody ever paid attention to her, and now that she was pregnant, she finally caught the eye of the hottest guy in school. The boy her best friend was after. Then again, Cleopatra was after any pole with a pulse. Still, Britney found herself smiling and nodding. She didn't know anything about football—she was more into soccer—so half of what he said didn't make sense, but it didn't matter. She was under the spell of his green eyes, his well-delineated brow and his heart-shaped lips.

The clinking of glasses alerted the audience to the evening speakers. A former White House chief of staff and another local celebrity would be bestowing an award on a former Republican senator from Arizona and a former Democratic congresswoman for the work they had done to defend the environment. These people were sure into the bipartisan thing. Big whoop. Britney wasn't listening. She had a plate of veal in front of her and a quagmire in her head: Sean, baby, Miguel Ángel. Sean, baby, Miguel Ángel.

Britney didn't feel a bit bad about not paying attention to the speakers. She knew the local politico well. His entire family had been guests of the Scozzaris a few times. But the other two folks, she had no idea. She didn't know who they were, so it was just the same if she didn't hear the speeches. She'd have to ask Tiffany why they were so important, anyway. Her big sister would have probably enjoyed this dinner more than Britney ever could.

"God, I hate these boring sermons," Sean whispered to Britney. "The only good thing about this evening is that I'm getting to know you better."

She turned to look at him and their faces were so close they almost kissed. She pulled back, a bit alarmed.

"Sorry, I didn't mean to scare you," he said.

"No, you didn't."

"Can I ask you something a bit personal?"

"Sure, go ahead."

"Why are you going out with that loser? Look at you, you're so beautiful. You could get any man you want."

"You really think so?" Britney said, feeling like the gates of heaven had opened and she was about to go through them.

"I'm not kidding you. Look at your silky hair, your beautiful eyes. You're truly gorgeous."

Tiffany insisted Britney was "good looking." Her friends always called her sexy. Her mother called her pretty. But nobody ever had called her gorgeous. Not even Miguel Ángel. And in the middle of a political awards dinner!

"Excuse me, I need to use the restroom," she said, tossing her napkin on the floor and darting out of the room.

In the bathroom, she examined her image in the mirror, trying to find the gorgeous diva of silky hair and beautiful eyes. Well, her eyes were pretty—blue and big. She tried to take care of her hair, buying expensive products and whatnot from the family's stylist in Carmel Valley. She had impeccable taste in fashion. Still, she wasn't quite convinced she had the kind of beauty that gets you the Sean Schrattenthalers of the world.

When she came back from her little excursion, she decided against going back to her seat. She headed for Cleopatra instead.

"I have to talk to you," Britney whispered in her ear. "It's urgent."

Cleopatra pulled out her chair noisily, attracting the attention of everyone at the table. Britney looked away to avoid Sean's eyes. The girls scurried across the room and emerged in the foyer. They would have stayed there, except that Cleopatra was going to use the occasion to light another cigarette. She practically dragged Britney to one of the glass doors overlooking the ocean.

Once outside, Cleopatra pulled out her pack of cigarettes and offered Britney one. She declined this time.

"Okay, so what is it now?"

"Sean Schrattenthaler, he looks interested."

"Yeah, I saw you, little whore. I'm here so I can be the one who gets to know him," Cleopatra grumbled, tapping her stiletto furiously on the parquet floor.

Britney lowered her eyes, a bit embarrassed. This was not what she had in mind when she came for dinner. "Cleo, he likes me. And I may like him, too."

"What about Miguel Ángel and the baby, huh?"

Yeah, she was pregnant. But maybe not for long.

CHAPTER 21

It was just past 10 p.m. when Coach unlocked the passenger side of his truck to let Miguel Ángel in. He then walked around the vehicle and opened the driver's side door. Once in, he rummaged through the clothes, boxing equipment, empty water bottles and bags in the narrow back seat, looking for some clothing. He found a pair of pants and a sweatshirt.

"Here, put some clothes on. You look like a beach bum, ha ha ha!" Coach was trying to make light of the situation, a sure sign of relief. Miguel Ángel didn't find it humorous. "Thanks, Coach," the boy said, shivering. "I thought they were gonna put me in jail or something."

"Don't mention it. All you have to do now is pay me for the bail I posted for you. But don't worry about it, it's only five thousand dollars."

"Five thousand dollars? Jesus, Coach, where am I going to find that money?"

"Just kidding, *m'ijo*," Coach said, letting out his loud and snorty laughter. "They didn't charge you with anything. They just let you go. We'll talk about it later. Hungry?"

Truth was, Miguel Ángel was starving. He hadn't eaten anything since lunch, and it was already late. He could eat the biggest burrito in the entire Alisal. "Yeah, I could use a taco or two. I'm starving."

"Okay. Where do you want to go?"

"Any *taquería*. As long as it's not Taco Bell," he said, and both laughed.

Coach drove to one of his favorite eateries on East Alisal Street. They made the best *chiles rellenos* in the entire city. After ordering and sitting at a table, Miguel Ángel faced the second interrogation of the day.

"Okay, now you're gonna tell me what you did, punk."

"You too, Coach? I thought you believed me. I swear to you, I didn't do anything."

"Look, Miguel Ángel, you can't fool me. I'm older than you are, and I know you must be up to no good. So let's hear it."

Miguel Ángel was a good boy in Coach's eyes. He was dedicated to his sport and had learned his lesson way back when he made him fight high as a kite. But he had a lot of pent-up anger. He was angry at his dad for having left him, angry at his stepfather for beating him, angry at his mother for letting them get away with it. Who knows how many other demons dwelled within him.

"I already told you. I went for my usual run, you know, minding my own business, when I see this *vato* face down on the dirt. I wanted to see who it was, you know, I got curious. So I look in his pocket to see if he had a wallet, and he did, but I didn't recognize the name. So I turned him over and I saw who it was."

"And? Did you recognize him?"

Miguel Ángel nodded, but didn't say anything. Just then, a waitress brought their burritos and chips. The famished fighter took two chips with salsa and then unwrapped one end of his burrito. He dumped half a cup of red sauce on it and took a huge bite. "*Ándale*, Miguel Ángel, I'm waiting," Coach urged him.

"It was Jarocho. Beto's homeboy."

"Ah," Coach said, shaking his head. "Have you seen Beto lately?"

Miguel Ángel hesitated. He had managed to keep the secret of Beto's gun from the cops and didn't want to spill the beans to Coach. "I ... saw him yesterday from afar, but I didn't talk to him. I'm trying to stay away from him, you know?"

"Don't lie to me, goddammit," Coach smashed his fist on the table. "Who do you think you're talking to, punk? What did you guys talk about? What the hell did he tell you? Did he know anything about Jarocho?"

The little color left in Miguel Ángel's face was completely drained after seeing Coach's reaction. He hadn't seen Coach get mad at him in a very long time.

"Chill, Coach. He didn't say anything about Jarocho or nothing. He wanted me to hide a package for him, and I told him I wouldn't do it, you know? He was waiting for me outside the gym last night, and that's why I came inside to go out with you through the back, so I wouldn't run into him, remember? But he was waiting for me when I got home, you know? I swear, Coach, I ain't hanging with him or no gang banger. I swear."

Miguel Ángel was sweating. That's why he could never tell Coach about Britney. He would have to confess to using Beto's car to visit her, and Coach would never approve of that.

Coach's eyes fell into Miguel Ángel's face, looking at him as if he were trying to penetrate his head with X-ray vision. The kid was nervous, but Coach didn't think he was lying. At least not completely. Coach had known him since he was eight, and he had been able to keep him out of gangs by scaring the bejesus out of him. He looked scared now, but was he telling the truth? With Miguel Ángel, as it was with all of his boxers, it was a leap of faith. Coach couldn't accuse him of anything until he had the proof, and he had no proof. Miguel Ángel had been training, his running shorts and shoes were on him when the cops picked him up. The boxer did come back through the front to ask for a ride last night. Coach had warned him to stay away from Beto, but the boys had grown up together. It was going to be difficult for Miguel Ángel to stay away.

At some point, you had to stop pushing the boys or you risked pushing them too hard and losing them forever.

"This package that Beto wanted you to stash, did he say what it was?" Coach finally said.

"No, and I didn't ask. But I told him I wasn't going to keep it for him," the young boxer said, shaking his head emphatically. Miguel Ángel had no problem lying, but he really couldn't do it to Coach, who knew him too well. But by now, the fear to face his Coach's anger was bigger than his fear of getting caught in a lie. He had to take the risk. Plus, if he told Coach he was hiding a gun under his mattress, all hell would break loose.

"Coach, I'm trying to stay away from Beto, but he looks for me. Says he has no other friends. And he's my homeboy."

"Look, I've lived in this town for a long, long time, and I can assure you, nothing good comes of having friends who are banging. They're the virus that has made many towns sick, not just Salinas, but everywhere. Los Angeles and New York . . . You have to stay away from them. If you hang out with wolves . . . "

"You'll learn how to howl. I know, I know," Miguel Ángel completed Coach's favorite anti-gang warning.

Coach first moved to Salinas when he was sixteen. Fresh out of the state correctional system, he was escaping a gang-ridden town that offered nothing but trouble to a kid full of energy like himself. His brother, a carpenter, gave him a job and a way to escape from guys like him with nothing to do but find trouble.

As a newcomer, he witnessed what was happening in the agricultural town without getting involved: young boys put in jail for petty theft, for smoking dope, coming out hardened criminals . . . After a stint in juvie, they came out ready to begin selling drugs, rob banks at gunpoint or carjack old ladies. The street criminals were supposed to send their earnings to their commanders, the top leaders of a budding mafia. Coach never got involved, but many of his friends were part of it. You could tell by the cars they drove and the money they spent. That's why it was so attractive to be part of the brotherhood. Its members always had money, unlike their farm worker parents who just squeaked by to make ends meet.

The new recruits would be taught the ways of this brotherhood and how to keep money flowing to the imprisoned higher-ups. The kids, boys as young as ten, would be taught how to use knives and guns, how to break into cars and homes and how to spot a possible mugging victim on the street. The teachings would become more sophisticated with time: first it was how to rip off a convenience store, later how to rob a bank.

The most profitable enterprise turned out to be the drug trade. Street soldiers would be assigned to their turf—a block, a building, a neighborhood—just like any salesman is assigned to a region. Selling into another's territory was a capital offense, the source of many gang-style killings in the town. Dealers had to stay in their territory or pay with their lives. Coach had seen many "traitors" disappear and their executioners go to jail, the lives of both families shattered. While one buried its loved one under six feet of dirt, the other entombed a young man alive behind concrete walls. The only stories about gang life with happy endings were those of bangers abandoning the life forever.

Miguel Ángel had heard this admonition many, many times. He heard it when he showed up high for practice and Coach decided to teach him a lesson. He heard it after Beto received his first and second warnings. He heard it after his friend was banned from the boxing program. And he heard it while sitting in a pew at the funeral he and Coach had attended together. He wasn't afraid to die, but he feared becoming paralyzed, a vegetable that needs to be pushed around like produce in a shopping cart. And if there was something Miguel Ángel wanted more than anything in the world, it was to make that old man proud. He saw that glint of pride when he'd won his bouts, a special radiance in Coach's face that maybe his father would have worn if he hadn't abandoned him.

Yeah, maybe he could deal with the banger life, but that would anger Coach, not make him proud. That, Miguel Ángel could not handle.

CHAPTER 22

Cleopatra did not let go of Britney for the rest of the night, so the magic of Shrattnelicious evaporated. Finally it was time to go, and Britney followed her dad to the car.

After the tortuous ride home, Britney was ready to escape into the haven of her bedroom, when the voice of Mr. Scozzari stopped her.

"Britney, come here. I want to talk to you. Let's go into the study."

"Now? Dad, it's almost midnight. I have school tomorrow."

"You'll sleep half an hour less, you won't die. Come here."

Britney took off her heels and followed her dad across the foyer, past the living room and the library toward his inner sanctum.

The office, a space her dad hardly ever used since he was rarely home, was furnished with mahogany cabinets and bookcases, which reached the eight-foot-high ceiling. On the far end of the room was her dad's desk, an antique he'd flown back from a trip to London. Mr. Scozzari did not sit down behind his desk. He walked toward the bar, where he poured himself a Scotch on the rocks.

"What do you want to drink, Brit?"

"I'm good," she said curtly. God, how long was this going to last, she wondered.

"Let me give you a glass of Chardonnay. You should begin to learn how to hold your liquor."

Brit opened her eyes and her mouth, quickly using her right hand to prevent any noise from escaping it. She remembered the first time her dad poured a glass of wine for Tiffany. It was during the family Christmas gathering, and all her cousins watched when the sixteen-year-old had her first official glass of wine. They were all fascinated at the sight of their uncle letting his teenage daughter drink.

This kind of news could not wait for the morning to be spread. Britney pulled her cell phone and, just as her dad was busy opening a bottle and pouring, she started texting Cleo. She had to let her know she was now considered an adult.

"Thanks, Dad," Britney said, suddenly feeling all grown up.

"I saw you chatting with Sean tonight. He seems interested in you. Do you like him?"

Oh, no, it was going to be a "boy" talk. Dad seldom made any effort to chat with her, so the attempts always made her uncomfortable. It was not natural. It was like a fogless summer day on the Monterey Peninsula. Britney felt her cheeks flush, her hands turn wet. This was not the kind of conversation she wanted to have with her father just now.

"I don't really know him, Dad," she stammered. "I'd never spoken with him before tonight. Is it okay if we talk about this some other time? I'm so sleepy."

"Brit, look, I know we don't have the best of relationships," Mr. Scozzari interrupted, waving a hand at Britney as if trying to make her concerns disappear. "I know I'm much to blame. I work very long days and have lots of social commitments, so I don't spend that much time with you. But I do want you to know something. I love you very much and I want the best for you. That's part of the reason why I work so hard, because I want to give you the best. You're going to a good school, you live in a nice house by the ocean, you travel the world with your sister and your mother, all because I want you to have all that. That means I have to work very hard to pay for it. And well, if I'm going to be very honest with you, I also enjoy my work quite a bit. I have good clients, a good law firm, a good reputation, all built by very hard work. I've done it for me, because I enjoy it, but also because I have you and your sister."

Britney was sitting in one of the leather chairs strategically placed at the foot of Mr. Scozzari's desk. He got up from his chair and grabbed her face to pull it close to his. He reeked of alcohol, but she was afraid to turn her face away. He was flustered enough. She just had to settle for squirming in her seat and hope Cleo would be awake and text her right back.

"That's why I didn't want your sister to be going out with that loser. Yes, he was going to go to Harvard or MIT or whatever, but he was still born into a family of losers. Whoever goes to school on a scholarship? Only those who can't afford to pay themselves: losers. If you don't have money to pay for yourself, you don't deserve to be there."

The phone in her hand buzzed with an incoming message. Britney pushed a button then took a peek. R U CRZY? The tiny screen flashed.

Her dad, oblivious to her phone, got up again and kept going. "And when a loser goes out into the world, all they want to do is 'improve their communities' or 'give back' or one of those heroic futilities that sound romantic and make Democrats happy. They want to 'help the disadvantaged' or 'speak for the voiceless,' even if they starve in the attempt. They choose careers like social work or teaching in an inner-city school, or drug counseling so they can help people. But they don't have the guts to go into business on their own because they have no vision, they can never see themselves as successful entrepreneurs. So they go work for the government because that's a steady paycheck, even if it's a pathetic one."

Now he was standing by one of his bookcases, his Scotch in his right hand, as if he were speaking before a jury box or at the board of supervisor's chamber. It was a show where he was the main attraction, all lights and attention on him. Britney was sinking deeper and deeper into her chair, punching keys on her cell phone whenever Mr. Scozzari turned his head away.

"Brit, you don't want to end up with somebody like that, a government bureaucrat with no chance to take you to see the world. Look at me. I've created a respected name in the community, a law firm with clients not just in California but all over the world. When people hear the name Scozzari, Gumball, Pfeiffer and York, they know they'll win. Because I'm a winner. I know what I want and I go after it, no matter what."

Britney realized her father had begun to slur his words. Perhaps it was best to stop texting and make for the door.

"Dad, it's getting late . . . "

"Shush. I'm not finished," he yelled, going back to the mini-bar. He poured himself another drink, swished it and turned to Britney as if trying to visualize the spot where he had stopped his monologue.

"People like me, like us, don't get here overnight. We have a vision. We dine with the powerful because we have something to offer. And people like the kid your sister was dating, they're not like us. They're an inferior breed, like a mutt that will never be best in show."

"I WANNA DIE," Britney wrote to Cleopatra.

"That's not the kind of man I want for you, Brit. I want to see you with somebody like Sean, the son of a visionary, a person who sees the future ahead of him and will not be afraid to go after it. I'm not trying to push you into marriage, or anything, God, no. You're only sixteen. But I know you're at a very vulnerable age. Wasn't Tiffany your age when she fell in love with that Mexican kid? God, that was pathetic. You should have seen his face when I brandished the gun in front of him. Ha. That was the funniest moment I've had in years!"

Mr. Scozzari was way past drunk.

"Dad, it's getting late. I better go to bed," she pleaded, pushing herself out of the chair.

"But before you go, tell me something," he said, dragging his words. "Do you have a boyfriend?"

"Nnn . . . no, Dad. Of course not," she said hesitantly.

"Mmmmm, you're lying. I may not spend time with you, but I'm still your father and I know you're lying. Is he a loser?"

"No, Dad, I don't have a boyfriend. I gotta go to sleep, okay?"

"Let me tell you one thing, Britney Marie. If I see you hanging out with a peasant, I'll rip his heart out while it's still beating. Mark my words."

CHAPTER 23

Miguel Ángel was hoping to find everyone asleep when he came home, but as soon as he saw the TV light shining through the window, he knew he had no chance.

"Brother, you're home," Mari Carmen ran to hug him and cling to his neck.

"About time, you punk," Blanca Rosa, the oldest girl, chided him.

"*M'ijito*, why are you here so late?" his mother pleaded.

"Enough! Leave me alone. I had things to do, all right?" Everyone turned to look at him as if he suddenly had grown horns. Whatever. It was not like they never saw him get angry.

"*M'ijito*, I made *chiles rellenos*, your favorite," his mother said. "Come, sit down to eat."

"I'm not hungry, ma," he said. "I'm going to take a shower."

Miguel Ángel thought he would be safe from the family scrutiny for a few minutes in the privacy of the bathroom. He decided to spend long minutes under the hot running water. But the temperature never rose above tepid and, before he even soaped his body, he heard a discreet knock, then the door opening.

"Miguel Ángel, can I come in? I really need to pee," he heard Víctor Manuel say.

That's how it was in his house. There was never any privacy, not even in the bathroom. As soon as one of the brothers walked in, another one wanted to have his turn.

"Yeah, come in," Miguel Ángel yelled. It was the rule. If you were taking a shower, the toilet was free for the taking. And no spying through the curtain.

He dried off while he was still in the shower, then got out and put on clean clothes. He put the sweat pants and T-shirt Coach had lent him in a plastic bag and placed them on top of a growing pile of dirty clothes.

Everyone was still awake when he walked out of the bathroom. Julia and Pablo, the star-crossed lovers of the soap opera "Cañaveral de Pasiones" were about to learn a terrible secret on the small screen.

"Miguel Ángel, *¿ya te sirvo?*" his mom asked. He wasn't hungry, and to be very honest, he wasn't a great fan of his mother's food either. But there was no way to say no to her. And food was so rare in the house these days, he was afraid to turn it down.

"Okay, I'll have one *chile relleno*," Miguel Ángel said.

His mother's face lit up. She put two steaming *chiles* on a plate, two heaping spoons of beans and two of rice, the spicy aroma of hot pepper and tomato sauce spreading through the apartment before the dish was on the table.

The young athlete was full, but as Coach said, he could always eat some more. He was, after all, training to be a champion.

"Can you read me a book, Miguel Ángel?" his youngest sister begged, trying to squeeze herself between the arms that attempted to eat cheese-stuffed *chiles*.

"Mari Carmen, you're going to get your book all greasy," her mother scolded her youngest daughter. "Go ask Ana Estela to read to you."

"Mom, I already read to her," Ana Estela yelled from the bedroom. "Tell Juan Carlos, he's done nothing all day."

"Shut up, carrot face. I'm busy here. You're the smart one, you read to her," Juan Carlos yelled back.

"Then ask Blanca Rosa, she's a good reader," Ana Estela yelled out.

Blanca Rosa, who was sitting right beside her older sister, jabbed her with an elbow.

"Ouch! Mom, look at Blanca Rosa. She punched me in the stomach!"

"I didn't punch you, liar," Blanca Rosa screamed. "I just pushed her a bit."

"*¡YA! ¡CÁLLENSE!*" their mother screamed from the kitchen. "Shut up, all of you. Let your brother eat in peace."

Oblivious to the racket around him, Miguel Ángel concentrated on his *chiles rellenos*. Delicious, after all. They were the best remedy against dead bodies on Old Stage Road and Packing Shed concerns.

"Your girlfriend *te estuvo llama y llama*," Blanca Rosa interrupted him.

"Yeah? What time did she call?"

"First around four. Then at four-thirty, then at four-forty-five, then at five, then at five-fifteen. She kept calling all afternoon. Then she stopped calling around seven."

There was a knock on the door. Mari Carmen darted toward it with the full intention to open it, but her mother stopped her.

"Hey, where are you going? You can't open the door, you know that. Let your brother get it."

Víctor Manuel, older than Mari Carmen by two years, was allowed to open the door under supervision. He pulled it toward him as far as the chain would allow and saw it was Beto. Víctor Manuel let him through.

"*Buenas, señora,*" Beto greeted Doña Lupita before talking to anyone else. He may have been a gang banger, but he had good manners.

"*Buenas, m'ijito.* Come in. Do you want a *chile relleno?*" she asked, already getting a plate for the unannounced guest.

"No, *señora.* I'm not hungry. I just had dinner," Beto said, tossing his yellow stress ball into the air.

Lupita placed a steaming *chile relleno* in front of him. "How's your *papá, m'ijo?*" she asked Beto. "And your sisters?"

"They're good, *señora.* My sister Adela just had another baby," he answered, attacking his *chile* without breathing.

"Another? How many does she have already?"

"This is going to be her third."

"My God. Back when I was young, you could understand why women had so many babies. We knew nothing about birth control or anything. But girls these days, they have no excuse. Three children!" she said, starting to laugh.

"Ma, it's none of your business how many kids Adela has. Look who's talking," Ana Estela said.

"Yeah, I already said I had an excuse. Nobody ever told me about birth control, nobody gave me pills or condoms. You have it so easy and you have no idea."

"Ma, what's a condom?" Mari Carmen asked, her big brown eyes fixed on her mother.

"It's the wrapper of a tootsie pop," Juan Carlos said, and they all laughed, except for his mother.

"*Chamacos*, it's almost midnight. You all have school tomorrow, so let's go to bed. *¡Ándenles!* Beto, I'm going to sleep, good night. This is your home, stay as long as you like."

"*Gracias, señora. Buenas noches.*"

"*Buenas noches.*"

The return of Beto so soon after asking Miguel Ángel to stash his brown paper bag could only mean one thing. He wanted it back. That was good, Miguel Ángel thought. He didn't want to have a loaded weapon around the young ones. But it was also a bad thing because he didn't want to retrieve the brown bag in front of his family. He didn't want to reveal his secret spot.

Beto didn't say anything about the package, though. He seemed worried, his lips pressed, his forehead furrowed.

"Did you see the news?" he asked Miguel Ángel.

"No, I just came back from the gym. Another gas station?"

Beto glared at him. Miguel Ángel lowered his gaze. "Sorry, man, I was joking. What's going on?"

"Jarocho got killed."

Beto couldn't have learned that from the news. The cops usually took at least a day to identify murder victims. He had just died this afternoon, so there was no way Beto got this from Channel 5.

"When?" he said, trying to sound casual. He would tell him about Jarocho, his contorted body facing the Gabilans, his afternoon with the cops and perhaps even the scolding he got courtesy of Coach. Yeah, Miguel Ángel would pass on the scolding to Beto. He was badly in need of one. But not in front of all the kids. They had all gone to bed, but they were not sleeping yet. He could hear them tossing and turning in their beds.

"Today, sometime," he said. "The news showed the body of this man killed on Old Stage Road. They didn't show the face, but they showed his pants and his tennis shoes. The same clothes Jarocho was wearing this morning. We were supposed to go over to Monterey this afternoon for some business, but he didn't show up. I went to look for him at his house, but nobody's seen him. I'm sure it's him, I can feel it."

"Are you sure? They never show nobody dead in the news. The pants and shoes mean nothing," Miguel Ángel said. "It could've been anybody."

"It was Jarocho, I know," was Beto's determined answer. The look in his eyes was a sign that he wasn't going to entertain any more doubts. He knew something he wasn't telling Miguel Ángel.

"Let's go outside," the boxer said, glancing nervously over his brothers' beds. They weren't making any more noise—their breathing was deep and even—but Miguel Ángel did not want to take any chances.

CHAPTER 24

Beto got behind the wheel of a brand new Escalade and lit a cigarette. Miguel Ángel admired the SUV but did not say anything, figuring it would give Beto an excuse to show off and press Miguel Ángel to joining him in whatever criminal endeavor he was involved in. "There's this *vato* everybody's been looking for," said Beto. "Gringo, the blonde one with blue eyes. I told you about him, remember? The one with the scar running down his left cheek."

Miguel Ángel remembered seeing Gringo and vaguely associated him with Jarocho. "Well, he said he was gonna clean up his act, wasn't gonna bang no more, and so we sort of left him alone."

Beto paused for a moment, enough to take a drag out of his cigarette and let out a column of smoke. With his right hand, he was throwing his stress ball into the air. Throw and catch, throw and catch.

"But check this out. One day, I was cruising on Soledad Street looking for my customers, and guess who I caught dealing? *Pinche* Gringo, he said he wanted to drop out, but all he wanted was to keep his earnings from the bosses."

"So then? What's going to happen?"

"Well, I went to talk to Jarocho, and he gave the green light. It's our territory, Miguel Ángel, and if we allow him to piss in our backyard, he's gonna piss in our living rooms next."

Miguel Ángel knew that whoever got to Gringo first would earn points in the gang, and a promotion within the ranks. The higher you are in the brotherhood, the more money you get to keep when it comes time to share the wealth. He shook his head. Miguel Ángel really cared for his friend, but his life was getting scarier by the minute.

"So what's next?"

"I'm not sure. But word out there is that Gringo found out Jarocho gave the green light on him, so he was looking to strike first," Beto whispered.

There was something funny about Beto tonight, something Miguel Ángel couldn't quite place. He seemed more restless, nervous. Beto rarely looked at Miguel Ángel when he told his stories, but this time he wasn't even looking straight ahead, he was looking to the other side. And the stress ball, it was going up in the air faster, more times. Something was not right.

What if somebody didn't like what Beto was doing and put a green light on him? What if Miguel Ángel was around when they tried to kill him? Would they get to him? He shook his head, as if his thoughts were unpleasant mosquitoes he could scare away.

"Gringo got to him first," Beto said, concluding his tale and letting out a sigh. He now was bouncing the ball against the windshield. Thump, thump, thump.

"We're gonna have to do something about that."

"What are you going to do?" Miguel Ángel asked softly.

"We can't let him get away with it. He's not only dis-respecting our territory, but now he's killed our boss. This type of shit is only paid with blood."

"Beto, you have to get out of this life. You're going to end up dead or in prison if you don't."

Beto took a drag in silence. He stared at Miguel Ángel for a long time, as if trying to unveil a secret hidden inside his friend's eyes. As if trying to say something urgent, something important, a truth that only his best friend could hear.

Miguel Ángel felt a cold snake slither down his spine. He turned away from Beto's gaze.

Outside their apartment building it was dark. Only the lights of a few apartments pierced the blackness, and only a few cars cruised up and down the street. There was litter on the sidewalks, weeds growing in the cracks and old cars parked back to back along the curb. The scribbled tag KL—Kilbreth Locos—was stamped on a few houses and fences marking their territory. "My friends in the gang, they're all I have," Beto finally said, with a hint of defeat in his voice. "If I leave, where do I go? You're my friend too, but you're different. You're in your own world, you go boxing and you go to school and you have your mom and your rich girlfriend and you can't just hang. And, you know, Coach even kicked me out of the Packing Shed."

"You got kicked out because you started dealing," Miguel Ángel interrupted.

"They've been there for me, man. Jarocho, he paid attention to me when nobody else would. When my *jefi-ta* died, even my pops stopped caring."

Beto's voice had a little tremor in it, and he stopped talking. He had finished his cigarette and now was tossing the happy ball side to side, from one hand to the other.

Miguel Ángel thought about the conversation he had with Coach. He wished Coach was here to repeat to Beto what he'd said earlier. He wished he knew how to speak like Coach so he could convince his friend that this road was a path to some real bad stuff. But he just looked ahead, beyond the white hood of the SUV, into the crushed plastic cups and water bottles strewn on the ground. His eyes followed the cars parked on the street to the next street, and to the next, until they rested on the foggy silhouette of the Gabilans.

"Brother, I need my gun," Beto said, his voice transformed from barely a whisper to a thunderous command.

"What are you going to do?"

"The less you know, the less you'll tell the police," he responded, still staring into the darkness of the street.

CHAPTER 25

"**W**hat are you afraid of?" Tiffany said, a tinge of exasperation in her voice.

"Shhhh!" Britney responded, her right index firmly pressing on her lips. "Get a megaphone and broadcast my problems to the world, will you?"

"All right, all right. What are you afraid of?" Tiffany said again, this time her voice so soft it was barely audible.

Britney rolled her eyes at her, and almost decided to ignore her, but Tiffany looked at her intently. Why in the world was she so persistent? Britney looked around, as if the answer to Tiffany's question were hidden behind the chimney of the Explorer's Center, sitting on the leather couches or hanging from the chandeliers. This was usually Britney's favorite place, so sunny and comfortable, even when the fog was embracing its large glass windows. But lately, no place made Britney feel comfortable, and the Explorer's Center was no exception.

Hoping to tell Tiffany all about her evening with Sean Schrattenthaler, Britney came looking for her sister at the Explorer's Center, also her favorite hangout. But Tiffany was not in the mood to hear Britney's adventures.

"I've made you an appointment at the clinic for Monday," Tiffany said as soon as Britney plopped herself down on the burgundy couch. "As soon as we're done with class, I'll drive you over to Monterey."

Britney froze. The impact of her interaction with Sean was such that she had forgotten all about Miguel Ángel and the unfortunate consequence of their encounters. Britney had spent the entire morning doodling, writing Sean's name and thinking about his lips, barely paying attention to class. The fantasy of Sean was definitely more pleasant than her present reality with Miguel Ángel.

Britney could always count on Tiffany to bring her back to reality, though.

"C'mon, Brit, what are you afraid of?"

Britney sank lower into the leather couch, not knowing what to respond. She was afraid of their father and how he'd react to the news. But if she didn't end the pregnancy, he for sure would find out, and she did not want to face his fury. She was afraid of his friends finding out and making fun of her. Britney and the loser. She would be the laughing stock of their school. And if Sean found out, he would definitely forget about her. They were not even together yet.

Her life would be ruined if she didn't go to college. But plenty of girls had babies and went on to study. She could too. Maybe her father would make her marry Miguel Ángel. That wouldn't be bad, but it would make it hard for them to buy a house at Pebble Beach. Maybe they could live in the Alisal, and have more children. What if, in ten years, she had no college degree and ten children?

Why, if she was so scared, was she also so hesitant? It wasn't religious reasons either. Grandma's teachings had always been important, but the idea that life begins at conception, that a sperm and an egg together, smaller than a pin's head were ready for life . . . Nah, she wasn't quite ready to buy that one either.

Then, what? What was holding her back, preventing her from going along with Tiffany and saying yes to the appointment?

"It's not like you want to marry Miguel Ángel or anything, right, sis?"

No, she didn't want to marry Miguel Ángel—not right now. But if Britney told him she was pregnant, and then told him she was going to end the pregnancy, he would never forgive her. Miguel Ángel always complained about his siblings, about how noisy they were and how they didn't let him do his homework, but he loved them. He always said he wanted to have children of his own.

That's what she was afraid of. Losing him.

"Of course I don't want to marry him," Britney finally said. "I just don't know what to do. I'm so confused."

"What are you confused about?" a voice she recognized as Sean Schrattenthaler's whispered close to her ear. "Maybe I can help you with something?"

"Oh, hi, Sean," Britney said, trembling like an autumn leaf. "This is my sister, Tiffany."

"Yeah, hi, Tiff," Sean said, waving a confident hand. "Well, I checked with my dad, and he said he won't need me for Labor Day. So . . . I can join you on your trip. Can you let your dad know?"

Britney's blood rushed out of her face, leaving her with no color on her cheeks and a queasy feeling in her stomach.

"Yeah, definitely, I'll let him know," she said softly, with no more room in her lungs to speak louder.

After following Sean's departure with her eyes, Britney turned to Tiffany and met her burning stare. "I wanted to tell you all about it, but you wouldn't listen."

"You're playing with fire, girl."

≫≫≫

The sisters were driving home from school when Britney saw the car Miguel Ángel used to borrow parked along the road.

"Tiff, drive slowly. I think that's Miguel Ángel."

As Tiffany's BMW slowly rolled past the car, Britney turned her head, looking to meet the driver's eyes. Honey colored, wide and adoring, just like she remembered them. But the spark of recognition was not as intense. Sean Schrattenthaler was still on her mind.

Miguel Ángel waved at her to pull over. Britney turned to her sister, who was already aiming the car at an empty space a few spots ahead.

"Tell mom I'm with Cleopatra. Thanks, sis."

"Don't come home too late," Tiffany said. "I thought you were in love with Schrattenthaler. That's what you just said."

"I'm not in love. I just met the guy," she said as she slammed the door.

Miguel Ángel was waiting for her by the passenger side. He gave her a brief kiss on the lips and opened the passenger's side door for her. "I called you all afternoon yesterday and your sister said you never came home from school. Where were you?"

Miguel Ángel waited until he had pulled out into the street to begin telling his tale. He started with the moment he ran into Jarocho's body and described how he got arrested and interrogated and how Coach saved him and lectured him. He almost mentioned Beto and the gun, but decided against it.

By the time he was done with the story, they had arrived at Asilomar, the beach where they hid their love from prying eyes. It was their spot to kiss and snuggle, to escape from friends, family and the world. Leaning against the rocks, feeling each other's skin, it was the best place to escape they had found.

Britney was thinking of no magic. Instead, she was looking at Miguel Ángel with amazement, her eyes wide open, as if trying to visualize everything he'd just told her. Dead body. Patrol car. Cops. Interrogation room. The images were crashing in her mind like the waves on the shore.

Instead of finding a secluded spot, Britney led Miguel Ángel to a path along the shore. She needed time to process the information. This was not just about her, her pregnancy and her sudden interest in Sean. This was about the boy she dreamed about. Suddenly, he didn't sound as innocent as she always believed him to be. Britney was slowly awakening from the daze she had been in all day.

"Did you hear what I just said?"

"I'm sorry, I have a lot in my mind. What did you say?"

"I said I'm glad that you're in my life. Everything else is all screwed up right now."

He stopped walking and pulled her close with one hand and held her face with the other. He was going to kiss her, but she resisted a little, the face of Sean flashing in her mind. And then, with the touch of his lips against hers and the electric discharge that ran through her body, Sean was momentarily forgotten.

Miguel Ángel began kissing her slowly, a sweet dance he liked to control. He gently pressed his lips against Britney's, carefully opening his mouth to suck in her breath, her smell. It was as if Miguel Ángel held Britney by the hand, pulled her onto the dance floor and made her respond to the rhythm of his own body. His tongue was the graceful dancer, and Britney's had no problem following the lead.

She felt his body turn warmer under her touch. His kisses became more passionate, his hands crawled under her sweater, searching for the softest parts of her skin. These were all places where he'd been before, but this time, a soft, quiet voice deep inside of her told her to stop. What was she thinking? She couldn't go on with a relationship like this. She was only sixteen, and she was pregnant.

"No," Britney mumbled, the palms of her hands softly pushing Miguel Ángel away.

"What's the matter, baby?" Miguel Ángel asked, his hazel eyes fixed into hers.

And it happened again. The love, the anguish, the mystery, the rage, the desire, all those feelings inside Miguel Ángel's eyes caught her one more time, trapped her like the spider its prey. They were her dark cave of promises and secrets, of hope and adventure, a place she found hard to resist.

When she failed to answer, Miguel Ángel kissed her lips again, and she stopped fighting. Their breathing became heavier, their movements transformed from slow and deliberate to frantic and hurried. There was a rumbling volcano about to explode inside his chest, his head, between his legs. Miguel Ángel began anticipating the sweet sensation of touching Britney all over her body.

At first, Britney was getting swept by the emotions of the surprise encounter. She'd missed Miguel Ángel so much, she tried so hard to reach him and felt as if he would just disappear. Then she remembered Sean again and all the confusing emotions he brought with him. "Stop!" Britney cried out, pushing him away with all her strength.

Miguel Ángel was taken aback by her show of force. He looked at her quizzically and pulled her closer. "What's wrong?"

"I, I, I don't know. I'm not feeling well," she said, again trying to push him away. "Maybe it's something I ate last night. And I have a lot of homework to do. And I don't know . . . I don't think this is right."

Miguel Ángel felt the air escape from his lungs. Being with Britney, feeling her touch was the solution to all his problems. Her presence made him disappear from the universe, from its joys and heartbreaks, from his brothers and his sisters and his mother. It didn't matter whether he lived in a tiny apartment or if the Packing Shed evaporated. Whether his mother wore silly hats or Coach yelled at him. Being with Britney made it all feel right. Her rejection stung more than a hundred lost bouts.

"C'mon Britney, you know how hard it is for me to get here. I don't even want to borrow Beto's car anymore, but I did it just to be with you."

Britney bit her lip. It would be the perfect moment to tell him everything. That she was pregnant and she was scared and confused. That she was afraid of what her father would do if he found out. That what they were doing was crazy.

"I'm so sorry, Miguel Ángel. I need to go home right now."

CHAPTER 26

Coach arrived earlier than usual at the gym. He wanted to have some time to think, time with his heavy bags all alone. He needed the release that only comes from punching sand-filled canvas bags. They were his best friends. They allowed him to pound them senseless and nevertheless still said goodnight at the end of the day. Bags never complained or required a cut man to stop the bleeding. Their strength was free, unconditional, caring. Any time, any day.

He was still trying to digest the meaning of Bruno's revelations. His program was facing obliteration not because it was bad, or because he had enemies, people he had managed to offend in the past. It was because he was standing on the wrong side of the political fence when the winds of change started blowing. Bruno was saying, his alliances would not make a difference. Friends could only help if they had power and if they wanted to use it.

Coach chose a pair of punching gloves and wraps from the cage. Like any skillful boxer, he wrapped his knuckles himself. Skill or not, there was nobody else around to help. He walked to a heavy bag, the closest to the mat, and began rolling on the balls of his feet as if facing a fighter. He threw his best punches, first right, then left, and found a block of cement waiting for him. It was like trying to stop a train with your fists. Maybe you could stop it eventually, but the moving beast wasn't going to leave you standing.

It wasn't fair, he thought. Punch, punch. Fifteen years of volunteering, and then this. Bang, bang. What about his kids, the twenty boys with no after-school programs? Jab, jab. Maybe it was time to let go, move on, do something else. He was retired. Maybe he should travel around the world with his wife. Punch, punch. The children needed him, he thought. Jab, jab. Somebody else would step in, he said to himself. Bam, bam.

Fifteen minutes later, he didn't feel the need to beat council members into a pulp any more. He would only have a little chat with them. Maybe he would give them a piece of his mind. Punch, punch.

His boys began to arrive. They saw him training, so they said a quick hello and ran directly to the mat to stretch. Their nimble bodies easily bent, their hands reaching their toes in no time.

∾∾∾

"Am I sparring today, Coach?"

The boxers had finished their required warm up and Coach was walking among them, stopping to instruct, advise and scold. Look, you're holding your arms too high, you look like a bird. Don't just punch—bob and weave. Gotta remember to duck your opponent. Move your feet, don't just stand like a statue.

And now Ryan, the youngest and most recent addition to the gym, was asking for the highest reward a trainee could aspire to. The first chance to hop into the ring. Coach looked down into Ryan's eyes, deep and fiery as a beach bonfire. The nine-year-old had been coming to the gym for exactly three months, and from the get-go he had made it clear to Coach there was nothing else in the world he wanted more than getting inside the ropes.

Ryan was eager, but coach wasn't sure he was ready. He had been running every day, training every afternoon and practicing all the combinations, exactly as instructed by Coach. But he was too anxious. Coach was afraid that, if let loose in the ring, he would go wild like a runaway horse.

"You're going to bleed up there. Are you ready for that?" Coach told Ryan, still looking hard into his eyes.

The boy nodded rapidly. "Yes, Coach, I know. But I'm not afraid. I'm ready."

"Bring me the wraps," Coach instructed, letting out a big sigh of resignation.

While it was true that Coach usually let the boxers get into the ring after three months of running, bag punching and shadowboxing, he liked to play a little with the timing depending on the fighter. Those who were too eager needed a bit more restraint, or they could hurt themselves. Each fighter was different, and Coach had to use some psychology to figure out what pushed his boys.

Ryan had a hard time handling disappointment. Too many adults in his life had broken too many promises, and Coach didn't want to add his name to the list. He would let him spar for one round and see how things went.

As he wrapped the boy's bony hands, Coach went over three months of training in five minutes. "Now, remember. When you're up there, just look at the other guy's chest, don't look at his face. Focus on the two-three combination: right jab, left cross, right hook. Move your feet and your head, don't just stand in one place. Keep your arms close to your body and, when you throw a punch, pull your arm right back and crouch back to position again."

The boy said nothing, only nodded through the set of instructions that Coach was rattling off.

"Mouse, get ready. You're going to help Ryan here."

"Yes, Coach," the eleven-year-old fighter said, running to the boxing cage for a pair of gloves.

Their helmets on and mouth pieces in place, the boys climbed into the ring and waited for the bell to start its next round. Soon, five or six kids surrounded the ring, each encouraging their favorite. A dozen water bottles stood sentinel, ready to be used at the sound of the bell. Since it was Ryan's first time, the crowd was rooting for him.

"Get him, Ryan, get him," they yelled. It was all part of the training. Ryan lunged at Mouse and tried to reach him with his long-practiced one-two combination, but Mouse used his arms to deflect the blows.

"Slow down, Ryan, you need to last three rounds. Mouse, try one of your combination punches, but go easy, okay."

After almost a minute of ducking and blocking punches, Mouse used a one-two combination of his own that sent Ryan butt first to the canvas. Ryan bounced back like a spring, but Coach could see his nose was bleeding. Just as he expected it. Coach waved Ryan to his corner and cleaned his nose with a towel soaked in bleach and water. It was barely a trickle. The trainer looked into his boxer's eyes, made sure the boy was okay, and waved him back into the ring.

The adrenaline rush that accompanies a fighter into the ring is hard to control, and inexperienced fighters get easily hurt when they haven't learned how. It makes them run out of gas quickly, throw stupid punches that land nowhere, forget how to move around to prevent them from getting hurt. It would take three to four months for Ryan to get used to the adrenaline in his system, but aside from the nose bleed of his first fight, he would be all right.

At the sound of the bell, both fighters approached Coach's corner, where he was ready to squirt their mouths with water.

"Here, Ryan, look at me. Are you okay? Can you go on?"

Ryan looked at Coach with the same intensity—and now a spark of fear—in his deep brown eyes. Coach held his gaze for about a minute—it was steady, focused. Maybe the kid could handle another round. Then he looked at his shaky hands.

"Okay, Ryan, you're done for the day. Come down here," he ordered the nine-year-old.

As he helped the young boxer take off his helmet and gloves, Coach continued with the lecture. Ryan, still quiet, had a mix of disappointment and relief in his face.

"You went at Mouse too fast, and that got you all worked up, see? You have to watch your opponent first, make sure you guess what he's going to try. You also have to pace yourself, remember? You have to last three rounds up there."

"Yes, Coach," Ryan nodded eagerly.

"All that emotion you feel, all that energy that's going up and down your body, that's called adrenaline. It helps you become faster, more alert, but you have to learn how to control it. Can you feel it?"

The boy nodded rapidly, a spark of recognition in his eyes.

"It feels weird now, but you'll get used to it. Go sit down with your head leaning back until the bleeding stops, and then do some shadowboxing. You have to be ready for tomorrow," Coach said, still looking into his boxer's eyes.

"Okay, Coach," Ryan responded and walked toward the chair Coach had pointed to without stopping.

ᔑᔑᔑ

Coach was on the fourth spar of the afternoon when Luis, one of his most promising and most inconsistent boxers, stopped by long enough to be noticed. He was covering his nose, and his left eye had a cut below the eyebrow. It was bleeding. There was blood all over his eye and on his white shirt.

"Let me see that," Coach said, turning away from ringside. "You won't need stitches, but you need to get it fixed right away. Let's see what we can do."

Coach went to find his first aid kit. He had the thirteen-year-old boy sit on a chair, and then he cleaned the wound on the eye and used surgical tape to make a bandage. He examined the nose. It didn't appear broken, although it was badly smashed. Coach made the boxer hold his head back and pinch it at the bridge. In the meantime, he cleaned the blood already drying around his mouth and on his cheeks.

"Stay like this for fifteen minutes," he told Luis when he was done. "It's going to hurt for a few days, but it doesn't look like it's broken, and you don't need a doctor sewing you up. What happened?"

"I was walking out of the store with my cousin when these two guys from school came up to us and asked us what we claimed. My cousin said, 'We don't claim nothing,' but he was wearing his 49ers shirt, you know? He's a big fan. So the guys tell him he's a liar, and they push him to the ground. I didn't want to see my cousin beat, so I jumped in to defend him. You should see how I left them, Coach. I showed them real good," the boy said, a painful smile showing on his face.

"You're not supposed to be fighting on the streets anymore, remember? You're supposed to be saving your energy for championships. What if you break your hands and then you can't compete? Is that what you want? All this training spoiled by a stupid street fight?"

"I couldn't help it, Coach. They were beating my cousin. Would you let your cousin get beat up?"

"I guess not. Is your cousin in a gang?"

"I don't know. I don't think so."

"And you? Are you getting into gangs?"

"No, Coach, I wouldn't do that."

"So what does this mean, eh?"

Coach had pulled out a red bandana hanging from Luis' rear. When the boy sat down, the piece of cloth almost reached the floor. He snagged it and shoved it into Luis' face.

"Coach, it's just un *pañuelo*. I need it to clean my sweat and everything."

"Don't give me that bullshit," Coach snarled, throwing the handkerchief on the ground and stomping on it before turning his back on the boy.

It was one of the first signs. Kids who joined gangs began displaying their colors: red or blue, Norteños or Sureños.

Coach looked at Luis as if he were reading a map and knew exactly where the roads originated and where they led. Children like him, with poor parents slaving away at underpaid jobs, with no role models in their surroundings and little hope to ever become anything in life, were drawn to the gang as a way to become somebody. It was the same everywhere: in Los Angeles, Boston, Chicago, in small towns and big cities all over the United States. The gang lifestyle, with the money and power that came from selling drugs, was like a mirage in the middle of a bankrupt desert.

It was time to bring in another expert to shake some sense into Luis. Coach marched over to Bruno's office. Coach paced near the pool tables while Bruno finished a phone conversation. Finally, he heard him beckoning.

"Hey, Coach, come on over."

"Bruno, help me out here. I have one of my fighters carrying a red bandana and saying he's not in gangs. Wanna talk to him?"

"Sure, I'll come over."

Both men walked over the training area. Coach ordered Luis to follow Bruno, who put a hand around the youngster's shoulders and brought him back to his office. They spent more than an hour talking, under the watchful eye of Coach, who was splitting his attention between the ring and Bruno's office.

When Luis returned to the training area, he walked by Coach without looking him in the eye. He walked into the cage and pulled out a jumping rope. He jumped for about two minutes before he put the rope back. Then he walked toward one of the speed bags. He did that for another two minutes, then moved on to his next exercise, as demanded by the buzzing bell. Completing their training in two-minute intervals reminded the fighters what they were training for.

Luis trained for about an hour—he usually stayed twice as long—before he announced he was leaving. Coach didn't say anything, just turned around and waved goodbye.

After the kid was gone, Coach gave instructions to the boxers up in the ring. Then he moseyed back to Bruno's office on the other side of the Packing Shed. The big boisterous man wasn't on the phone this time. He seemed to be concentrating on adding up some numbers with a calculator. He raised his head when he heard Coach approach his office.

"You too want to leave the gang?" he asked, a wide smile on his even wider face. "It's gonna cost you. . . . "

"So what did the kid say?"

"The usual. 'I'm just hanging with my homeboys, they're in the gangs but I'm not. I dress like them because it's cool.' 'I like red, it's a good color.' 'A tattoo means you have friends, not that you're in a gang.' Man, I've heard the same explanations for twenty years."

Coach sat on a chair next to Bruno's desk. He had the look of a wounded bull, a bleeding brute that couldn't believe the sword had gone through his flank and was almost touching his heart. He'd suffered many of those and knew exactly how they felt. And even though the pain was a familiar one, it took on a different meaning each time. He was on the verge of losing a kid again. He'd saved many, but he'd lost more than he cared to remember. It was a painful recognition, a bitter feeling. Every time he recovered from a heartbreak, from losing a kid to the gang or to a gunshot, he always hoped he'd never have to go through it again.

"Have I lost him?"

"Nah, not yet," Bruno said, his carefree tone almost too jovial for the occasion. "He's a good kid, he'll turn around. He's not deep into it yet. You just have to watch out for his bullshit, that's all."

Coach lowered his head and bit his lips. For a few minutes, he was silent.

"How do you do it, Bruno? You've been at it for almost as long as I have, and sometimes, man, I just want to throw in the towel and say I've had it. Yesterday Miguel Ángel, today Luis. Who's gonna do this to me tomorrow?"

"We don't know that, man. But the problem is, there are not enough people like us here to help them all, so we can't abandon them. Yeah, you get discouraged because one or two kids leave the program, but so what? There are twenty who are still here. That's twenty who are not smoking dope, who are not killing each other on the street. Twenty is a good number, if you ask me."

"But it's not enough, Bruno. We could do so much more."

"We're doing what we can, man, and if there were more people like you, they could take another twenty under their wing. And another guy like me could take another twenty. So we need like five thousand of us to take the whole city's children. Heck, we need a whole army. It's not just here in Salinas, you know that. Wherever there's drugs, there's gangs. And maybe those who are home watching soap operas are the ones who should feel guilty, not you man. We're doing what we can, we're only human."

Coach shook his head and rubbed his forehead with his left hand. How ironic! More people like them were needed and here they were, hoping not to be put out on the streets in the next few months. The people who were needed, now without a place to go. The group that ran the arts program had been put out in the streets by the city a few months ago. Why would they do the same to his boxing program, to Bruno's anti-gang counseling? It didn't make sense. It just didn't make any sense.

"Bruno, I want to talk to one of those politico friends of yours, somebody who can help us out of this mess. Plug me in, man."

"Well, I've already spoken with Agnes, but she's trying to be very cautious. She can't promise anything, but she's always been very supportive of my program. Maybe you should introduce yourself."

"I think I should, Bruno," the old man said, staring into the Packing Shed's welcome sign: No colors allowed here. "Maybe I'll bring one of my fighters with me."

CHAPTER 27

Britney showered and changed her clothes as soon as she got home. Then she walked over to Tiffany's room.

"Tiffany? Are you there?"

"Come in," she said. "It's open."

She found her sister lying on her back, reading a vampire novel. Tiffany could be so unoriginal.

"How did it go?"

"Where's Mom?" Britney asked, trying to avoid the question.

"She left about half an hour ago. She had some meeting."

"Tiff, do you think Miguel Ángel is a loser?"

Tiffany lowered her book and placed it on her stomach. She looked at her sister's wrinkled forehead, a sure sign of stress. She didn't want to make it any harder on her.

"How can I tell? I don't know the guy. You know him better. Is he a loser?"

"Dad lectured me last night about how we deserve to get better boyfriends than a loser like . . . Manolo. He said he wants me to get together with a guy like Sean Schrattenthaler, or other clients' children. That we are going to have a future and someone like Miguel Ángel won't. Do you think that Manolo has a future? Or Miguel Ángel?"

"Well, everybody has a future, but just what kind of a future, that's the difference. I suppose it's harder for a guy like Miguel Ángel to have a future like yours or mine. We're going to attend the best schools in the country and meet lots of important people. Will Miguel Ángel attend one of the best schools? If he's lucky, he'll go to community college or maybe San Jose State. We'll go to Brown or Stanford. Manolo got a scholarship to MIT, so he may be different. If he studies hard, he may get a very good job. But sometimes it's not how hard you study, it's who you know. If you don't have influential friends or contacts, it's going to be more difficult to get ahead. Maybe that's what Dad was talking about."

"But does that make you a better person? Going to Harvard or MIT or Stanford? If you go to community college, are you a loser?"

"No, it just means you don't have our kind of money, and you probably won't be able to spend your summer vacations in the Bahamas or drive a BMW or buy an Armani suit."

"But people like Miguel Ángel, or Manolo, they're kind and sweet boys. I just can't believe they're losers."

"But they can't buy you nice gifts. Look at what I got for Valentine's," she said, caressing a gold necklace. "Manolo gave roses, a book of poetry and letters. I mean, they were romantic and all, but you can't take your letters to a party. You can't show your letters to your friends. Well, you can. I did, and all my friends gave me a hard time about them. I was heartbroken and all, but really, when it comes down to it, if you're going to be with somebody, you better be with someone who can afford to keep you in the lifestyle you're accustomed to, or even better."

Miguel Ángel was sweet and gentle, and Britney loved recreating in her mind the moments they spent together. Over and over and over again. But she didn't know if that meant she was in love. And her new attraction to Sean made her doubt it. What would Miguel Ángel do if he found out? Would he beat him like a punching bag?

Britney had to stop seeing Miguel Ángel. She couldn't go on with this. But she missed him. She missed his eyes, his lips, his hands. He made her feel so good, so loved, so beautiful. It was intoxicating, and she was addicted.

The thought scared her. She shot up from the bed and decided she had to run.

"I gotta go. I'll see you later."

"Wait. Where are you going? Wanna come with me and my friends to the movies? We're going to see *Disturbia* in Roxanne's home theater."

The idea of spending an evening with her sister's friends was not exactly what Britney wanted. She'd rather stay home listening to music and thinking about the whole mess she had gotten herself into. But she didn't want to be alone either.

"Okay, I'll go. When are you leaving?"

"In an hour or so. You can start changing clothes now."

"Ha ha ha, you're so funny."

CHAPTER 28

"Keep it Gangsta" by Snoop Dog was playing in Beto's stereo, the amplified sound making the Escalade rattle like an ill-constructed bridge under the weight of lettuce-loaded trucks. Beto's idea of having a good time was riding around town with the windows down and the sound of the stereo up, way up. That's how the girls noticed him and his sparkling white chariot.

After dropping Britney off, Miguel Ángel had returned to Salinas to bring back his friend's SUV. He had missed training the day before, so he was determined to train twice as hard today. He was already running late. Coach would be upset. And he was getting a headache, so he stretched his left arm to the stereo's dial and lowered the volume, following immediately with a question.

"How can we save the Packing Shed?" Miguel Ángel asked, hoping Beto would overlook his trespass.

Beto turned his head and glowered at Miguel Ángel.

"Man, I have no idea. Want me to ask my homies if they have a place Coach can rent?"

Miguel Ángel wanted absolutely nothing to do with Beto's *vatos*. "Never mind. Let me ask you something else. Do you think Britney would ever marry me?"

"You're joking, right?" Beto said, his look of anger quickly becoming one of disdain. Beto rolled his eyes as he turned his face away from Miguel Ángel. "Man, those women are like the stars at night. They're to be admired, to be studied. But you don't marry a star, not if you're not one of them. And my friend, you're not one of them. Sheesh, what does she see in you anyway . . . "

Miguel Ángel let out a loud sigh. Deep down he knew Beto was right, but he didn't really want to admit it. What if he was wrong? What if he could marry Britney? He was going to be a champ, right? He was going to win the Olympics in London, just like Mohammed Ali had won the Olympics in Rome. He was going to turn pro and start defeating big names and win lots of endorsements. Soon, he would be a star, just like Britney, and he could buy her a house in Pebble Beach, like the one she had right now. But he would buy one for his mother first, one with a room for each of his siblings.

On the corner of East Alisal and Sanborn, as they waited to make a left turn, a red Lincoln Navigator stopped next to them and began honking. Miguel Ángel turned to look at the driver. He looked familiar. Beto pushed his body up to see, and he recognized one of his homies.

"Beto, Jarocho was offed," the man said, his voice trembling. "We're gonna meet at the office. Where are you going?"

"I just need to drop my homey here," he said, yelling past Miguel Ángel. "I'll catch you there."

The light turned green and both cars sped, the Navigator going straight and Beto's Escalade turning left.

The encounter left a bitter taste in Miguel Ángel's mouth. Sometime in the last couple of days, Miguel Ángel's image of the gang and Beto began to take a nosedive. He had always been tolerant of bangers, respectful even. All the *vatos* who joined were guys no different than Miguel Ángel. They came from the same neighborhoods, their mothers all worked in the fields, their fathers were *borrachos* or not around. They were not the evil people Coach described. And really, banging was just fun—sure, old people didn't think filling walls with graffiti or smoking weed was harmless, but Miguel Ángel didn't see what the big deal was either.

Besides, we all have a right to make our choices, Miguel Ángel would tell himself. If Beto's choice was to join a gang, so be it. But lately, the choices Beto was making didn't seem harmless anymore. The more Miguel Ángel saw Beto and what he was getting into, the more scared he got. The robbery, the gun, now this meeting with his homies. What if he ended up dead by the side of Old Stage Road, just like Jarocho?

Miguel Ángel didn't want to say anything, but for the first time since he met Beto, he was afraid for his homeboy. It was as if the sight of Jarocho had unveiled a new reality for him, as if the possibility of death for his best friend had gone from ghost to human. Yes, Miguel Ángel had seen the calm waxen face of death in a casket. But seeing Jarocho's cadaver was different. He had been abandoned by the side of the road, like a dog you want to get rid of. There were no flowers, no candles, no sobbing, and the cruelty of death smacked him right in the face. This could be Beto's fate.

Miguel Ángel feared nothing he could say would keep Beto away from the gang. He also was beginning to realize nothing good could come out of it. Coach had told him many times that the "generals" in prison, the guys who issued the rules and decided who would die and who would live, just used the *vatos* for their dirty businesses and later dumped them. It never made sense to Miguel Ángel before. Now it all started to take shape. Beto was being majorly stubborn. STOOOOPID.

They didn't speak again until they were outside the Packing Shed, Snoop humming his tunes in the background.

Before jumping out, Miguel Ángel said, "What are you going to do, bro?"

"This is war, man. We either kill or get killed. There's no choice."

"You can choose not to be in a gang, Beto."

"It's too late for that," Beto said, and he drove away.

Miguel Ángel picked up his bag from the ground, wondering if this was the last time he'd see his friend alive. The thought made him shiver. He shook his head and tried to displace his fears with the sights and sounds of the Packing Shed: the rumble of the kids fighting for a pool cue, the recreation employee calmly walking from behind the counter to broker peace. Three boys and two girls were running behind a basketball, throwing it at the hoops whenever they got their hands on it. It was a chaos that filled him, that made him feel at home . . . a home he could be on the verge of losing.

Coach was hitting a speed bag, his back turned to the door. Still, the old man could tell Miguel Ángel had arrived.

"Glad you could make an appearance," Coach greeted the young boxer. "About time you start training, champ."

The boy dropped his bag inside the cage, next to the bags of the other fighters. He stretched his legs on the mat for a few minutes, worrying about what Beto was about to do. He had been out of juvie for no more than three months, and Miguel Ángel was so glad he was out. Yet, he wanted to get away from him. He knew Beto was a bad influence, and whatever he was doing, it was bound to end up really bad.

But Beto was his friend. They had walked together to and from school for all those years. Ever since Beto had jumped in to defend him in the street fight long ago, they'd become inseparable, like true blood brothers. You don't turn your back on your family, you just don't.

He picked up the jump rope. Britney had been beautiful today, but she seemed distracted. Her kisses were cold, her eyes looking into the distance, not into his eyes. There was something wrong, but Miguel Ángel could not figure out what.

The speed bag was next. Here he would have to concentrate. No more Britney or Beto or Mom or schoolwork. It was just him and the red bouncer, his hands, his face and his little hanging friend, the speed-building wonder.

Coach walked over to him and began talking, interrupting his thoughts.

"You're letting your arms drop too low. Bring them up higher, so your fists don't have to go too far," he said, moving Miguel Ángel's elbow to the position he wanted the boy to have. "There, just punch like that. It'll be easier."

"Okay, Coach," he said, trying to concentrate on the new position encouraged by Coach. The old man stood watching for a few minutes before moving on to the next boxer.

The gym settled into a lull of jumps and punches, interrupted only by the periodic buzz of the bell and the loud trumpets and trombones of Banda el Recodo. The boxers moved from bag to bag, from ring to rope, from speedball to treadmill to shadowboxing without stopping for instructions, only exchanging a few words here and there with their fellow boxers.

In the routine and chaos of the gym, Miguel Ángel felt a little peace returning to him, a feeling of well being that was as satisfying as the milk he drank first thing in the morning. It was a peace that inundated him and made him whole, a peace he only found when he ran, when he read and, sometimes, when praying in church. And lately, when he was with Britney.

Each punch made him stronger. Shadowboxing made him quick, even if it was only an imaginary foe he was fighting. That's how he practiced his one-two combination, that's how he went over and over his jabs and hooks until he could use them with perfection against his opponents.

If he was going to be a champ, he needed to be strong, quick and have lots of stamina. Most importantly, he had to believe he could win. That's what Coach always told him. His next fight was at least a month away, but he had to start preparing right now. He was going to be the toughest, quickest, strongest boxer, and he was going to win all his bouts.

Two hours later, he was done. He took off his gloves, unwrapped his fists and packed his bag. He waved good-bye to Coach, who stopped his chat with another fighter to see him.

"You're leaving? Want a ride?"

"That's okay, Coach. I want to walk today."

"Okay, see you tomorrow."

The late August afternoon was cooling down with the winds blowing in from the ocean. Miguel Ángel pulled his black hood over his head and charged on North Sanborn against the wind. It was a wonder to him that at almost nine at night the sky could still be so clear, the Gabilans still so visible. He walked past a young mother pushing a twin stroller with a child on one of the seats and bundled blankets on the other. Across the street, outside the Laundromat, a couple of wary men wearing dusty jeans talked while waiting for their clothes to wash. The siren of a police car drifted from the south. It's far, he thought. But police cars were never far enough.

I hope it's not Beto in trouble, he thought.

Outside his apartment building, a throng of kids were chasing each other in the patio. They were playing the most popular game in the neighborhood, "La Migra." A kid chosen at random was the INS officer who captured the immigrants who were without papers. As long as the kids had a hand on Doña Martina's garage door, they were safe. But before reaching the door, they had to get past the *migra* officer, who had to trap them and bring them to jail, which was the garbage dumpster at the side of the apartment building. It was a game Miguel Ángel had played when he was little. *La migra* was their boogeyman, the devil they had to cheat if they wanted to reach the Promised Land.

His mother and siblings were about to sit down to eat. Even before anyone told him what was cooking, Miguel Ángel already knew. The spicy-chocolaty smells of chicken mole inundated the entire apartment. Mari Carmen screamed in joy and jumped to his neck as a greeting.

"Migue, you're home!" she said, smacking a big kiss on his cheek.

"*M'ijo, ven, siéntate a cenar.* I made the *mole* you like so much. It came out really tasty," his mother said, lifting her head so she could see him from under her red hat.

Miguel Ángel and his siblings crowded around the tiny table to eat the hot chocolaty dish, while their hunched-up mother stayed by the stove heating up tortillas. No sooner had she dropped a steaming maize disc in the basket, when six hungry hands reached for it.

After dinner, they sat at Miguel Ángel's bed to watch TV. They were hooked on "La Otra," the breathless story of Bernarda, the lover of a dying, rich man, and her two illegitimate daughters. The young women would inherit the money of the rich man when he died, but his only legitimate child was fighting for the inheritance, even though his father wasn't even dead.

When "La Otra" was over, their mother began shepherding the children to bed.

"Mari Carmen, Juan Carlos, Víctor Manuel, you need to brush your teeth. And then get in bed."

"Mom, we don't have to go to school tomorrow. Can we watch TV a little longer?"

In the end, their mother went to sleep in the apartment's only bedroom while all the kids stayed up watching TV. Miguel Ángel pulled out one of his Muhammad Ali books and opened it to a random page.

Cassius grew up in a time when blacks were forced to stay apart from whites. He and Rudy had to go to a school for blacks. Like most other blacks in Louisville then, the Clays were quite poor. There was no school bus for black kids, and the Clays didn't have enough money to pay bus fare for both boys. So they usually had to walk to and from school. Young Cassius announced that he wanted to be rich one day, but his father told him he could never be rich because his skin was not white. Although he was basically a happy child, Cassius sometimes cried himself to sleep over what his people had to suffer.

CHAPTER 29

The cool morning fog had not dissipated when Miguel Ángel got into Coach's beat-up truck and took off toward South Salinas, the wealthy part of town, the area where people drove instead of walked and where hardly any women could be seen pushing strollers.

Perhaps their mission made Miguel Ángel more aware of the landscape, of the vast differences between the Alisal and the world he was about to enter. Coach drove on East Alisal across town, past the beauty shops, food markets and clothing stores that defined the East Side; past the field workers coming home from a half-day's work. The women wore embroidered white hand-kerchiefs to cover their faces, hairpins symmetrically aligned across the fold. With no school Saturday, their children would probably be home by themselves, free to roam the streets and cause mischief.

The early phone call had startled Miguel Ángel and everyone else in the family.

"Get ready," Coach told him. "I'll pick you up in five minutes."

Miguel Ángel almost gave Coach an excuse, but he couldn't. He didn't really feel like going to talk to a politician, much less to an old white lady who probably was scared of coming to the Alisal. But it was hard to say no to Coach. Plus, the Packing Shed meant a lot, to both of them.

Coach turned south on Pajaro Street. The avenue bypassed downtown with squat, commercial and office buildings and led directly to South Salinas, where the houses were markedly different than those in Alisal. No crowded apartment buildings here, only large homes with irrigated lawns, well-trimmed rose bushes and naked ladies. There were only a few people on the streets, either young joggers or old walkers parading their dogs. No pushcarts, no strollers. The magnolia trees emerged from the fog like visions in a dream and gave the old neighborhood an eerie look, as if Miguel Ángel could get trapped and never return to the Alisal.

When they arrived in the home of Agnes, Coach parked the truck, and they stepped out.

"Ready, champ?" Coach asked.

"Ready, Coach," Miguel Ángel said, craning his neck left and right.

"Good morning, come in," the would-be-mayor said after she opened the door. "It's good to see you. I was just about to have breakfast, but I can chat with you for a few minutes."

From the home entrance, Miguel Ángel could hear the chatter in the adjacent room. The smell of butter and bacon wafted from the kitchen and wrapped itself around hundreds of dolls lined up on the entrance bookshelves. Miguel Ángel looked at this old white lady, gently smiling at him, and found himself thinking about Ita. Without much thought, he followed her and Coach toward a small office.

The small room had a tiny desk and two chairs in front of it. Rather than behind her desk, she sat in front of them—no barrier between the mayor-to-be and her future constituents.

Coach avoided politicians. He always said he had no use for their empty promises or shifty personalities. Miguel Ángel was surprised Coach even asked him to come to the candidate's house. But Agnes didn't strike Miguel Ángel as shifty or empty. She was not trying to grab the microphone to say what she wanted. She was going to let Coach do the talking.

For some reason, that made Miguel Ángel feel good.

"I don't know if you know what's happening at the Packing Shed, but I want to see if there's something you can do about it. I've never really asked for favors from anybody, all I want is for my boxers to have a place to train," Coach said.

Coach talked about the hours he'd put in training young boys, the equipment he'd bought to improve the place. It was a hobby in a way, he said, but a hobby that gave children something to do. No, not all of the children ended up champions, not all of them wanted to put in the time and energy. But at least they were not roaming the streets, learning the ways of the gangs and crime.

Then he told her about the rumors. Was it true that he was being punished because Bruno supported her? And if she got into office, could she promise he was not going to get kicked out?

Miguel Ángel was startled. It was the first he'd heard of this, and he didn't like it. He was about to say something, but he turned to look at Agnes and thought better of it.

"Ma'am, I don't want anything for me. I'm an old man, I'm retired, I can go find another hobby if I want to. But

I believe, deep down in my heart, that those kids need me," Coach went on.

"Mr. Ramos, I've heard an awful lot about you over the years, and I'm sure glad you decided to come visit me. But I'm going to be very honest with you. I don't want this issue politicized. I believe we have to look out for our children and our youth, not play politics and backstabbing.

"Be that as it may, I'm in no position to make promises. I know you care about the Packing Shed and how much work you've put into it. I promise to get you appropriate recognition by the city for what you're doing. We should write you a well-earned commendation."

"What's a commendation going to do?" Miguel Ángel exploded. "I can't train on a commendation. We need a gym, we need punching bags."

Coach bolted from his seat and turned to Miguel Ángel.

"Calm down, champ," he yelled. "Sit down and show some respect."

"Serious, Coach? What did you bring me here for, then? So I can listen to this crap?"

"Young man, sit down," Agnes said calmly. "I want to hear what you have to say."

All Miguel Ángel wanted to do in that minute was run back to the Alisal. He closed his eyes, grinded his teeth, craned his neck and tried to calm down. "I'm sorry, ma'am," he mumbled. "I'm under a lot of stress right now. We don't want to lose the Packing Shed." Agnes walked around the desk, poured herself a glass of water and offered some to Coach and Miguel Ángel. They declined. She then walked back again to her chair and sat down.

"We need this place," Miguel Ángel pleaded. "Is there anything you can do to help us?"

Agnes stared at Miguel Ángel for what felt like an eternity. She took another sip of water, then finally spoke. "I can't promise that you'll stay at the Packing Shed. I can't do that, young man, and it has nothing to do with your program, Mr. Ramos. What you're doing is commendable, and if we only had one hundred residents as committed as you are to our youth, this would be a very different place.

"If I start making promises here and there, and later on they compromise the overall health of the entire city, I'm going to have to break those promises. I don't want to do that."

Miguel Ángel dropped his head to his chest. Coach let out a sigh and rearranged himself on the chair.

Agnes went on with her speech, but Miguel Ángel stopped listening. There were plenty of adults in his life who had let him down, and he wasn't interested in hearing yet another one.

CHAPTER 30

The small room trapped a strong smell of fried onion and warm tortillas. From the window, Britney could see dozens of children chasing after footballs, brown kids with silver teeth and short, black hair. By the stove, where boiling milk was spilling over, a rattan cradle held a small baby. The baby began crying, softly at first, but its cries grew louder and louder. Britney ran from her bed to pick it up and try to calm it down, but the baby wouldn't stop. She tried the lullaby Rosa used with her when she was little, the one the old nanny still used whenever Britney cried on her shoulder. But that didn't work. The baby kept on crying, louder each time.

Miguel Ángel walked in. He yelled at her, "What's the matter with you? Can't you hear the baby crying?" He sat down on a chair, took off his work boots and his greasy overalls. Soon after Miguel Ángel, four children followed: three boys and a girl, their clothes ripped and stained, all blonde and blue-eyed, asking for food.

"Mom, we're hungry," they demanded. "What's for dinner?"

But besides the boiling milk, there was nothing on the stove. Britney went to open the tiny refrigerator next to the kitchen sink and all she found was a six-pack of beer.

Miguel Ángel yelled at her: "Give me one. Maybe there's something you can do after all."

"Mom, I'm hungry!"

"Me too!"

"Me too!"

"Are you going to make something?"

"We want some tacos."

"Can you make me some nachos?"

"Can you make me spaghetti?"

"Can you make me *chilaquiles*?"

The noise upset the baby even further, and Britney ran to the cradle to pick it up. She rocked it, trying to hush it, but its wails grew even louder.

"Did you check her diaper? Maybe it's wet. Why don't you think of these things? Why do I have to tell you how to do everything?" Miguel Ángel yelled at her, taking another swig of his beer.

Britney put the baby on the table, unwrapped the blankets to change the diaper. But instead of finding the baby's milky white belly, the young mother came face to face with a bloody old man, a wrinkled, red devil that let out a sinister laugh. Britney grabbed the baby under the arms and threw it against the door.

She woke up sweating and crying. She grabbed the phone and dialed Miguel Ángel's number.

CHAPTER 31

Early morning runs were always good to help Miguel Ángel get rid of pent-up anxiety, and today's was a particularly good one. Hardly any cars on the road, lots of birds flying above, he didn't even notice the garbage on the road. By the time he made it back into the apartment, he had already forgotten everything about that old politician lady. The magic didn't last long.

"For you, Miguel Ángel," bossy Ana Estela announced after answering the phone.

"Miguel Ángel, I need to see you right away," Britney cried at the other end of the line.

"Baby, what's wrong?"

"I had this horrible dream."

"Calm down, baby, I'll come to see you as soon as I'm done, okay? Don't cry, honey, please." The line was dead.

Britney's voice sounded so panicked Miguel Ángel didn't even want to shower. But he didn't want to see her all sweaty and stinky, so he rushed to the bathroom. Locked.

"It's busy," Víctor Manuel yelled from inside.

"Dude, get out. I need to shower now."

"Wait. I'm busy."

Miguel Ángel pounded the door.

"Get out now, it's urgent!"

"Sheesh. You can't even go to the bathroom in peace in this house," Víctor Manuel said, as he walked out still zipping up his pants.

"Gross! Did you wash your hands?" Ana Estela asked.

"Didn't you see how he was rushing me?"

Miguel Ángel ignored the rest of the conversation. He jumped in the shower, got out and got dressed in about a third of the time it usually took him. Now the problem would be how to get to the Peninsula. He didn't want to ask Beto to lend him the Escalade. Something was going to happen, something always happened when gang bangers declared war, and he didn't want to be near his friend if suddenly he ran into his enemies.

He'd have to take the bus. It would take him two hours to get there, and with his head tied in knots, it was certainly going to feel like an eternity.

The bus left from East Alisal and Sanborn at around 2:15, almost half hour after he walked out of his house and a lifetime since he began waiting. At the downtown bus station, he boarded Route 11 of the Salinas-Monterey Transit bus line, which would take an hour to reach Monterey. The bus was almost empty, but he refused to sit down. Instead, he walked to the back of the bus and began jumping lightly on the balls of his feet, as if waiting to enter the boxing ring. Never mind the beautiful hills that everyone always seemed to admire. Right now, the hills on Highway 68 were just an obstacle to meeting his girlfriend. Maybe she was at their spot already. That dream must have been awful. She'd never called him crying like that before. Maybe she dreamed that he died? That her father found out about him? That they broke up? Or worse, that Miguel Ángel would never be a champ?

The bus wasn't traveling very fast, yet the trip was making him dizzy. He sat down, and from the window he admired the hills of Toro Park, where dozens of contented cows munched on the dry grass and the turkey vultures flew so low Miguel Ángel could touch them if he stretched his arm up. An older, gray-haired woman sitting two rows in front of him told the woman sitting next to her, "*Mira qué bonitas se ven las montañas.*"

"Yeah, the hills look beautiful," the younger woman responded, absentmindedly, without raising her eyes from her furiously texting fingers.

I hear you, sister. The mountains are pretty, but not when you're admiring them from the bus, he thought.

Miguel Ángel decided to shut his ears to the chatter and concentrate on his girl. Yes, her voice sounded panicked, but he knew hers was a problem he could solve. There was nothing a champ like him couldn't do. Cool in crisis, cool in crisis. Whatever it was, he would fix it. Then they would even find a cool hiding place to make out. Dang, why was the frigging bus taking so long.

The tortuous bus ride took more than an hour and a half to reach its ultimate destination in Pacific Grove.

Miguel Ángel found Britney sitting on a bench overlooking the shore, the Central Coast's gateway to the Pacific Ocean. He withheld his first impulse to run to hug her and instead stayed still for a second, admiring her long, golden hair cascading behind the bench. Even from the back, she looked like a movie star.

They were too young to marry, but his own mother had married at fourteen. Britney was sixteen now, so maybe it was possible. He could drop out of high school, take a job and rent a small apartment for the two of them. He would train evenings and weekends.

"Hi, honey." Miguel Ángel hugged her from the back and gave her a kiss on her right cheek. "Have you been waiting for long? I'm sorry, the buses take forever."

Her eyes were red and swollen, and her nose looked pink and raw from all the wiping. She tried to smile, but all she could manage was a grimace. The salty ocean breeze pushed her hair past her face, and he tried to pull it back with his fingers. She looked like a child who had just broken her mother's precious vase and knew she was in for a scolding.

"I don't know how to tell you this," she began. "The night when we first . . . remember you said you'd pull out. . . . Miguel Ángel, I'm pregnant," she said, and immediately began sobbing.

The boy drew her close and hugged her, his mind drawing a blank. Pregnant. A baby. With this beautiful girl, the love of his life. Maybe a boy. He was speechless. What do you do when you have a baby? You're supposed to be happy, right?

"That's great news, honey. Right? Why are you so sad?"

Her sobs became wails now, her desperation mounting on realizing perhaps he wouldn't be as supportive of her decision as she expected.

"I can't have this baby. Don't you get it? I'm too young, I have to go to college. I have a future."

He drew away. All his life, he had seen the announcement of a new life coming to this world as the ultimate happiness. Even when his younger brothers were born, even when he had so many misgivings about them—never any food in the fridge, never enough clothes to hand down—his mother was always happy. A child was always something to be desired. Celebrated.

"I . . . I don't get it," he murmured. "You don't want to have a baby? But you're pregnant already. What do you want to do?"

Britney didn't answer. Instead, she lowered her head and bit her lips.

Then it hit him. She wanted an abortion. She wanted to end the life they had created together. The realization felt like a blow to his solar plexus, like the ones he got from the older boxers who wanted to teach him a lesson.

"You want to . . . You don't want to have it? You want to have an abortion? Is that what you want?"

Britney nodded firmly, thick tears rolling down her cheeks.

"But why? Don't you love me? Don't you want to be with me? Don't you want to have my baby?"

The girl had managed to control her crying, but after Miguel Ángel's questions, her muzzled sobs grew louder again.

She looked into his thin, earnest face, and saw an ocean of love that she knew she couldn't brave to navigate. It was too wide, too choppy, too intense. As long as she had a beautiful view of the sea, she had no desire to enter its waters.

"I'm only sixteen," she mumbled. "I have my whole life ahead. I can't stop right now to have babies."

And I don't want to end up with lots of kids, living in a smelly apartment and seeing you change into a jerk, she wanted to say, but stopped herself. It was a dream, a bad dream to be sure, and she knew Miguel Ángel would never become the ogre of her nightmares. At least she hoped not.

Miguel Ángel looked into the ocean. There were lovers walking on the beach, holding hands, stopping casually to give each other a kiss. There was low tide, and the waves were gently lapping against the sand. The foam rolled in and out, and two otters anchored in some weeds rolled with the waves and played with each other.

The first time he had seen the ocean was a few months ago, when Britney asked him to come see her near her house. He had never seen anything so vast, so open. The Gabilans were magnificent, but they had a limit: when they touched the sky, they stopped. The ocean had no edge, it just kept going and going for miles until it fused with the heavens and became one. Just the way it happened when he and Britney had made love.

When he first saw the ocean, with Britney standing next to him, he thought he would always think of its impatient waters joyfully, because they would remind him of his sweet princess and the delicious times they spent together.

Life could be so cruel.

This wasn't fair. If Britney didn't want to have their baby, it was because she didn't want to be with him, she didn't trust him, she wanted no link to him. She didn't want to have his baby.

The elation he felt on seeing Britney turned into anger, a heat that started in his belly and spread to the rest of his body. In that moment of transformation, Miguel Ángel saw himself hitting Britney across the face with such force that she landed on the sand far away from the bench where they were sitting. He'd become just like the men he'd seen abuse his mother, the drunks who demanded respect and obedience at all cost. In his vision, Britney rubbed her reddened cheek and began screaming for help. He would be arrested and taken to jail for spousal abuse, just like Mari Carmen's father was.

He would serve time in prison for hitting his girlfriend, a rich girl who could probably afford a pricey attorney. A lifetime of consequences just for slapping a brat, a girl he thought loved him, but didn't.

He wouldn't do it. He closed his fists, his eyes and ears to all the voices of rage. Cool in crisis, just like Ali. Cool in crisis. Your opponent hits you in the pit of your stomach, and you don't become angry, you don't waste your energy trying to pummel him. You go over your strategy, remind yourself of your ultimate goal, and keep your head on your shoulders. Keep your cool, man. Keep your cool.

"Do you need help? Money?" he said, fighting the tears that were brimming behind his eyelids.

"I don't know. I'm going to ask my sister to take me to the doctor on Monday."

"I can take you if you want me to."

"No, it's okay. I'll ask her. It'll be better."

"Okay, then. I need to go home. See you."

"But you just got here. Don't you want to talk?"

"We have nothing to talk about," he said, getting up from the bench. "You've made your decision. *Adiós.*"

A soft voice in her head told her to follow him, to hug him and ask him to stay, to cradle him like she would a baby. A louder voice told her not to bother, he looked too determined to be convinced to stay. He was a proud guy, she thought. A poor proud boy, the kind her father described in his midnight tirade.

CHAPTER 32

So this is how it feels to lose your soul. In one fell swoop, a dark hand reaches into your stomach, pulls out the happiness, the hope and the illusion, and drains you empty. You are still here, but nothing you cherish is within sight. There is no space in your mind for plans or dreams. All that's left is the last moment with your loved one, a film projector from hell playing over and over the scene that ripped your soul apart.

Britney was gone. His baby was gone. They had arrived like a surprise summer rain, and just as quickly they had evaporated.

He walked back to the bus stop, but didn't wait for the next one to come. Like a robot, he began walking, not thinking about the distance he had to travel. The waves, furiously lapping at the rocks, seemed to be lashing out at him. The seagulls fighting for scraps of food, the casual runners going up Lighthouse Boulevard, they were mocking him, telling him, "You've been so stupid." It was all an illusion. How could you ever believe you could grab a star? Isn't that what Beto said? Stars are to be admired, not to be plucked from the heavens and kept in a one-bedroom apartment at the Alisal. Britney was a star, and Miguel Ángel could never have her, no matter how much he loved her. How could he be so stupid?

The summer fog was rolling in, but he didn't feel the cold. He strolled past Pacific Grove and into Monterey by the Aquarium. He noticed people eyed him suspiciously. People like him—dark-skinned men with cropped hair and wearing hoodies—weren't exactly the tourist type. He walked by Cannery Row and its luxury shops—the golf clothing, the chocolate store—that were a far cry from the sardine canneries Steinbeck had described in his novel. He walked by Fisherman's Wharf, where there were hardly any fishermen left; and Window on the Bay, with its joggers and roller skaters, kayakers and surfers. Miguel Ángel's head was throbbing with questions, stabbing him once and again with the piercing thought of Britney's actions. Why? Why did she have to do this? His mind would play the fateful moment over and over and over, blinding him to the cars, to the beauty of the ocean and beaches that attracted tourists from all over the world.

In Seaside, he took the bus. It was crowded with young men and women, as brown as his mother, his cousins, his friends at school. They were so much like his neighbors. They probably would laugh at him if they knew what Britney had just done to him. And you thought you could fly and steal a star? Did you think the moon is made of cheese too?

He never planned on having a baby. Or breaking up with Britney. Or hooking up with her, for that matter. Meeting her had been a lucky event, a comet that appears in the sky once every hundred years. So he just stood there, watching it go by across the heavens, being lucky enough to grab it by its tail and enjoy the ride.

Sometimes, he would think about having a family with her. Heck, that's what he was thinking about on the way over. Yes, it would be wonderful to have a family. It'd be a chance to show the world how to treat a woman, his woman and their kids. He would never hit Britney or abandon her, like his father had done to his mother. Like so many men had done to his mother. It never occurred to him that Britney would be the one to leave him. He'd never seen his mother reject anybody.

But she was really pregnant. There was a baby inside of her that he had created, and he would never get to see it. She wanted to have a future, that's what she told him. And that future did not include a child, or Miguel Ángel.

When the bus reached the Salinas station, he rushed to the bathroom and made it to one of the stalls just in time to throw up.

A few hours after leaving Britney, Miguel Ángel arrived home. He found Ana Estela doing homework at the kitchen table, in a tiny space squeezed among piles of bills, clean pots and empty grocery bags. He sat down in front of her and watched her read and take notes for a while. She had the same look she always took on when she was trying to ignore him.

Finally, she looked up from her papers. "What's eating you, brother? You seem upset."

"Nothing," he said.

She looked at him intently. Her lips parted, but then she shook her head and went back to her homework.

After a long silence, he spoke again. "Do you believe we have a future?"

She stopped and raised her head, a quizzical look in her eyes. That was a weird question coming from him, and Miguel Ángel knew it.

"Of course we have a future. What kind of question is that? You're going to the Olympics to win a gold medal.

You're going to get lots of endorsements from Everlast and Nike and Golden Boy Promotions. And I'm going to become a lawyer to defend farm workers. Our brothers and sisters will go to college, make money and buy a house for Mom. That sounds like a good future to me."

"But what if it doesn't happen? What if I don't qualify for the Olympics and there's no medal and no endorsements? What if you don't get accepted to law school, but get pregnant and have to get married to support your baby? What if none of us can go to college and can't buy Mom nothing? What if she has to pick lettuce for a living for the rest of her life?"

"What if an airplane falls out of the sky on our apartment? What if an earthquake rips the earth and swallows us whole? Miguel Ángel, you can't be worried about what ifs because they're just that, what ifs. We're not going about life just hoping I can go to college and you can go to the Olympics. We're working hard to get there. It's not as if we're hoping to win the lottery, we're working hard to get somewhere. What if it doesn't happen? Well, that could be, but at least we tried. If we didn't try, if I didn't study or you didn't train, our chances to get into law school or the Olympics would be really tiny."

There was a coolness about his sister's words that made him feel refreshed and also upset. "That's what mom always says: 'If you work hard, good things will follow,'" he snapped. "But look at her. She works hard, and all she ever gets are backaches and leftover lettuce."

"You can't compare what Mom's gone through with what you or I can do. She had no chance to go to school, began having kids when she was young, and had no help raising all of us. But she came to this country hoping to give us a better life. That's why we'll have a future. It's

Mom's gift to us. That's why we can't mess up, you can't get into gangs and I can't just go out there and get pregnant. It would ruin our future."

Ana Estela was now using Britney's words. He glared at his sister with anger, got up from the chair and left the apartment, slamming the door on his way out.

CHAPTER 33

Under the torrent of hot water, Britney was hoping to wash away yet another restless night. She closed her eyes and let the water pound her eyelids, her cheeks, her lips. As if the water had entered her bloodstream, Britney felt a surge of new energy running through her veins, strengthening the resolve she'd found in the early hours of the morning.

The sun was barely coming up, when the twilight gave the pines surrounding their home an eerie appearance, and the ocean was nothing more than a dark mirror with no power of reflection. Britney had come out onto the balcony to feel the ocean breeze, look into the horizon and let the sound of the waves pounding the shore calm her doubts.

Precisely what she feared the most had happened. Miguel Ángel had walked away from her, leaving her alone on the beach, sobbing, feeling miserably abandoned. She had tried to reach him the rest of the evening, wanted to tell him she was sorry, but his sister said over and over again he wasn't home. Eventually, nobody answered the phone anymore.

Staring at the photos she had taken of him—running, clowning around, shadow boxing—she cried all evening, the soft sounds of her whimpers accompanying her misery.

But when she woke up in the early morning hours—again with a start—she had a new resolve. She was not going to let him go. Miguel Ángel was her first love, the first boy who took her seriously, and she wasn't ready to give that up. They would get back together. And if she needed to have a baby to convince him, so be it. It was in the twilight, when the pitch-black sky was turning electric blue, that Britney felt her resolve grow stronger.

But strength dissolved like a sand castle under a summer wave when she saw her mother sitting on the edge of her bed, holding in her hand what appeared to be a . . . pregnancy test stick?

"Mom, what are you doing here?" Britney asked, feeling the pounding of her heart.

All her mother did was wave the test stick in front of her face, like a teacher waving a disapproving finger to a naughty student. "Is there something you need to tell me, Britney Marie?"

"I . . . don't . . . think . . . so . . . Mom," Britney responded, digging in her head for possible explanations, trying to figure out how the blessed stick ended up in her mother's French-manicured fingers.

"Britney, I'm not your father," her mother said calmly, still waving the stupid stick. "I'm not going to beat you up or exile you to Avelino. You've been acting really weird lately. Does this mean what I think it means?"

How did Mom recover the pregnancy test? Who told her—Tiffany, Rosa? Maybe Britney could lay the blame on Tiffany. How long could she hold on to a lie if she decided to tell one?

Britney looked at her mother long and hard, at those green eyes that could easily be Tiffany's, they were so similar, at her arched, perfectly trimmed eyebrows and the carefully delineated lips. For the first time, Britney saw something in her mother's eyes she'd never seen before: a glint of sadness, a well of despair that, much like Miguel Ángel's eyes, threatened to swallow her whole.

All the resolve was gone now, the sand castle flattened by the tide, reduced to a shapeless pile of sand. The girl collapsed on her mother's lap.

"I'm so sorry, Mom, so very sorry," Britney sobbed uncontrollably. "I never thought . . . never wanted to . . . "

Using her mother's knees as a cushion, as a handkerchief, Britney cried and cried until she felt there were no more tears left in her eyes. How could she have been so stupid? There was no way she was going to be able to hide her pregnancy forever. Her mother didn't speak, only stroked her hair. Were it not for the weight of her hand and the scent of her perfume, Britney could have sworn she'd disappeared.

Finally, her mother pulled her face up.

"Come up, sit here, Brit," her mother said sweetly. "We're going to work this out. Tell me everything. Who's the father?"

The girl told her everything. How she felt ignored by boys, how she met Miguel Ángel and how much she cared for him.

When Britney was done, her mother got up, took a tissue from the night stand and wiped Britney's face like she would a little child.

"Enough tears, sweetheart, crying is not going to solve the problem. Besides, your dad may hear you and wonder what's wrong. He can never find out about this."

"But, Mom . . . I was thinking . . . maybe . . . I should keep the baby . . . "

Mrs. Scozzari covered her mouth with her right hand, muffling a chuckle. She narrowed her eyes, as if trying to regain her focus, and then began speaking again in a professorial voice. Britney could tell her mother was terrified.

"First of all, Britney, just because you're pregnant doesn't mean what you have in there is a baby," her mother said. "A baby is a fully formed human being who can breathe and eat on his own, a creature with responsible adults willing to take care of it."

"But, Mom, Nonna used to say that life is sacred and that . . . "

"You know who says all life is sacred? The same people who let Hitler kill millions of Jews, that's who. A bunch of hypocrites, that's who. I wish your Nonna had never filled your head with those superstitions."

"But, Mom . . . "

"Shhh, listen, Britney. You are only sixteen, and you have your whole life ahead of you, a life that will be full of wonderful experiences and difficult choices. Will you go to SC or Princeton? Will you drive a BMW or a Mercedes? Will you buy your wedding gown in New York or Madrid? But these are choices that you'll never have to face if you decide to continue with your pregnancy."

"Mom, you make it sound as if having children was the worst thing in the world," Britney said, her voice betraying her disappointment.

"No, honey, that's not what I mean at all. I love you and Tiffany very much," she said, holding her daughter's face with both her hands. "But your dad and I were ready for you. We were married, he had a job and we knew we wanted to form a family."

Her mother pulled Britney back to the bed again, inviting her to sit. "If your father finds out, he'll kick you out of the house, and you know it. How are you going to feed a child? What's going to happen with college?"

Mrs. Scozzari took a break as if to observe Britney's reaction, to let her words sink in. Britney didn't respond, keeping her head down, her fingers doodling imaginary circlets on her jeans.

"I may be distant sometimes, but I'm still your mother, and there's no way I'm going to let you ruin your life when you're only sixteen," she said firmly. "Nothing good can come out of being attached to that boy. Your dad is right about that. All they know how to do is kill each other. That's why nobody cares about all those gangsters."

"But, Mom, Miguel Ángel is not a gangster, he's a boxer," Britney complained.

"Whatever he is, you're never going to see him again."

"Okay, Mom," Britney mumbled, crossing the fingers of her right hand behind her back.

CHAPTER 34

Sunday was Miguel Ángel's favorite day of the week. It was the family's only day to be just that, a family, to spend time with no work, no cries, no worries. Yeah, his heart felt as if the neighbor's dog had chewed it up, but at least he didn't have to be in school or in their crowded apartment.

When Miguel Ángel arrived at St. Mary's, Mass had already started. He walked up the right hallway looking for his mother in their usual pew: the fifth one from the front. Mari Carmen was saving a spot for him at the edge of the bench, and she scooted closer to Ana Estela to make room for him. He had come home late after their chat, and they hadn't spoken to each other since. Ana Estela gave him a long, quizzical look. The one she always had when she was about to interrogate him. There was nothing to say, he thought. Britney is not having my baby, and there's nothing to say.

"Brothers and sisters," Father Emilio began his sermon. "We just heard on the news of the terrible tragedy of another one of our brothers getting killed by gang violence. We don't know why our brother Raúl Versamin was killed. All we know is that his body was found at the edge of a road, his life taken from him too early. He was only twenty-seven.

"We don't know what our brother did in life. It's not our job to judge him. That's the job of our Lord Jesus Christ, who will see him and decide if he's worthy of His infinite mercy. But I wanted to mention Raúl because the violence of his death, and I presume its suddenness, gives us an opportunity to reflect not just about our lives, but the life of our community. Brothers and sisters, we're allowing these crimes to happen. Somebody out there, perhaps somebody who's sitting right here right now, knows what happened. That person is not coming to the police with information that may lead to the killer, so that person is then an accomplice to murder.

"Now, I know what you're going to tell me. You're going to say, 'We don't trust the police. If they find out we live here illegally, they'll take us to jail.' Well, let me tell you, brothers and sisters, that in moments like this, when Jesus, Our Lord, is asking of us to do what's right, we can't be thinking about our own well being. Was He thinking about His well being when He gave His life for us on that cross?

"My dear brothers and sisters, we have to be an instrument of God's peace by stepping forward and letting those who commit crimes against His children know that we're not willing to tolerate it. And if you would not tolerate that your children lie or steal, why would you tolerate that they kill? This is the moment when you stand up to anybody who believes they're protecting a friend and let them know they're committing a sin against God. Let us praise the Lord."

The words of Father Emilio bounced around in Miguel Ángel's mind like bats in a cave. "We have to be an instrument of peace." He wasn't very religious; that role he left to his sister and mother. But he didn't like hurting anybody. Boxing was one thing. You get into the ring with somebody who's trained, who knows how to punch and bounce on the balls of their feet. But shooting somebody in the back didn't seem honorable.

Killing a baby, that wasn't honorable. But the baby wasn't born yet, so maybe it didn't count. He was mad at Britney and at first, he wanted to punch her. That's probably what his stepfathers felt when they hit his mother. But that wasn't right, and he felt good about himself for having the courage to walk away without giving her a purple eye. Britney seemed so scared, and his own sister had said she would not want to have a baby now so she wouldn't mess up her future. Maybe it wasn't right, then, to make Britney have a baby if she didn't want it.

He looked at the stained glass windows of the Stations of the Cross. His mom always told him churches in Mexico were darker, taller, more like real churches should look. Gringo churches were plainer, simpler, and lacked the solemnity of the ancient temples in her old country. One day, when he was famous and had a lot of money, he'd travel to see what they really looked like.

"Are you going to take Communion, Miguel Ángel?" Mari Carmen's voice brought him back from Mexican churches and the idealized memories of his mother.

"No, I can't take Communion," he answered. "I haven't confessed."

Miguel Ángel and Mari Carmen stayed behind with Víctor Manuel. He had not done his First Communion yet, so he wasn't allowed to take the sacred wafer. His mom and Ana Estela, Blanca Rosa and Juan Carlos squeezed through the pew to join the line.

He stopped paying attention to the Mass. All he could think about was Britney and her pregnancy.

When the parishioners began pouring out of St. Mary's, the vendors were already waiting for their clients. Dozens of people crowded around for corn on the cob, *paletas*, *chicharrones*, *churros* and cotton candy. Miguel Ángel's favorite part of the Mass was when it ended.

The children surrounded their mother and Miguel Ángel to get money to buy their munchies. After getting their snacks, they sat down next to their mother, who had found a bench with enough space for the children to surround her. Miguel Ángel sat on the ground in front of her, munching on a corn on the cob and wiping the dribbling butter with a napkin.

Between nibbles from his corn, he raised his eyes to look at his mother. She was concentrating on her spicy *churritos*, licking her fingers after each one disappeared into her mouth. She had her hair tightly pulled in a bun, a few strands of silver already making an appearance on her temples and on the crown of her head. She was only thirty-three, but the marks left by six children were evident.

She was so pretty, Miguel Ángel thought, and so elegant in her red hat. Her olive skin had become darker after all those years working under the sun, and her strenuous but non-aerobic job gathering lettuce and broccoli had contributed to her bulging belly. She had big, brown eyes with a mischievous spark in them and a wide, round nose with flaring nostrils. When she laughed, you could see her three silver-lined teeth sparkle. Víctor Manuel, the comedian of the house, was telling her jokes. They all loved her laughter, so they competed against one another to see who could elicit it.

"Ma, how come you didn't become a movie star?" Miguel Ángel asked. "You're so pretty."

"*Ay, m'ijo*, the things you say," the woman said, laughing like a teenager. "I got married too young."

"Would you have liked to become a movie star?"

"We all want to be famous, or rich, but some of us aren't that lucky. But you are going to be a great fighter one day. You'll be famous like a movie star. What more can I ask for? Then you can get me that big house you're always telling me about."

"I'm going to buy you everything you want, Mami," the boy said earnestly before turning his face away. If any clouds of doubt shadowed his face, he didn't want his mother to notice.

CHAPTER 35

If Sunday was a day for God, it was also a day for shopping. After finishing their snacks, the clan followed their mother to the grocery store. She had gotten paid the day before, so after setting money aside for rent, rides, babysitter and debts, she took a hundred dollars to stock up. The family walked out of the Mexican supermarket carrying at least one plastic bag each of tomatoes, tortillas, potatoes, bread, cheese, dry beans, powdered milk and other staples to hold them over for two weeks, if they were lucky. If not, there was always the food bank.

They walked several blocks to their apartment, and when they got home, they saw the neighbors firing up a grill, ready to start another Sunday ritual. A soccer game was playing on a TV propped up on a stack of empty broccoli crates. A stereo placed on the ground was tuned to the same soccer game. It was the "classic" América vs. Chivas, the arch-rivals in Mexico's soccer circuit.

"*Buenas tardes*," greeted Don Rufino, the building's chef-in-residence greeted the family. "Bring something to barbeque. We're having a good party here."

Don Rufino was the foreman of a crew that mostly harvested broccoli. He was a large, good-natured man, who'd built the reputation of being a good boss. Many foremen were known for being abusive with the harvesters, always pushing them to finish the production quicker and many times cheating them out of their pay. Not Rufino. With his big mustache and round belly, Rufino looked like a Mexican Santa Claus. His wife had died a few years back, leaving him to take care of four young children. For many years, he had been nothing but devoted to them. He rarely went out drinking with his friends and instead took his children to the movies or shopping. Lately, though, he'd begun paying attention to Miguel Ángel's mother.

"*Buenas tardes*, Don Rufino," she returned the greeting.

"Come on over, we'll soon have a feast, Lupita. My goodness, you look so elegant today."

"Don Rufino, you're always such a flatterer. We're going to put the stuff away and we'll be right out," Lupita, their mother, said, already walking up the stairs. Rufino followed her with his eyes until she disappeared behind the apartment's door.

While the oldest kids helped put the groceries away the younger ones stayed outside to play. Miguel Ángel was looking at her with a bit of jealousy. He had noticed how Rufino had made advances toward his mom, but this was the first time he saw his mom actually respond. The thought of another stepfather in his life did not amuse him. He'd already had two, and even though he had often wished he had a father, he didn't want to have another creep in his life. He didn't need a role model—he had Coach.

"Mom, why are you flirting with Rufino?"

"Ah, *muchacho*, don't say that. I was not flirting with him, I was just being nice. What are you supposed to do if somebody says you look elegant? Am I supposed to slap him?"

"No, but just say thank you and move on. You don't need to give your hand and leave it there for like a century!"

"C'mon, *m'ijo*, don't exaggerate. I'm not flirting. Besides, Don Rufino is a very nice man, and he probably has lots of prospects elsewhere. He's not going to notice me. I'm not the woman I used to be. Look at me, I'm thirty-three-years old and have six children. Who's going to pay me any attention?"

"Mom, I already told you, you're beautiful. And besides, you don't need a man. You have me!"

She placed the last bag of beans in the cabinet above the stove before turning around to face her oldest child. "*M'ijo*, listen. I know you want to be the man of the house because you don't have a father, but you're still my son. You can't be my *compañero*, but I need one."

Miguel Ángel drew a deep breath and turned away without a word. He took three steps to his bunk and jumped on the bed. He lied down on his back and stared at the honeycomb wires that supported the mattress above him. After a long while, he pulled out his Muhammad Ali papers and dug out his favorite quote: "The fight is won or lost far away from witnesses—behind the lines, in the gym, and out there on the road, long before I dance under those lights."

Maybe it was just as well he wasn't going to have Britney around anymore. Miguel Ángel had turned seventeen in May, had one Golden Glove championship, had sixty wins and four losses. He was behind, he thought, but there was another year to catch up. Other than that, he was almost there with Ali. He ran several miles every day, trained for at least two hours, and he didn't smoke or drink, and he had just passed a big test: He had remained cool in a crisis and had not reacted to Britney's news about the baby. It'd be long before Miguel Ángel had his time under the lights, but he was getting there. Even though he didn't like what his mother told him about needing a *compañero*, he didn't scream or yell. Maybe his mother was right. Maybe she needed a man, somebody other than her oldest son.

What would Britney be doing right now? He got the phone off the cradle and began dialing her number, but before he punched the last digit, he hung up. He needed to go punch some bags instead. Too bad the gym wasn't open on Sunday.

"I was looking for you. Can you read me a book?" Mari Carmen asked as she opened the door of the apartment. She ran to him and jumped on the bed, throwing her arms around her big brother.

"Which book do you want me to read you, huh? *Amos and Boris*?"

"Yeah, that's my favorite."

CHAPTER 36

The soccer game had ended, so Don Rufino had turned off the TV and changed the stereo to a Mexican music station. The trombones and trumpets of Banda el Recodo, "the mother of all bands," made the apartment building shake. Rufino had had a couple of beers and was still grilling steaks and corn—food that was disappearing faster than he could cook it.

Lupita was standing nearby, laughing at Rufino's jokes and helping pass around the plates. Neighbors, men and women, couples and singles, were sitting around a picnic table somebody had brought from one of the apartments. The men leaned against the fence, one foot propped against it. They were wearing their Sunday best: cowboy boots and hats, long leather jackets, silver buckles paying homage to their hometowns of Michoacán, Jalisco, Guanajuato. In a few hours, they would pick up their girlfriends to go dancing to the most happening place in the entire city of Salinas.

The kids were playing soccer on the street. They had started their game on the patio, but after the ball almost knocked the barbeque to the floor, Rufino chased them to the street. There were other kids playing there too, with their skateboards and their bicycles, making the neighbors drive slowly when passing by.

Rufino called to Miguel Ángel when he was walking down the stairs. "Miguel Ángel, there will be nothing left if you don't come soon."

As much as the boy wanted to remain holed up in his room, he could not resist the juicy smell of *carne asada* wafting in from the patio. He found a place to stand between Rufino and his mother and saw her place a couple of tortillas on the grill. Rufino managed to reach in front of him and lay two steaks on the tortillas. On the improvised picnic table there were three kinds of salsas, chopped onions, cilantro and limes. Lupita sprinkled onions and cilantro on the meat and handed the plates to her son.

He took a chair at the picnic table, next to a young girl nursing a baby under a light blue blanket. Roxana. They took government class together. She had stopped going to school about one week before the end of their junior year.

Miguel Ángel had managed to keep his mind from drifting to Britney and her pregnancy for a little while. But now, sitting next to this young mother—maybe his girlfriend's age—he couldn't ignore it any longer. He glanced at Roxana out of the corner of his eye, hoping she wouldn't catch him staring. She looked so peaceful ogling the little bundle under the blanket.

He was perplexed. Roxana had a baby, but Britney wouldn't. Was it religion? He'd seen Roxana at church. Britney mostly went to Mass on Christmas and New Year's Eve.

Stupid brat. She didn't even ask his opinion. Maybe he wanted to quit school and look for a job to support his child. He could easily get a full-time job at a grocery store. There were dozens of girls who had their babies and then went back to school. Britney could surely do that. He could rent the trailer in his neighbors' backyard so they could make a home to welcome the baby.

Maybe he was staring after all. Roxana turned to him, and their eyes met.

"Hi," he said.

"Hi," she responded, turning her face back to her baby. "Haven't seen you around. Still going to school?"

"You're the one who's not going," he chided her. "Are you going back?"

"Yeah, I'm signing up for the alternative high school in the spring, but the baby's too little right now. They want her to be at least three months old."

"How old is she now?"

"Six weeks."

Miguel Ángel grunted an acknowledgement before starting to eat his steak. Between chews and chews, he was looking at the girls out of the corner of his eye. His former classmate was so young. She could just as easily be cradling a doll. He wondered if a young girl could be a good mother.

"Where's the father?" he asked her.

"Oh, he doesn't want to have anything to do with us. Says he's not the father."

"Is he?" he asked, and immediately felt his cheeks flush.

She raised her head and gave him the most piercing look he'd seen in a long time. And then she unleashed a fury he could have never imagined this sweet, young mother had in store.

"You guys think you're such men, trying to convince us to have sex because 'You love me' and that's how 'I'm going to prove I love you.' Right? And then you don't want to wear a condom because it's like 'eating the candy still with the wrapper on.' And then, if you end up pregnant, oh well, 'It's not my fault, because if I could convince you to have sex, maybe others did too, so how do I know I'm the father.' Right? You're all filth."

She got up and tried to get away, but Miguel Ángel held her by the arm, pleading with her.

"No, Roxana, don't leave. I'm sorry, I didn't mean no offense, really. Hey, listen, let me tell you something. Come here."

Everyone in the patio had stopped to look at them. The old men, the children, they were all staring. But as soon as he pulled her to talk to her in private, they all returned to their *carne asada* tacos.

He whispered in her ear his painful secret. The girl looked at him, as if trying to guess if he was lying. After a few seconds, she sat down again.

"How do I know you're telling me the truth?" she asked him. "As far as I can tell, all men lie."

"I don't lie. Lies only get you in trouble. Besides, I have nothing to gain. It's not like I want to get into your pants or anything. I have enough problems already," he said, almost as if talking to himself.

Roxana seemed to consider this for a long while before she spoke again. "What are you going to do?"

"Nothing, I guess. She's made a decision, and I ain't gonna stop her. But I swear, I would have taken care of that baby. I would have raised it, played with him, the whole nine yards. I wasn't gonna leave my baby the way my dad left me."

"That's nice," she said, a painful smile on her face. "I do have to go in now. I have to change her diaper."

"Can I hold her a bit before you go?"

"She's a bit wet. Is that okay?"

"Sure, let me."

The baby sure was light, maybe lighter than his boxing gloves. She had a smattering of black hair on top of her head, and her wide-open eyes were looking at him first, then at her mother and at the neighbors who were looking down on them from the second floor. She had that sweet sweaty smell of all brandnew people, of talcum powder and milk. She was a blank book with all her pages yet to be filled. What would life write on them?

"What's her name?" he asked.

"Esperanza," the mother said, beaming. Hope.

Roxana looked content, but also exhausted. A baby like hers needed care around the clock: feeding, changing diapers, feeding some more, putting her to sleep. The dark shadows under the young mother's eyes revealed many sleepless nights. That was probably what Britney was running away from. She did not want to be chained to a baby, so she could stay out with her friends and go skiing near her cabin in the mountains. Or maybe what she wanted was go to the university and get a good-paying job.

"Thanks," he said, suddenly feeling frustrated and returning the infant to her mother's arms.

"No problem," she answered, embracing the baby before walking up the stairs to her parents' apartment.

Miguel Ángel finished his tacos while taking in the scene: his mother flirting with Rufino, the guys eying the female neighbors and the young women walking up and down the patio so the guys could take better notice. He turned around and saw some of the children playing on the street. It was a scene he had witnessed hundreds of times and now felt different, as if he were just a spirit passing by, as if he didn't belong there. He was a stranger among his people. He didn't like drinking or chit-chatting with the neighbors like his mother did or playing soccer like his brothers. This wasn't his home anymore. It was a strange land full of people who didn't understand how much he was suffering. Nobody understood how hard it was to let Britney go, how much he wanted to understand her because, deep down, he suspected she was right. They were in no position to have a baby. They were too young. Britney knew that, but he was too stubborn to accept it.

Miguel Ángel felt the urge to leave, to escape. Maybe call Coach to have him open the gym.

"*M'ijo*, why don't you go upstairs now and do your homework?"

At first, he thought it was his mother, but he raised his head and saw her still engrossed in playful banter with Rufino. He turned around and saw Ita, this time wearing cowboy boots, blue jeans and a white blouse with tiny embroidered hummingbirds, roosters and cows. With her braids tied with a ribbon on her head, she looked like Frida Kahlo.

"Ita, where've you been? I needed you yesterday," the boy whispered.

"Sorry, your grandma and I had very important matters to discuss. Let's go to your room and talk about it," Ita said, moving her head toward the apartment. "Too much noise out here."

Before he could get up, another voice reached out to him. "Hey, Miguel Ángel, what you up to?" It was Beto, approaching the patio.

"Nothing much. What's with you?" Miguel Ángel responded as they bumped fists.

"Nothing. Going for a ride and thought I'd come see you. Wanna come for a while?"

"*Muchacho*," Ita interrupted, slamming her foot on the ground. "You and I are supposed to have a talk, remember? Tell him you're busy."

Miguel Ángel shook his head. Ita had never given him this kind of order—not in front of other people. He wanted to go up with her, but he found it so hard to say no to Beto. He would understand his problems with Britney. Miguel Ángel wondered if he ever was going to manage to stay away from his gang-banging friend. Maybe if he moved to his mother's ranch in Michoacán.

"I want to do some reading, Beto. I have homework to do."

"Yeah, that's it, *chamaco*," Ita egged him on. "You have homework to do and Ita to talk to."

"It won't be a long ride, just downtown and back," Beto said, a prayer in his eyes. "I just need someone to talk to."

Miguel Ángel lowered his head and swung it slowly side to side. He could go for a couple of hours, just in time to come back and finish that essay for English class. But writing was tough, and if he stayed up late, he would not be able to get up in time for training.

Miguel Ángel looked at Beto for a second, then turned to Ita, who was tapping her shiny brown boots on the patio concrete. He didn't want to let her down.

"I'm sorry Beto, I have to . . . "

His words trailed off as he discovered the bouncy figure of Britney slamming the door of Cleopatra's sports car and running in his direction.

"Miguel Ángel, we need to talk," she announced. Her tone left no room for rebuttal.

"Con una fregada," Ita mumbled, fishing in her pants' pockets and pulling out a cigarette and lighter.

Miguel Ángel stared at Britney, his thoughts so confused, they seemed to tie up his tongue. He turned his head to Ita, to Beto and back to Britney, speechless.

The air had turned still. The neighbors had stopped talking, or so it seemed to Miguel Ángel, and the rambunctious kids were now watching a drama they didn't understand, as if catching a random episode of an ongoing soap opera. His mother, no longer enraptured by Don Rufino, began walking in Miguel Ángel's direction.

"Britney, come with us," Miguel Ángel jumped from the bench and pulled his girlfriend by the arm. "We can talk while Beto does his business."

Miguel Ángel almost pushed Britney into the back of Beto's SUV. He was getting into the passenger seat, when Miguel Ángel felt a tug on his shirt.

"Why are you ignoring me, Miguel Ángel?" his mother demanded. "Where are you going?"

"I'm just going for a ride with Beto. I'll be right back," the boy replied, slamming the door on his mother's face.

CHAPTER 37

As soon as Miguel Ángel closed the Escalade door, Beto announced the ride wasn't going to be as short as he originally promised. "Man, these people owe me some money down in Greenflas. You're down, right?"

Beto and his tricks. What bothered Miguel Ángel the most was falling for them over and over again. Worse, this time he had Britney to deal with. He lowered his head and rested his forehead in his right hand.

"Beto, I swear, I have lots of homework. Coach made me talk to this white lady yesterday, and . . . " he stopped. He turned around and faced Britney, rolled up in a ball in the back seat. "I'm sorry, girl. I didn't want my mom to ask questions."

Looking like a wounded deer, Britney shook her head, her long blonde hair hiding her face from her boyfriend. Ex-boyfriend.

"We won't take long, right?" she finally managed to say. "I promised Cleopatra it would only be a few minutes."

The ride from Salinas to Greenfield, forty miles south through Green Valley, could take anywhere between thirty to forty minutes, depending on how many produce trucks hauling lettuce, strawberries or broccoli were hogging the road. Before responding, Miguel Ángel looked for Beto's gaze, but he was restless, changing the dial from one station to another without picking one.

"How long is this gonna take, Beto?" Miguel Ángel asked.

"It won't take long, I swear. We'll get there in fifteen minutes, so the whole round trip will take us like half an hour. I need you to do me a big favor."

You could only get from Salinas to Greenfield in fifteen minutes if you were flying a helicopter. Miguel Ángel had ridden before with Beto and knew his friend had a lead foot.

The sun was setting but it was still light enough outside for the crops to be visible. Although it was late in the summer, it was the peak of the growing season and the fields were lush with produce, their aroma rising from the earth like spirits being summoned to the heavens.

Miguel Ángel did not dare turn back to face Britney again. He didn't understand why she had come. When he walked home after their fight, he swore to never see her again. Now, here she was, curled up like an iceberg lettuce in the bottom drawer of the refrigerator. Had she changed her mind about the abortion? Miguel Ángel would save all his questions until they were alone.

The rows of vegetables were running fast along the highway, going deep into the mountains, as if they connected the Gabilans to the east and the Santa Lucias to the west with long, stretched cornrows. Enormous patches of land were only interrupted by supply stores, seed companies, cities along Highway 101 and a smattering of nurseries. Beyond that, the fields were infinite, uninterrupted, a dream of fertility and production that brought richness to the Salinas Valley but misery and exhaustion to the harvesters. His mother knew this all too well.

✥✥✥

"Greenfield? R u going nuts?" Britney's iPhone screen flashed.

She didn't reply. Cleopatra was right, she was going crazy. What possessed her to ask, to beg, her best friend to drive her to Salinas on a Sunday, when the family was supposed to be spending time together? She should have stayed away from Miguel Ángel, especially so soon after the break up. After her mother's talk.

Britney did not understand what had made her get into the car. But she'd done it so many times, it only felt natural, even if Cleopatra was waiting for her.

She started biting her nails, a habit she thought she had kicked. The idea of staying away from Miguel Ángel was unbearable. She had to see him again. She couldn't stop thinking about him, his shattered face when she told him she was not going to have the baby. Maybe if she explained to him what their lives would be like with a baby right now, he would change his mind and support her decision.

Despite what her mother had told her, and yes, what a relief it was she knew, Britney wanted Miguel Ángel's support. She needed his acceptance. His love. Yes, the decision was made, yes, mother and sister were support-ive, but still. Still, did she need to include Miguel Ángel? It was her body, her life, right? She was the one who would have to carry a baby for nine months, live with the responsibility her whole life. He could just up and leave if he wanted to.

Would he?

She shook her head. It didn't matter what Miguel Ángel would do. Britney was not having a child.

❧❧❧

The ride to Greenfield took twenty-five minutes but since no one spoke, it felt like an eternity to Miguel Ángel. They took the first exit to the small downtown area, where he immediately saw a few women and children walking on the street. The short, dark indigenous people from Oaxaca.

After parking the Escalade at the entrance to a mobile home park, Beto turned to Miguel Ángel. "We need to talk, Miguel Ángel. You need to do me a favor."

Puzzled, Miguel Ángel turned to Britney, sitting in the back seat with her headphones on, but followed Beto out of the car without a word. Beto was already opening the SUV's back door. He showed Miguel Ángel a box with small bags of something that looked like sea salt, then slammed the door shut to keep Britney from hearing him.

"What is it, man?" Miguel Ángel asked.

"See that green house by the red car? I need to make a delivery, but the cops are watching. They know who I am, so I can't be doing it. I need you to make it for me. I'll give you five hundred bucks."

Miguel Ángel shook his head in disbelief. He could not believe Beto was asking him to do this again. And the amount of money, his family really could use it.

"You're nuts," Miguel Ángel said, finally reacting. "We've gone over this before, and you know I'm not doing this. What's the matter with you?"

"If you don't do this, we've come all the way here for nothing."

"Why didn't you ask me before? I wouldn't have come if you'd said anything."

"Because that dumb blonde of yours jumped in the car, and I'm not gonna talk business in front of her."

"That dumb blonde, as you're calling her, is going to have my baby, you idiot," Miguel Ángel yelled, grabbing Beto by the collar.

"Wow, man, that's frigging huge. The more reason for you to start making some real money," Beto said, pushing Miguel Ángel away.

"You just don't understand, do you? I'm not getting into your business, and that's that. If you want to waste your life, that's your problem. That ain't me."

"You think you're better than me? You think you're going to be this great boxer and become a millionaire and all that? Well, I have news for you. You're wrong. All we have at the Alisal is this," Beto said, pulling out a bag of white powder and shaking it in front of Miguel Ángel's face. "This is it, and you're throwing it away."

"What's gotten into you, Beto? We've talked about this. Your deal is not for me."

"Never mind, great boxer. If you don't do this delivery, I will. I didn't come all this way for nothing."

Beto opened the back door, stuffed his pockets with some bags, shut it back again and stomped away toward the red car parked outside the green house. At first he looked as if he was just going to march all the way, but then Miguel Ángel saw him hide behind the cars, sneaking away like a cat in the night. He'll take forever, Miguel Ángel thought as he got back inside the SUV and slammed the door shut.

"What happened?" Britney asked.

Without turning to see her, Miguel Ángel reached to the car stereo to change the station. He struggled to concentrate on the music, trying to push Beto from his mind.

But it was hard. It wasn't the first time that his friend had insinuated he should get into the gang business, but this was brazen. And it was the first time he offered money. It was something Miguel Ángel was not expecting. Five hundred bucks. More than his mother saw in a week. He pushed the "scan" button, the "tune" button, the pre-set channels, but nothing he liked—or that soothed his nerves—would come out. Greenfield was so far from the Peninsula, the signal probably didn't even get there. Giving up, he shut the stereo off and turned to Britney.

"I thought you didn't want to see me no more," he said, gritting his teeth, prying his thoughts away from Beto and his offer.

In her head, Britney had rehearsed her speech over and over again. Truth was, she didn't really know what she would say when she saw him. All she knew is that she wanted to see him.

"Miguel Ángel . . . I . . . I'm confused," she said, tears streaming down her cheeks. "I'm so scared. We're so young . . . "

"You're gonna cry again?" Miguel Ángel said, running his fingers through his hair. "Stop crying, woman, for God sakes!" he yelled.

With this, Britney's quiet sobs became uncontrollable wails. Miguel Ángel's head went spinning. Exactly what he didn't need right now. Beto, Greenfield, the delivery, the trip, his mother, Rufino, Ita's warning, and now this. He felt like smacking her around, like his stepfather used to do to him when he cried as a little boy. But he clenched his fists and restrained himself. Glaring at her, he stormed out of the car. If he could, he would run back to Salinas. But there was no way he would leave Britney alone with Beto. All he could hope for now was that she not be crying when he came back. So he paced up and down alongside the car like a caged lion, hoping to burn some of the energy that was devouring him.

When he felt calm, Miguel Ángel got into the back seat of the car, next to Britney, and took her in his arms. She tried to push him away at first, but truly, this was what she'd come for. To have him hold her, kiss her. Giving in, she buried her wet nose in Miguel Ángel's neck, his musky scent immediately bringing her comfort.

"I miss you so much," she whispered.

"I miss you too, baby," he said. In the depth of Britney's blue eyes, he forgot about their fight, the pregnancy, Beto and Greenfield.

CHAPTER 38

"**M**iguel Ángel, I don't want to have a baby, but I don't want to lose you either. Can you understand that?" Britney asked, stroking her lover's hair while taking in his scent.

Miguel Ángel didn't answer. Beto's delivery was more than a block away, but he would be returning soon. His head on her chest, he could hear the drumming of her heart. It was so quiet he could feel the steady boom-boom reverberating throughout his body, as if her *corazón* was not just pumping her blood, but his as well. "I could get a job. We could get married, have the baby . . . "

"I don't think that's a good idea."

"Why not? I can work evenings and weekends, and train in the mornings."

"Do you know how much you have to pay in rent for a one-bedroom apartment in Pacific Grove?"

"No, I don't," Miguel Ángel responded icily.

"About fifteen hundred a month. And there's no way I can come live with your family—there's no room—or in Salinas," Britney said.

"Not big enough, huh?" Miguel Ángel said, smirking, wondering how much he could make if he joined in Beto's enterprise. Three deliveries and he would have enough for the rent.

"Hey, man, come out. I need to talk to you," a loud knock came through the window.

Not again, Miguel Ángel thought. But maybe it'd be for the best. He'd come out and order Beto to start driving them back to Salinas.

"The place is surrounded, man," Beto exploded as soon as Miguel Ángel stepped out. "I can't get near the stupid house. You're going to have to help me."

"Did you forget my girlfriend's in your car? I'm not doing this, fool, and that's that. We need to leave now."

"Miguel Ángel, if we don't make this delivery, we're in big trouble!"

"We? What do you mean 'we'? This is all your doing, don't try to bring me into your business. I already told you, I don't want any part of it."

"If you're really going to be a father, you'd do a lot better this way, Miguel Ángel."

"Listen, man, I know it's tough in the 'hood and that there's no jobs and shit, but I don't want your problems. I don't want to end up dead by the side of the road."

"But that's not going to happen to you, I swear man. Haven't I always defended you?"

"How can you defend me when there's all these killings going on? Is the green light still on Gringo?"

"It sure is, man. But he's probably out of town. If he dealt with Jarocho, he can't be that stupid to stick around."

Britney poked her head through the window.

"What are you guys talking about? Can we go now? I need to get home, or my Dad's gonna kill me."

Beto threw a side glance at Miguel Ángel. An order.

"Let's go, man," Miguel Ángel said.

Beto stomped out his cigarette and got in the SUV. True to his word, Beto flew on the freeway. City and car lights sped by like fireflies. Miguel Ángel knew better than to say anything, his friend was going to do what he was going to do. The needle on the speedometer hit 100 mph, and Beto didn't seem to notice.

"Beto, if Gringo offed Jarocho . . . What if he's still in town? Aren't you supposed to be looking for him? What if he's looking for you guys?" Miguel Ángel whispered. He wanted to know but he also wanted to distract Beto and make him slow down. Make him forget about his offer. And whatever he said, it could not be heard by Britney. Fortunately, she'd put her headphones back on and seemed oblivious to their conversation.

"He's probably not around. He can't risk it, you know," Beto responded through clenched teeth, his foot firmly planted on the gas pedal.

"But what if he wasn't the one? What if it was somebody else who killed him?"

"Man, what's gotten into you? I thought you didn't want to have anything to do with this. Did you forget we have company?"

"Okay, okay, I'm sorry. I just want to know, that's all. What do the police say?"

"Who knows? We don't know what the police is up to. We don't know where Gringo is. But if he gets caught, we'll find out."

As they approached the lights of Salinas, the fences began slowing down on the side of the road, the signs were passing them at lower speeds. It had gotten quite darker, and there were lots more cops in the city. No use getting in trouble with the law just for speeding.

At the first Salinas exit, Beto left the freeway and drove toward a convenience store. "I need some cigarettes. Want anything?"

"No, thanks. Girl, you want anything?" Miguel Ángel asked Britney as she pulled her earbuds off.

"I want to go home, that's what I want," she said, frantically typing into her phone keypad. "Wait, wait. I want some water. A big bottle. Or maybe a Diet Coke. They have Red Bull, don't they? Maybe just Evian . . . "

Beto rolled his eyes, stepped out down from the SUV and slammed the door behind him.

Britney's eyes welled up, a gesture Miguel Ángel was much too familiar with for his taste.

"C'mon, let's go get the water ourselves, okay? No need to cry," he told her.

❦ ❦ ❦

Miguel Ángel was right, she was crying way too much. Maybe Tiffany was right and she should be watching movies or playing with her computer at home. Everything she did felt wrong, and when she tried to correct it, everything got worse.

Britney tucked her iPhone in the front pocket of her skirt and began a slow stroll among the aisles. Convenience stores brought back memories of car trips, the few journeys the family took by car eons ago. If traveling to Los Angeles, they would stop in Paso Robles for a bathroom break and a quick bite to eat. Britney liked to look at the stuffed animals overflowing in stacked-up crates, the sodas perfectly lined up, like soldiers in an ancient battle ready at the front. Those were fun times, Britney thought, when Dad didn't seem to be so much in a hurry all the time and his temper wasn't about to explode at the flip of a coin.

In the food aisle, Britney ran her fingers over the edges of several bags of chips, as if the rough sensation could reveal the taste inside. Baked? Deep fried? With vinegar? Corn? Sea salt? Miguel Ángel had turned her onto *chicharrones*, the ones made of flour. She still had no stomach for real pork skin.

She wasn't hungry. All she needed was something to drink, but she felt glued to the floor, as if suddenly roots had sprung from the entire Salinas Valley and wrapped her around the ankles, making her unmovable. Stuck. She loved Miguel Ángel, didn't she? And she wanted to please him, right? But her mother and sister were right: This was not about her boyfriend, it was about her own life. What's more important, she asked herself, as she ran her fingers through the cold plastic bottles, to please her dad, her boyfriend or do what was best for herself? What was best for her own future?

"Ready, honey?" Miguel Ángel's voice behind her surprised her.

She jumped around quickly and met her lover's eyes so close to hers, his full lips so near hers. She couldn't resist. She lifted her head, he lowered his, and soon they were locked in a passionate kiss.

"Miguel Ángel, I thought your girlfriend was in a hurry," Beto yelled from the entrance, his voice dripping with jealousy. "I'll wait for you guys in the truck."

❧❧❧

With his right hand, Miguel Ángel led Britney to the cashier's line while rubbing his left index on his lips. He could still feel the burning sensation her mouth always left on his—strong as habanero, sweet as *atole*. Maybe it was wrong of Miguel Ángel to always compare Britney's kisses to the taste of food, but he felt so nourished by them, there was no other way for him to describe them.

This escapade with Beto had given Miguel Ángel a whole new perspective about the situation. Britney belonged in a completely different world, a world that required a lot more money. He watched her move along the food aisles, her long hair floating down her back like a curtain of monarch butterflies in the forest of his mother's Michoacán. She was a princess, a beacon in an ocean of darkness, and he never ever wanted that light to be extinguished. As long as Miguel Ángel lived in a cramped one-bedroom apartment with his mother and five siblings, as long as he trained to be a world champion, he could not take on another responsibility. Being a father right now was not a good idea.

Unless, of course, he were willing to start selling drugs. He shook his head and forced himself to think of something else.

Roxana was right. Guys got their girlfriends pregnant, but never took on any of the responsibilities. Miguel Ángel wanted to think he would be different, but deep down, he knew he wasn't up for it. If Britney had a baby, she would end up with most of the work. She would be the one changing diapers. She'd be the one to feed the baby, rock her to sleep. College would have to be postponed, or maybe cancelled forever. Her life would never be the same. And unless he won a marquee fight next month, he was in no position to support her and a baby.

Or maybe her dad would make her give the baby up. He had heard crazy stories about Mr. Scozzari, and he was willing to believe he'd do anything.

It didn't matter what Mr. Scozzari would do. Miguel Ángel had to give Britney up. He shook his head and seemed for the first time to notice the cashier, an older woman who appeared to be talking to herself and was taking forever to punch keys in the register. The line was barely moving, and Miguel Ángel could see Beto outside the store pacing up and down, smoking a cigarette. He was on the phone, talking, gesturing wildly and shaking his head. It was hard to tell if it was the phone call or the wait that was making his friend anxious.

There was something that was coming sharper into focus for Miguel Ángel. This gang life was not as innocent as he once tried to believe. Beto was not only in deep trouble, now he was trying to bring him further into the gang operation. If Miguel Ángel didn't want to get smeared by it, he would have to cut their ties. *Pronto, muchacho, pronto*, as Coach and Ita would say.

A red pick-up pulled into the parking lot, on the opposite side of Beto's Escalade. Out of nowhere, a bulky man wearing a black hoodie emerged from the shadows and approached the passenger of the red pick-up, giving him a black, shiny object. Miguel Ángel had seen him before, but where? The hood cast a shadow in his eyes, but he could still make out the nose, the lips, the chin. The scar on the left cheek.

Gringo.

"Let's get out of here," he ordered Britney, grabbing her by the arm and pulling her out of the cashier's line.

"Wait a second, honey, I need my drink," she said, pouting, holding steadfast to her place. "It will only be a minute."

Gringo and the two men in the pick-up raised their heads in Miguel Ángel's direction. They stared at him briefly and then went on with their conversation. Miguel Ángel froze. He looked away, trying not to attract attention to himself, or to Beto, still pacing in the parking lot.

Just then, Beto snapped the cell phone shut, shoved it into his front jean pocket and charged toward the store entrance.

"Are you guys *finally* ready to go? I have business to take care of," Beto said, poking his head into the store.

Miguel Ángel felt the blood draining from his face. Get the heck back to the car, he wanted to scream, forgetting about the water for Britney and the weird cashier. The commotion grabbed Gringo's attention, and he was now looking back toward Miguel Ángel. Without thinking, Miguel Ángel leapt to Beto's side, pushing him away from the door, from Gringo and the red pick-up and gesturing toward the Escalade, as if the frantic gesticulations could somehow deliver his friend from danger.

"Get in the car, Beto, get in the car!" Miguel Ángel shouted. From the corner of his eye, Miguel Ángel could see Gringo moving away from the red pick-up and toward them, his hands stuffed into the front pockets of his hoodie. His palms sweaty, his eyes glazed, Miguel Ángel turned to look for Britney, who was now running toward him from the store. Just as she was reaching the group, a black sports car skidded into the parking lot. From the black car jumped a tall, white haired man, wearing khakis and light blue polo shirt. His nostrils were flared and his eyes were drilling holes into Britney. Oblivious, the girl continued prancing to Miguel Ángel. Before Miguel Ángel could reach her, the tall man grabbed Britney's arm and pulled her to him.

"Un-frigging-believable," the man yelled. "With a frigging Mexican. A frigging beaner. Get in the car, Britney Marie, right now!"

"What you doing, man?" Miguel Ángel screamed right over the man's voice. "You can't treat her like this."

"You stupid punk, get away from me," Scozzari bellowed, turning to Miguel Ángel and smashing a fist on his nose.

Miguel Ángel's body twisted in the air and landed on the hood of the Alfa Romeo. "If I catch you near my daughter again, I'll blow your brains out, you hear me!"

Scozzari shoved Britney into the passenger seat of the tiny sports car, slammed the door shut and stomped to the driver's side. Miguel Ángel was thrown off again, this time onto the asphalt, when the Alfa Romeo screeched out of the parking lot.

Miguel Ángel sat down and touched his face to assess the damage. He wiped the blood flowing from his nose with the sleeve of his sweatshirt, glancing at Beto, who was now hovering near him. Gringo and the red pick-up were gone.

"Maybe you should see a doctor, man," Beto said.

"Nah, let's just go home," Miguel Ángel said, feeling more like he wanted to kill somebody.

CHAPTER 39

"You have to help me get her," Miguel Ángel said after an eternity of silence.

"What?"

"You heard me, homes. I'm going to take Britney away."

"You're joking, right?"

"I'm dead serious. I'm gonna snatch her and bring her home."

It was the first Miguel Ángel had spoken since the incident at the convenience store. So instead of going back to Alisal, Beto bolted onto the freeway, got as far as Chualar and hauled back on River Road. He got back on the 101 to Northridge Mall and then cruised around residential streets. Miguel Ángel held his fists up close to his face, as if ready to land a punch on an invisible opponent.

The entire scene was giving him a headache. Britney prancing towards him, Scozzari grabbing and jerking her around, him defending the girl, Scozzari punching him, the car peeling away. He tried to make sense of it, but his head pounded with hurt.

In his veins ran the urge to do something. But what? Punch Scozzari in the face? Send him an invitation to spar? Ask Beto for his gun so he could . . . what? Every idea that popped into his head seemed ridiculous, and he quickly skipped onto the next one.

Britney loved him, of that he was sure, so he couldn't hurt the father of the girl he loved. And she wanted to be with him, or she wouldn't have come looking for him. So maybe the answer wasn't to beat him to a pulp, but to take Britney away from him.

"You've lost your mind, dude," Beto said. "By now, your future father-in-law has already hired an army to protect the princess and his castle. How are you even going to reach her? You don't even have a cell phone."

"I'll call her from home before leaving. I'll tell her to wait for me by the beach, in our usual spot. If she doesn't have time to pack, we can come back later, when he's not around."

"This is crazy, man. You've really lost it this time."

Miguel Ángel sank back in the seat without responding. He didn't want to let Beto talk him out of his idea. He reached for the stereo again and began shoving its buttons, not waiting for an actual station to play music.

As they approached his apartment, Miguel Ángel noticed a red pick-up truck parked a few houses away. He craned his neck to see who was inside. Nobody. A cold chill ran down his back, but shaking his head, he tried to dismiss any fears.

Beto circled around the block once before finally deciding to park in a tiny space between a rusty Honda and a driveway. The entire rear end was sticking out, but Beto didn't seem to care. Miguel Ángel got out before his friend and started walking to the apartment. A hooded figure came out from behind the red pick-up and charged toward the boxer. From the front pockets of his sweatshirt, a black shiny object emerged. Before Miguel Ángel had time to react, a squeaky, familiar voice made his head turn.

"Miguel Ángel, you're home."

Bang, bang, bang.

Miguel Ángel grabbed Mari Carmen by the waist and threw her to the ground. He tried to cover her tiny body with his, expecting the hail of bullets to continue, not daring to raise his head to get a good look at the shooter. But all he could hear now were frenzied screams: *"Llamen a la policía."* "Somebody got shot."

Then, he heard his sister's whimpering.

"Miguel Ángel, are you okay?" Beto called out from his refuge behind a car.

"I'm fine. Mari Carmen, get up, let's get out of here," Miguel Ángel said.

No answer.

Miguel Ángel felt a hot, sticky substance on his fingers before actually seeing the blood escaping from his sister's back.

CHAPTER 40

It was scary enough that Britney's father didn't speak the entire trip back home, not even when she begged him to stop to let her throw up. It got downright frightening when he barreled into the house and went straight upstairs and to her bedroom. There were already three suitcases and several dresses scattered on the floor when Britney caught up with him. He was possessed, getting clothes off their hangers, opening drawers and emptying their contents, running his arms on shelves and dumping everything on the carpet.

"What's going on here, Mom?" Britney wanted to know.

"Tony, have you gone mad?"

"You know what your daughter's doing?" Scozzari barked, turning to shake his wife. "She's going out with a Mexican. With a thug! She's running to Salinas every chance she gets to be with this punk. Britney Marie, my own daughter. And you probably knew about this!

"I've given them everything," he said, going back to the closet and the clothes. "And this is how they repay me, hanging out with losers. But I've had it. Take all your crap with you. I never want to see you again."

"But, Tony, how do you know all this? Britney would never . . . "

"Shut up," Scozzari pushed his wife so hard she fell to the floor, but that didn't stop him. "I found her with him, that's how. I made Cleopatra tell me everything. How she drives her to Salinas, how that good-for-nothing thug borrows a friend's car to come see her. Right under our noses. And it's all your fault, Anne Marie. You're never home, you never even know what your daughter is doing."

Tiffany ran to her mother, while Britney turned to her dad, trying to stop him. Instead, he slapped her with such force, she also fell to the ground, hitting her back on one of the suitcases. Her father now turned his full anger towards Britney, giving her one strong kick on her side, then freezing in place.

Britney, who had seen her mother endure countless beatings, could not believe it was her turn. She saw her father, the man who gave her life and could terrify her more than death, towering above her, ready to strike her again. She saw his clenched fists, his lips tightly pressed in a barely discernible line, watching her with immeasurable anger. Disappointment. Contempt.

It was the last thing she saw before losing consciousness.

CHAPTER 41

Miguel Ángel now had a chance to learn what adults meant when they said they hated hospitals. It wasn't the smell of disinfectant, the uncomfortable seats or the lifeless, white walls. Or the stupid medical shows with the blonde, skinny people in them—so unlike his neighbors at the Alisal. It was the mind-numbing, painful, unbearable wait.

Not long ago, Miguel Ángel remembered hospitals as a place of happiness, and marveled at adults who complained endlessly of hating hospitals. Every time he'd visited one, it had been for the birth of one of his siblings: Juan Carlos, the loudest baby Miguel Ángel ever heard; Víctor Manuel, so quiet he never even cried; Blanca Rosa with her big, round eyes looking at everything from the doctors to her toys. And the baby, the tiniest creature Miguel Ángel had ever seen. Mari Carmen was a preemie, and everyone was scared she would not make it, or would have health problems down the road. And here she was, the sweetest sister he could have ever hoped for. Fighting for her life.

Miguel Ángel was slumped on a chair, his body almost parallel to the floor, his legs forming a straight line as if he were a coffee table where sorrows could be placed like vases full of flowers.

Mari Carmen had gone into surgery more than two hours ago. It was almost midnight, and all Miguel Ángel could do was wait and relive the moments that had brought him to this cold, bright, oppressive emergency room.

Feeling the blood on Mari Carmen's clothes was like stepping into a time machine. Everything that happened from then on was both clear and blurry, like a movie you've seen hundreds of times being fast-forwarded: the shooter running away, the sirens, the cops, the ambulance, the screaming neighbors. The paramedics took Mari Carmen to the hospital. A young, skinny white woman with a long ponytail gave Miguel Ángel a quick check up and determined he didn't need an ambulance ride. Beto rounded up all of Miguel Ángel's dumfounded siblings, his hysterical mother, and drove them first to the Salinas public hospital, then to another up north. He finally figured out why all gunshot victims are sent by helicopter to hospitals in San José or San Francisco: there's no trauma center in Salinas.

Two bullets had entered Mari Carmen through the back, and that's all the doctors would tell his mom. They would know more when the five- or six-hour surgery was over. Pray. Wipe his mother's tears. Think. Wait.

For the first hour he couldn't sit still. He walked up and down the narrow spaces between chairs, the halls, bouncing on the balls of his feet, trying to keep his hands in the pouch of his sweatshirt, the cold away from his body. He wanted to raise his fists and punch somebody. He wanted to fight. Whoever.

"Ma, do you need anything?" Miguel Ángel asked his mother, who seemed to have fallen under a spell. Her eyes were like two darkened windows, boarded up, keeping the light from going in or coming out.

"No, *m'ijo*. I don't want anything," she mumbled without looking at him.

After the fifth time asking—and getting the same answer—Miguel Ángel dropped into a chair and became the human coffee table. Calm on the outside, as if he were ready to face an opponent in the ring, but raging inside.

The young boxer was trying to figure out how this had happened. How his little sister, his Pan con Mantequilla, ended up in the hospital. Did the bullets strike her when he lifted her for a kiss? Perhaps it all started further back, when he got into Beto's car in the afternoon. Or when he refused to stop seeing his gangster friend. Why Mari Carmen, why not him? If Gringo wanted to kill him, why hurt a little girl? Rage began flowing through Miguel Ángel's veins. Is this what *vatos* called honor? To shoot at a five-year-old? Mari Carmen never hurt anybody. She was just a sweet little girl who wanted hugs and stories.

The more he thought about her, about the way she held the spoon with her left hand and jumped on him to greet him, the harder he felt his fists tighten. His ideas were all tangled up, like the jump ropes before the afternoon practice. Everything Beto had told him about the gang always made these guys sound honorable, even worthy of admiration. All they sought was respect he'd say: respect for themselves, their families, their communities. Yeah, Coach was totally against them, but still, Beto would insist.

Beto's ideas had begun to lose appeal a few days ago, when Miguel Ángel saw Jarocho's dead body on Old Stage Road. There was no honor in killing another human being. Beating somebody in the ring is one thing—you need to work hard at it. What honor is there in pulling a trigger? No need to train, no need to concentrate, no need to guess your opponent's moves and beat them.

As if pushed by an invisible force, Miguel Ángel jumped from his seat, turned to a hall and attacked a wall as he would a punching bag. Against the immovable wall, Miguel Ángel's arm, his entire body bounced back. He fell on the ground with a loud thump and hit his face. By the time he began to get up, his mother was already by his side.

"What happened, *m'ijo?*" the ashen-faced woman asked.

"I fell, Ma. *Estoy bien*," he said, hiding his knuckles from his mother, biting his lips not to scream. "Come, sit down."

This, Miguel Ángel did not expect. This rush of anger, this desperate desire to hurt something. Somebody. This is not what he had learned as a boxer. He had to remain cool, he told himself. He rubbed his right fist and bit his lip until it felt numb.

Everything he'd learned about the gang was second hand: from Beto, from Coach. Maybe it was time to learn about the gang on his own. Maybe what he needed right now was to take matters into his own hands and make Gringo pay for hurting Mari Carmen. Maybe what he needed was to put a bullet between Gringo's eyes. That would be the honorable thing to do. To shoot back at somebody who disrespected him. Somebody who almost killed his little sister.

Miguel Ángel shook his head forcefully. No, Mari Carmen wasn't going to die. That was the one thought he had been trying to keep out of his mind the entire time. Pan con Mantequilla wasn't going to die.

He stood up and walked up to his mother again. She was slumped in a chair, her wide-brimmed red hat covering her face. Still, she reached out to his injured hand, pulled it toward her and shook her head. Miguel Ángel had seen his mother's eyes swollen before, and he couldn't stand it. It was as if a poisonous seed planted in his belly sprouted and began growing all over his body, like ivy threatening to choke him. He walked away from her, from the television set and the uncomfortable hospital seats.

By the soda machine, he ran into Beto.

"One hour and forty minutes, Miguel Ángel," Beto exclaimed, his hands in the air as if declaring himself champion of the world. "Am I smoking or what?"

The drive from San Jose to Salinas usually took a solid hour—and driving into the Alisal at least 15 minutes. Beto must have been flying when he took Miguel Ángel's siblings back home.

"I told you to be careful with my brothers in your car, *pinche vato*."

Miguel Ángel pushed Beto into the wall, a fist raised in the air, ready to come down. Beto raised his arms to cover his face.

"What's your problem, man? I was doing you a favor, and now you want to beat me up?"

Beto broke free and started to walk away, but Miguel Ángel's voice stopped him.

"I need a gun, Beto."

"I thought you didn't want anything to do with this life," Beto said, turning briefly to look at his friend.

"I'm totally serious." Miguel Ángel grabbed Beto by the arm. "I'm gonna need your gun."

CHAPTER 42

The first thing that Britney noticed was the buzzing fluorescent lights. She noticed their sound, the humming of a tiny motor, then the light shining bright on her eyes. She opened them slowly, her eyelids so heavy it was as if she were pushing them with all the muscles of her body. She blinked a few times, trying to put the white ceiling in focus.

About three months before meeting Miguel Ángel, Britney had helped Cleopatra celebrate her birthday with massive amounts of tequila: shot after shot until they couldn't get up for school the next day. What Britney remembered the most was how much fun they both had, and how much she'd suffered the next day. Her entire body had ached, her mind wrapped in a fog as thick as her winter blanket. It was the most disconcerting feeling in her life. A bit like she was feeling just now. Plus, an intense amount of pain radiating from her entire body.

A nearby computer was making a whirring sound. It wasn't loud at all, but Britney felt so awful, it might as well have been piercing her eardrums. She slowly opened her eyes and turned her head to the side, trying to find the source of the whirring noise.

Britney became aware of muffled sobs. She met her sister's eyes, a tissue held close to her nose. She blinked a few times until Tiffany came into focus.

"What's going on?" Britney whispered. "Where am I?"

"Nana heard the scandal and called the cops. Dad got arrested, but you had passed out already. They got the paramedics and they brought you here. How do you feel?"

"Don't know. Numb, I guess," Britney said, turning away from her sister.

Britney tried to remember the last thing she saw before she had lost consciousness, but when she closed her eyes, her mind went black. She remembered the tense car trip from Salinas, her father's angry breath on her face, the blows and the shoves. Then nothing.

"How did he find me?" Britney asked, looking for her sister's face.

"Your GPS. Any phone can have it," Tiffany responded, shaking her head in exasperation.

Britney closed her eyes again. She should have known. There was no way she was going to hide a boyfriend from her dad. He had warned her, repeatedly, not to go out with a Mexican. Tiffany did, and look what happened.

Everything ached. Her legs, knees, hips, bones, muscles. Her eyes hurt. She felt as if she had been run over by a steamroller. As if one of Miguel Ángel's friends had mistaken her for a punching bag. Actually, that's exactly what happened. Somebody had taken her for a punching bag, except the culprit wasn't a poor Mexican from Miguel Ángel's barrio.

She opened her eyes again and surveyed the room. There was a clock right in front of her, a TV propped

against the wall to her right and a Thomas Kinkaid paint-
ing. The sun peered through her window, which over-
looked a pine forest. Tiffany was looking at her without
speaking.

"What time is it?" Britney finally spoke.

Tiffany rolled her eyes. "It's right in front of you, sis.
Seven-thirty a.m."

"Where's Mom?"

"She went to bail Dad out. . . . He called her at four
a.m. He said that's when he finally got his call, and
didn't remember his lawyer's number. She rushed out the
door. She said to tell you she'd be right back."

Britney closed her eyes again. This hurt even more.

"What if he comes back with her?" Britney trembled.
"What do you think he's gonna do? Finish the job?"

"Stop that, Britney. He's gonna bring you a box of
Godiva cherry cordials."

Like he always did for Mom.

"Seriously, Tiff. You think he's going to send me to
New Jersey?"

"I think so. Britney, maybe this is not the time to talk
about this, but you have to stop seeing Miguel Ángel.
Next time, Dad's gonna kill him."

Britney had heard that warning so many times and,
for the first time, she realized she had never believed her
father was capable of something like that. Until today.
Yes, her father could kill her, or Miguel Ángel, or both, if
he was crossed again.

Two days ago, when she had met Miguel Ángel in
Asilomar, she was ready to let go of him. She had gone
with the full intention to dump him. And she did. Then
she went home and cried so much, she felt there were no
more tears left in her body. So she came back to see him,

find him, beg him to take her. He did, and the whole world felt better.

Mother had convinced her to dump Miguel Ángel, so why wasn't she dumping her husband? Yeah, Miguel Ángel wasn't rich, but he would never hit her. Britney believed that with all her heart. Miguel Ángel would never hit her.

Who was she fooling? Britney could never be with Miguel Ángel. It was just impossible. But Miguel Ángel loved her. She loved him. It was the first time she truly loved a guy, and she didn't want to give that up.

Maybe it was time.

A quiet knock on the door made the girls turn. A preppy-looking guy walked in, smelling of the after-shave sold at upscale department stores. White coat, a stethoscope around his neck, a writing tablet in his hand were the dead giveaway for his profession.

"How are you feeling?" he asked. Without waiting for her to answer, he touched her forehead, looked for her chart at the foot of the table and took some notes.

"Crappy," she finally said.

"Can you be more specific?" he asked without a hint of humor in his voice.

"I feel like my dad just beat the crap out of me," she responded. "Like somebody's punching bag. Like a man twice my size just pummeled me with his fists."

"All right, all right, I get it," the preppy doctor said, throwing his hands in the air. "You have contusions on most of your body, and a broken rib. Fortunately, it didn't puncture the lung. It'll take about two months to heal, and you'll need plenty of rest . . . but you'll be fine.

"Can I talk to you in private for a second," he asked Britney, motioning Tiffany toward the door.

"It's okay, she's my sister," Britney said. "She knows everything."

"All right, then," he said, taking in a deep breath. "You miscarried."

"What?" Britney cried out, shaking her head.

"I'm sorry. Early pregnancies, when exposed to trauma, can end like that," he said, lowering his head.

Britney turned away from the doctor. She didn't want him to see her tears.

CHAPTER 43

Things have gone too far, Beto thought as he looked into the dimly lit street. He had to put an end to this. But how? He didn't want to get a gun for Miguel Ángel. That was dumb. But Beto knew how stubborn his homeboy could be.

He was sitting in the Escalade, his windows rolled down, smoking a cigarette, his yellow, smudged squeeze ball in his right fist. It was past nine, past the time people ventured out of their homes. A few streetlights illuminated the trimmed lawns and newer model cars. From where he was parked, he could see Gringo's freshly painted house.

He had to come up with something to tell his boss. Obviously, he couldn't tell him that his homie wanted to kill him. That nearly killing his little sister had pushed him over the edge. Truth was, Beto didn't understand what Gringo was doing at Miguel Ángel's apartment, why he was pointing a gun at his homeboy, why he shot at Mari Carmen. Beto was avoiding his phone calls, too.

He flicked the cigarette butt, pulled another one from his pocket and lit it. He couldn't avoid Gringo forever. Or Miguel Ángel. Sooner or later, he would have to deal with both of them.

Just then, he felt a cold touch to his right temple and heard the well-known click of a gun being cocked.

"Get out of your chariot, you slimy jerk," Gringo said with a steely voice. "Slowly, don't make me shoot you."

Beto opened his door and stepped out. He looked up at Gringo and stared at the deep red scar that crossed his left cheek. His steely, dark green eyes had the familiar coldness. Gringo was capable of anything.

"Walk to my house. Don't make no crazy moves, homes. I'll have my gun ready to use."

Beto tried to push his hands into his front pockets, but soon felt a poke in his back.

"Nah, hold your hands where I can see them," Gringo said, pulling Beto's arms to his back.

Beto felt his heart pounding. His guts were clothes tumbling inside a dryer. He felt a drop of sweat trickle down from his neck. He had to do something. Quick.

"Gringo, let me explain," he muttered.

"Shut up," Gringo yelled. "Keep walking."

Gringo marched closely behind Beto, almost pushing him. It wasn't even half a block from the Escalade to Gringo's house, but to Beto it felt like the walk took forever.

"Go in," Gringo barked when they got to the house. "It's open."

Beto turned the doorknob and pushed in. It was dark inside, so he took cautious steps. Once fully inside, he spun around and tackled Gringo to the ground, trying to pull the gun out of his hand. Gringo thrashed around and attempted to push Beto away, but couldn't overcome the surprise. With Gringo's gun in his hand, Beto jumped up and pointed it at his boss.

"What's your problem?" Beto yelled, aiming the Glock. "I don't call you back and suddenly you want to kill me?"

"Don't be an idiot. I don't want to kill you. Or maybe I do. Your buddy Miguel Ángel's making me nervous, and I don't know about you," Gringo said, slowly lowering his arms. "Gimme my gun back."

"What you mean, you don't know about me? Haven't I showed you respect? Loyalty? All my earnings going to you mean nothing? What the hell?" Beto yelled, still aiming the Glock.

"Look, you've just been working for me three months, and you've known your homeboy all your life. I've been testing you. I didn't want to tell you that when I recruited you, but now things are getting weird. Your buddy was at the police station for a long time the other day. You know what that means? He's a *chivato*."

"Don't be stupid, he's not a rat. But you hit his little sister. Now he's pissed and he wants to kill you. He wants to borrow my gun to kill you. What the hell am I gonna do?"

Gringo eyed Beto intently, turned around and walked toward the kitchen. Beto followed, no longer aiming the gun. Gringo opened the fridge and took out two Coronas, found an opener in his key ring, took off the caps and offered one to Beto. They clinked and drank silently.

Gringo lived in a four-bedroom house in a part of town where shootings were a rarity and where people felt safe walking at night. He had painted it a few weeks earlier, and he worked hard at keeping the lawn trimmed. Gringo attended church every Sunday, and the congregation loved him. He had been a hard-core gang member in his youth, but in the eyes of his pastor and other church-goers, Gringo was reformed.

"I've been thinking about this a lot, Beto. You, homes, have to deal with your buddy."

Beto jerked around and the bottle slipped from his hands, crashing against the floor, making a mess. "No way, man, that ain't gonna happen," he yelled. "He's my homie. I can't. I just can't."

Gringo didn't move for a while, keeping his eyes on Beto. He lifted his beer deliberately, placed it on his lips and took a small sip. He wiped his mouth with the back of his hand and belched.

"I don't think you have a choice, homes. Your friend has to go."

"What do you mean my friend has to go? He's my buddy, my homeboy. He hasn't done anything."

Gringo lowered his head and shook it side to side. "Tsk, tsk, tsk. You know the rules, Beto, my man. All we ask of you is loyalty. And willingness to prove you'll do anything for the cause. This is your chance to show you're serious, to show you really want to move up. It's a test. And if you don't pass it, it's going to cost you."

"What do you mean? He's no rat. There's tons of *sureños* I can get rid of, you know I will."

"I've made my decision, *carnal*. You know I would have killed him myself if his little sister hadn't gotten in the way."

"So, why me? Why don't you do it yourself?"

"You need to pass this test, *vato*. And if I need to keep repeating myself, that means you're not ready. That means maybe you're the one who needs to go," Gringo said, his eyes boring into Beto's.

Beto was speechless. He had seen what Gringo was capable of, he had heard stories about his ruthlessness. Savage beatings, cold-blooded executions. Suddenly, he began to feel light-headed, and the room began spinning around him. He had to hold on to the kitchen counter to keep from falling. A wave of regret hit him. He should have never joined the gang, like Coach used to warn him. He should have never worked for Gringo.

It was too late for that. It was his life or Miguel Ángel's now.

Beto didn't speak for a long time. He lowered his gaze, studying the broken bottle, the amber pool of beer. He felt cold and dizzy, ready to pass out any minute.

"Do you have a time or specific place in mind?" Beto finally asked his boss.

"Just get it done. I trust you."

CHAPTER 44

The bell rang but could not stop the punch headed for Miguel Ángel's jaw. The blow spun him around, throwing him into the ropes. He flipped back, ready to attack, but Coach's voice froze him.

"The bell, the bell."

Miguel Ángel shook his head and dropped his hands. Bumped his gloves with Pablo. He had never beaten Miguel Ángel before. Nobody in this gym had ever beaten him. It was the second time this week. He wiped the sweat off his brow with the back of his left arm, came down from the ring and walked straight into the bathroom, ignoring the water Coach was offering.

The entire week had been torture. Deep down, he wanted to resume his life as if nothing had happened, as if everything was normal. But he couldn't. His little sister was still in the hospital. He needed to go to school and he needed to train. It was as if the Salinas River had flooded and mudded up his entire life. Or as if the Big Earthquake, the one everyone feared would destroy California, had finally hit. How could he go back to his daily routine when his life was upside down? His mother needed to work. Her bosses told her she could miss a few days, but she would eventually get fired, so she went back to the fields. Miguel Ángel stayed off from school, spent a couple of nights with his sister at the hospital. He had tried to go back to the gym, but got beat by a fighter much less experienced.

Then there was the issue of the Packing Shed. And Gringo.

Deep in thought, he used his teeth to untie his gloves and wrestled to pull them off. He didn't even bother to unwrap his hands. He opened the cold water faucet and stuck his head in the sink, getting as close to the stream as he could. He splashed his face, his head, let the water trickle down his back. Maybe the water would wake him up from this nightmare.

"You can't fight if you're distracted, you know that," Coach's voice brought him back to reality. "You leave all your problems outside the ring."

"I know, I know," Miguel Ángel mumbled, refusing to come out from under the stream of water.

Coach shut off the faucet, offered Miguel Ángel a towel and pulled him close to examine him. No blood in the whites of his eyes.

"Take a couple of weeks off until things settle down."

"I can't, Coach," Miguel Ángel said, his voice trailing off.

"Take care of your sister and your mother. This ring isn't going anywhere." Coach walked out of the bathroom before Miguel Ángel could respond.

"What about the Packing Shed?" Miguel Ángel screamed.

Coach kept walking without turning back.

Miguel Ángel turned back to the sink again, but instead of opening up the faucet, he stared at it for a long time. Miguel Ángel raised his head and looked at his image in the smudged, cracked mirror. There was a bit of swelling on his left jaw, and the bruise on his left eye from the fight three days ago was still plenty purple. Pretty soon he would have to be wearing a mask to hide all his battle scars.

He pressed his forehead against the cold mirror and lowered his gaze again. At some point, all this had to end, right? Right?

"Remember how I warned you not to go out with Beto that night, *m'ijo*?"

His great-grandmother hadn't been back to see him for a while. Other times he missed her like crazy. This time, he hadn't even noticed.

"Yeah, I remember, Ita," he said without raising his head. Without even looking at her, Miguel Ángel could see the scrunched up angry look on her face and the cigarette dangling from her lips. "I'm sorry."

"Sorry my big fat liver. All I want is for you to listen to me. So listen now. Go home. You hear me? Go home right now."

"So what's gonna happen now, Ita?"

"Nothing's gonna happen to you if you go home. So chop chop. Pack your bags and get going. *Ándale*."

Miguel Ángel dragged his feet out the bathroom to look for his sweats and his bag. Everyone in the gym was gathered around the ring, their eyes fixed on two scrawny boys sparring, their screams so loud they drowned the rap music playing on the old, grimy boom box. Nobody seemed to notice when he scurried out. Only Coach glanced his way and gave him a knowing look.

The fog was already thickly laid on the ground, the cars' shadows passing by. Though getting dark, the street was alive with bundled up moms pushing their children on their strollers and food vendors announcing their tamales. The usually comforting scene was annoying Miguel Ángel. He drew a big breath and began walking home. Half a block up the street, the familiar white Escalade pulled up to him.

"Get in," Beto ordered.

Miguel Ángel grabbed the door handle and was about to pull it, but hesitated for a minute. Ita warned him to go home. The last time he ignored her pleas, he got in so much trouble. His heart began beating faster, his hands to sweat.

"I'm just going home, man. I'm tired, I've had a long week."

"What, you mad at me?"

Miguel Ángel shrugged his shoulders, as if he didn't care. "I'm just tired, okay. Some other time."

"Are you afraid or something? I've got what you asked for . . . "

Miguel Ángel paused for a second. He did ask for Beto's gun. The gun to kill Gringo. Ignoring the nagging voices, he finally got in the truck.

"You haven't been around, man. What's up?" Miguel Ángel said, yelling over the gangster music on Beto's stereo.

"Sorry, dude, I was busy. Trying to get what you asked for."

Miguel Ángel pushed back against the seat. A week ago he had felt so sure about Gringo and the gun, but now he wasn't sure anymore.

"I don't know, Beto. Things are so screwed up right now."

"You don't know what? You don't want to avenge your little sister?"

Miguel Ángel shook his head without saying anything. There were so many voices in his head: Ita warning him, Coach scolding him, even his mother was there with her floppy red hat and a menacing finger.

"I'm not gonna tell you what to do, man," Beto said, pulling back into the street. "I'll just get you the gun. You do whatever you want with it."

Beto turned the stereo up again and pulled his yellow stress ball from the truck's coin tray. If it'd been a turnip, he surely would have squeezed blood from it, Miguel Ángel thought.

Miguel Ángel turned around to talk to his friend, but it was as if his lips were glued. His friend. The friend who was going to put a gun in his hands. The friend who was going to make it easy to take a path to prison or the cemetery.

"Where's the gun?" Miguel Ángel said. "I thought you had it with you."

"My homie's keeping it for me at his house. He's not too far."

The sun had disappeared completely and it was getting chillier, darker. Miguel Ángel's heart was beating faster, the sure sign that something wasn't right. Take me home, he wanted to say. I don't need a gun. I don't want a gun. I don't want to be a gang banger.

"Wait for me here," Beto said after pulling into a driveway. It was two-story, brand-new home on a recently finished housing development at the edge of town. The lawns were green and nicely trimmed, there was no garbage on the street, no broken cars parked on the sidewalks. Miguel Ángel had heard the houses were selling for hundreds of thousands of dollars. How do farm workers afford these? His mother never could, not in a million years.

Beto came back quickly, got in with a slam of the door. "No luck, my brother," he said, starting up the car again. "His mom said he's with his dad. Let's go find him."

"You know what? I have a lot of homework to do," Miguel Ángel muttered. "Just take me home. We'll do this some other time."

"Don't tell me you're scared," Beto sneered. "The mighty Miguel Ángel is chickening out, tsk tsk."

"Don't be an idiot. I'm not scared," Miguel Ángel shot back. "I've been missing a lot of school, I need to catch up."

"The homie just lives down the street, man," Beto said, lowering his voice and biting his lip. "It'll only take five minutes."

Best to keep quiet, Miguel Ángel decided, so he stopped talking. The dim lights of the Alisal gave way to the utter darkness of county roads where Beto was heading. It was the same route Miguel Ángel traveled during his training runs, he knew it well. But it was different to see from inside the truck: no cigarette butts, no candy wrappers. Only the hills shrouded in fog, the fields taking a break from the day's work. It was a magical place, any time of day.

It was also the place where gangsters liked to dump bodies. Where Miguel Ángel found Jarocho dead.

"This friend of yours, what's he called?" Miguel Ángel said, a loud warning ringing in his ears.

"Jaime," Beto said without turning. "They call him Enano."

"You've never said anything about him. Did he go to Frank Paul?"

"Nah, he's from Greenfield."

"So how you know he'll be at his dad's?"

"Man, you're nervous, aren't you?" Beto turned to his friend with a grin on his face. "Don't sweat it, man. It's all cool."

Miguel Ángel squeezed the seat under his legs and grinded his teeth. He felt the anger and frustration growing, going to his head like a gas that would make it explode.

Except for the lights of a few small ranches and a car or two that drove by, the road was pitch black. The place where gangsters are killed, where bodies are dumped. It was chillier now that the sunlight had disappeared completely. Miguel Ángel sank lower in his seat and pushed his fists further down in his pockets.

"Here we are," Beto announced, pulling over to the side of the road. "I told you it'd be five minutes. Come meet Jaime."

"Why are you bringing me here, Beto? How come there's no road here?" Miguel Ángel asked as he got down from the Escalade.

"Oh, I'm using the side entrance. The house's behind that line of trees."

"There's no lights there, Beto," Miguel Ángel said. "I really don't like how this looks."

"C'mon, you can't see them from here, but they're home, don't worry. I'll be right behind you."

They walked on a narrow trail surrounded by bushes and trees, dark as the black cover of strawberry fields. The only sound around them seemed to come from their feet stomping on the ground and fallen twigs.

Suddenly, the eerie click of a gun and its steely touch reached Miguel Ángel's ear. He stopped, raised his hands and felt as if a cold hand was gripping his throat.

"I don't want to do this, man," Beto whimpered. "But I have no choice."

Miguel Ángel slowly turned around, not wanting to give Beto cause to fire the gun. It was really him, holding the Beretta that Miguel Ángel had hidden in a paper bag no more than a week ago. The trees, the sky, the stars began to spin around Miguel Ángel, and he felt he was going to throw up.

"Don't give me that, Beto," Miguel Ángel said, getting over the shock. "We always have choices."

The gun trembled in Beto's hand, but he tried to hold Miguel Ángel's gaze. For a second, Miguel Ángel felt as if he were floating. He hovered up above, looking at himself and his friend, face to face, on a dark trail leading to the Gabilans. A cold drop of sweat trickled down Miguel Ángel's neck, making him shiver. His eyes pleaded for mercy, but his lips were zipped. He couldn't believe his friend was really going to kill him, as if he were nothing but a street thug.

It was true, then, that your whole life flashed back to you when you were about to die. In Miguel Ángel's case, all the scenes were with Beto in them: when he first brought a gun to the gym, when Coach kicked him of out the Packing Shed, when they ate the burritos they stole from the Ramírez twins. Ita warned him all along. Miguel Ángel didn't listen.

Beto pulled the trigger back with one slow, deliberate move, but then his hand lowered to his side as if the weight of the gun was too much to carry. His eyes glistened and, still staring at Miguel Ángel, he dropped to his knees.

"I can't do it," he whimpered, burying his head in his hands.

"You stupid bastard," a voice from the shadows emerged. "I knew I couldn't trust you."

The sound of a gunshot pierced the air. Beto slumped to the ground, blood gushing from the back of his neck. Miguel Ángel rushed to his friend, screaming like a wounded animal. "Beto, no no no!" the boxer howled. He turned Beto around, saw blood coming out of his mouth too, but no light in his eyes.

From the trees lining the path, the shadow of Gringo emerged, still holding the gun in his hand, his head covered by the hood of his dark sweatshirt. Miguel Ángel froze, his eyes fixed on his friend's killer, on the guy who had almost killed his sister. But it was as if some invisible hand was covering his mouth. Try as he might, no words came out.

Gringo stared at Miguel Ángel for what felt like a long time. The calm silence of the night was only disturbed by a barn owl hooting, the soft rustling of the leaves pushed by the wind. Gringo took two steps closer to Miguel Ángel and delivered a threat more chilling than the foggy night.

"I'm actually glad Beto didn't follow my orders. You know why?" Gringo said coolly, packing his gun inside his belt. "Because I really wanted to get rid of him. He was growing too weak, and he just showed me he wasn't ready for bigger things. I should kill you too, but you know what? I'm going to let you live. First of all, you're a civilian, and civilians should be left alone if they leave us alone. Plus, now you're gonna fear me, and I like that. You just witnessed what I'm capable of. And if you rat on me, shooting your sister won't be a mistake next time."

The gangster turned around and left just as he arrived, his footsteps barely making a sound.

Miguel Ángel cradled Beto's body, staring into his life-less eyes, as if he could breathe some of his energy into his friend's. Beto's blood was abandoning his body and taking away all hope with it. What do you do when you hold your friend in your arms, dead? Do you call 911? Do you escape so they don't blame you for his murder? Or do you punch him for trying to kill you first?

For a long time, all Miguel Ángel could do was weep.

CHAPTER 45

Miguel Ángel thought he was acquainted with death. After all, he had attended funerals, he had found Jarocho, he had seen Federico in his casket dressed as an angel and heard his mother's wails. He was a pro, wasn't he?

No, he wasn't. Nothing could prepare him to attend Beto's funeral. Miguel Ángel realized he wasn't as ready as he originally believed the moment he set foot in the mortuary. He felt as if an earthquake had just hit. Had it not been for Coach, who held his arm and helped steady him, Miguel Ángel would for sure have hit the ground.

Coach led him to the pew closest to the front. After shaking hands with Beto's dad and other relatives, they sat down in front of Beto's casket.

His friend had been dead for about a week, and Miguel Ángel still felt numb, still clung to the belief that Beto would walk through the door any day now and announce it was all a joke.

It wasn't, and Miguel Ángel knew it.

After Gringo left that night, Miguel Ángel cradled Beto until there was no more energy in the boxer's body. Finally, he got up, tucked Beto's gun in his belt, convinced this time he was going to use it against Gringo. He went out onto the road and began walking down the deserted Old Stage Road. From one of the few remaining pay phones, he called 911.

"Somebody got shot on Old Stage Road," he said before hanging up.

But he didn't go home. He went back near Beto, to see who would come get him. Hiding behind a fence nearby he saw the police, the ambulance, the yellow tape put up by the cops. Even local TV news teams showed up with their bright stadium lights and reporters doing live shots. Live vultures, nothing less. Nobody saw him in his hiding place, and Miguel Ángel wondered if the cops would find his prints in the car, pick him up and blame him for it all. The scene would replay in his mind over and over and over a thousand times until he thought he'd become ill. He couldn't sleep that night. He would not be able to sleep for many nights to come.

Miguel Ángel recognized all of Beto's relatives: his aunts, his cousins, his friends from school. His home-boys. He was close enough to the casket to hear what everyone said about him. What a good a boy he was, what a fun guy he was, how much he'd suffered without a mother. His dad just sitting there, staring into nothing. Once in a while, he'd draw his hand to his eyes, discreetly wiping his tears.

"Man, this is unreal," said Luis, the boxer that had just gotten a scolding from Coach for having a red bandana. "I just saw Beto at a friend's house last week. We were just kicking it, having a smoke, you know? I can't believe all of this is happening."

Miguel Ángel just nodded. Beto being dead was not the only part that was unreal for the young boxer. The photos on the memorial board looked like ghosts from lives past. The mourners—friends, complete strangers, women wearing tight bright dresses and high heels—could have been from China, so foreign they made Miguel Ángel feel.

Time froze and yet moved quickly, the seconds merging into minutes, into hours. Miguel Ángel felt as if he were inhabiting someone else's body, as if none of what he was watching were true. From the corner of his eyes, Miguel Ángel made out the terrifying shape of a vicious killer. Wearing sunglasses and a black suit, Gringo actually showed up to shake the hand of Beto's dad, offering condolences. A wave of nausea rose through Miguel Ángel's stomach, climbed up his throat, left him with a bitter taste in his mouth. He grabbed on to the pew as if for dear life. Then his hands moved to the back of his pants, where he was carrying Beto's piece. His hands trembled.

Coach noticed the sudden paleness on Miguel Ángel's face and squeezed the boxer's arm.

"You okay? Should I bring you some water?"

"I'm fine, Coach."

Miguel Ángel felt far from fine. His palms were getting damp, and his stomach was getting even more upset. Through the dark sunglasses, Miguel Ángel could feel the gangster's eyes drilling into his, warning him to stay away.

The minutes turned into hours and finally, after the service was over, the funeral director announced the doors would be closing in fifteen minutes. Slowly, Beto's aunts and uncles approached the casket one last time to place flowers onto his chest, to bid farewell. His dad had to be held up by family members when he almost lost his footing.

As Miguel Ángel walked out of the funeral home, he saw a familiar female sitting in the last pew. She was completely dressed in black, her blonde hair shining among a sea of black manes. She raised her head and their eyes met.

"Can we talk, please?" Britney pleaded.

"I'll be outside," Coach said, walking away.

Miguel Ángel sat down next to the girl. The funeral home was nearly empty by then. The closest person was a few pews away, and Miguel Ángel felt relieved. They would be able to talk with some privacy.

But the words did not come out easily, for either one of them.

"I'm so sorry," they finally said at the same time. Miguel Ángel would have started laughing were it not for Britney actually starting to sob loudly. The boxer drew her to him and tried to hold her hard. But he knew of her stay at the hospital, so his embrace was gentle.

They held for a long time. After a while, Britney broke away.

"My Dad's sending me to New Jersey," she told him. "There's a boarding school a couple of hours away from his brother's house, so I'll be able to visit them on the weekends. He's so angry he's still not talking to me, and he's even more upset because the case was referred to child protective services. They want to make sure we're not being abused. I'm so scared, Miguel Ángel. I don't want to move away."

Britney began sobbing again, and Miguel Ángel realized it was much easier to console her when he wasn't the one causing her pain. But there was nothing he could say. He had a million thoughts in his head and no words would come out. How much he loved her. How easy it was to forget his troubles when she sat beside him. How much he would miss her. Yet, all he did was stroke her hair, take in her smell. Remember briefly how wonderful it had been to have her in his life and how painful the separation had been. And would continue to be.

"Will you call me? Can we stay in touch?"

"I don't know, Miguel Ángel. I don't think we should. I'm so confused. I shouldn't even be here. The doctor told me I needed lots of rest."

"Of course. The baby, huh?"

"The baby's gone. That's why I came. I wanted to tell you in person."

"How?"

"The doctors are not sure. Maybe it was the stress, maybe when I fell after my dad pushed me. It was too much."

Miguel Ángel thought it wasn't possible to feel anymore, and yet, here it was, another blow that left him numb. No more child. He was expecting this would happen, but he was surprised at how much it hurt, nonetheless.

"I have to go," Britney said. "Cleopatra's waiting for me."

"She's such a good friend," Miguel Ángel said. "Tell her I said hi."

"I will. You take care, okay?"

"Wait," Miguel Ángel said, pulling her close to him again, looking for her lips with his, wanting to trap her forever in a kiss.

"Bye," she said, getting up and wiping away her tears.

"Bye," he said, walking behind her, looking for Coach. He was standing by his truck, arms crossed and staring into the mountains.

"Want to go get something to eat?" Coach asked.

"I'm okay. I think I'm going to walk back home," Miguel Ángel said.

Coach gave him the look that said "You can't fool me," but he didn't say anything. He slapped his back a couple of times, got into his truck and drove away.

❧ ❧ ❧

Miguel Ángel did not start walking right away. Instead, he sat outside the mortuary for a long time, watching cars drive by and people walking on the streets. The sun had just set, and the marine layer was quickly blanketing Salinas and eating away the remaining sunlight from the sky. It was getting chilly.

In a few hours, Beto would be no more. He would be cremated, just like his mother. Yeah, his family was Catholic and believed in burials, but they were also poor farm workers with no money to buy a plot or send the body to Mexico.

Either way, Miguel Ángel would never see him again. They would never go driving around the Alisal or speed along the Salinas Valley. They'd never again eat tacos *de lengua* or super wet burritos—Beto's favorites. He would never again feel the comfort of having someone look out for him.

A nagging question had been popping into Miguel Ángel's head ever since Beto was killed, but he managed to suppress it with urgent thoughts about the funeral and Mari Carmen's health. This time, with the funeral over and a world of choices ahead of him, Miguel Ángel couldn't help but think of it and the ones that follow right after. "Why Beto?" was quickly replaced by "Why did Beto want to kill me?"

Miguel Ángel got up and began walking, not toward home, but in the opposite way. He headed downtown, without a destination in mind, just wanting to escape. The air had cooled under the evening fog, but the dropping temperature did not bother him. The cold air felt good on Miguel Ángel's face, perhaps the only comfort he was aware of at this time of pain and confusion. It was, as he had discovered with many other sensations, different. The coolness felt sharper, as if caused by millions of tiny needles poking his face. With touch, sight, taste, Miguel Ángel was discovering his world was vastly more different now than when Beto lived in it.

The sights didn't look the same either. He walked by the post office, the courthouse and the county government building. Not too long ago, he had come to the Salinas City Hall to defend the Packing Shed. The buildings were still all on the same lots, had the same colors and yet looked transformed. Pain, Miguel Ángel realized, changes not just you, but everything around you as well. He suspected he didn't even know yet how much Beto's killing had changed him, would continue to transform him.

As if walking away from his demons, Miguel Ángel kept marching forward. As if running toward an answer.

Why did his friend have to die? Why did Beto try to kill him? Why did Gringo kill Beto instead? Why, why, why. The questions came at him like punches he could not evade, throwing him off balance again and again.

Ever since his mother died, all Beto had ever wanted was to find that sense of belonging he had lost. He thought he had found it among his homies, the friends who taught him how to snatch purses from old ladies and sell drugs in Chinatown. The friends who taught him how to make easy money.

But what's the use of creating a family, like Beto had, if they're going to kill you one day? Miguel Ángel knew this was something that happened not just to Beto. He'd seen it over and over again. If you pissed off your bosses, your so-called family, you'd end up dead.

Jeez, with his family, the worst he would expect would be his mother not talking to him for the entire weekend. Which was actually not such a bad deal.

After walking past Hartnell College and those big houses on the south side that looked like mansions compared to his tiny apartment, Miguel Ángel arrived at the edge of the city, where the houses disappeared and the vast, open fields seemed to devour light. He glanced at his watch. He had been walking for just about half an hour, what felt like a century. But he wasn't done, the demons were still behind him, the answers somewhere ahead. On the other edge of town, perhaps? Miguel Ángel turned south, determined to keep walking until he could not feel his feet any longer.

Salinas was weird. On his side of town, there were so many people, sometimes it felt like they all slept one on top of the other, like stacks of tortillas in the supermarket. On this side of town there was hardly anybody, no people walking in the streets—especially not on the road next to the fields—no women pushing strollers, no taco vendors.

Maybe if Beto had been born on this side of town, in a house with emerald green lawns and magnolia trees, things would have been different. If his parents had never left Mexico and raised their family down there, maybe things would have been different. Maybe Beto would have never asked him to sell drugs.

How different would things have been for Beto if his mother had stayed in Mexico? In the little ranch with no running water and no electricity? Would life have been, as his mother had told him many times, very difficult? Or would he have already gotten used to it?

He was getting thirsty, so he walked into the supermarket on the southernmost corner of Salinas, the real edge of town. He noticed a guy in a suit, a lawyer type, eyeing him as he approached the bottled water section. The type of look he always got at shopping centers, every time he was away from the Alisal. Miguel Ángel got his water, paid and left the store.

As Miguel Ángel rested on the sidewalk drinking his water, he was reminded of the weapon he'd been carrying all night. What was he going to do with Beto's gun? Was he going to do the honorable thing and avenge his friend's death and his sister's injuries, kill Gringo and show him he wasn't going to be messed with? Where could Gringo be found?

It wasn't fair, Miguel Ángel thought, as he got up and kicked the ground. All the training, all the effort he'd put into staying away from this gang bullshit, and now he was being dragged into it. Dragged into making a decision he didn't want to.

Damn you, Beto. Why did you have to do this to me?

Suddenly, the rage he was feeling toward Beto ignited like a fuel that needed to be burned up, his body a revved-up engine that had to be released or else explode. Instead of turning back toward the city, he turned onto Highway 68 and kept marching on.

Miguel Ángel wasn't bothered by the cars speeding by, the fumes, the garbage strewn on the road. This road he had traveled so many times by car, by bus, looked immensely different from the ground, vast and open like the ocean. The cold did not bother him. It was the poison in his body that was affecting him the most. His friend since kids, the guy who was supposed to defend him, almost killed him. But he didn't. Miguel Ángel had been replaying Gringo's words in his head over and over again. Beto had orders he could not complete.

That wasn't what was making Miguel Ángel angry, though. Coach had warned him endlessly to stay away from Beto and his increasingly dangerous lifestyle, and Miguel Ángel couldn't avoid it. Instead, he wanted Beto to change, to stay away from his gangbanging buddies, but he also refused. So whose fault was it? Beto's for finding refuge among those guys, or Miguel Ángel's for not staying away?

"*M'ijo*, turn around," the familiar voice came from among the trees on the edge of the road. "It's time for you to go home."

"I need answers, Ita," he said, stopping and turning around to face her. "I don't want to go home and run into Gringo."

"You don't have to run into anybody. Just go home and get some rest."

"I can't, Ita. If I turn around right now, I'm just going to go straight to kill Gringo."

"If you keep walking on this road, the one getting killed is going to be you," Ita yelled. "Either that or the cops are going to haul you back to jail with that thing you have tucked in your pants."

"Ita, don't you understand? I need to kill Gringo to avenge Beto. That's the way things have to be," Miguel Ángel yelled back.

"You're the one that doesn't understand!" Ita now screamed. "You don't solve problems by killing people."

"You're telling me that, the woman who ran with the revolutionaries?"

"That was different," Ita yelled back. "We were defending our rights to have our own land and grow our own crops. All you guys do is talk about this honor crap. Where's the honor in killing each other when there's practically nothing at stake?"

Miguel Ángel was searching for a quick and logical answer, when Ita simply vanished, like the genie in the movie.

But Ita had a point. If Miguel Ángel got caught with a weapon in his belt, he would be in real trouble. The options did not look appealing, though. He was nearing the end of Toro Park, almost half the distance he needed to travel if he was going to see Britney again.

That was the moment he realized what his real goal was: to see Britney one last time. It wouldn't matter if he got caught walking on the highway, a gun tucked in his belt and put away. He had no soul left. Beto's betrayal had taken that away. His baby was no more. Miguel Ángel, the guy who had been taught to be an honorable fighter, was now thinking about killing somebody. Wouldn't it be better if the police took him away now instead?

He had been walking for three hours, and even though the foggy mist that traditionally covered Salinas now was fully blanketing the road, he still wasn't feeling cold. If he kept walking, it would probably be hours before he reached the Monterey Peninsula. He was a bit hungry, but he wasn't tired. He could keep walking.

He paused to pull the water bottle from the pouch of his hoodie and drink. He looked at the rolling hills of Toro Park, the golden slopes Steinbeck had called "Pastures of Heaven." If Beto were here, he'd be pulling out a joint and having a drag. "They are beautiful, man, ¿qué no?" he would say. Miguel Ángel shook his head and wiped away a tear.

Miguel Ángel had to avenge Beto. He had no choice. He was his friend since he was in third grade, and he wasn't going to let his death go unpunished. Even if he wanted to drag him into the gang.

From the corner of his eyes, he saw the red and blue flashing lights of a patrol car coming his direction, following another speeding car. He was on a particularly narrow edge of the road, a place where there was little room to hide. Still, he walked up the hill hugging the road and hid behind an oak. His heart was thumping in his chest, drowning out all sounds of cicadas, cars and police patrols. Ita was right, I need to go back home now, he thought.

It's been like this all along, he thought. Ita gives me advice and I refuse to take it. Why would Beto listen to me if I don't listen to my own great-grandmother?

A few minutes passed, when Miguel Ángel climbed back from behind the tree. Once on the ground, he looked in both directions, trying to decide which way to go.

Salinas would still hold the same things for him: the same food, the same music, his family. In Monterey, he might have a chance to make up with Britney, find a new life with her. More than anything right now, he needed a promise of new life, something to hang on to, or run the risk of drowning.

He marched on, defying the speeding cars, the wind hitting his face and the occasional rustling of leaves— deer? Rabbits? Miguel Ángel had been walking for more than four hours by now, but a force he did not know before kept pushing him forward in spite of the growing grumblings of his stomach, his swollen feet and, little by little, his sleepiness.

But once he turned onto Canyon del Rey, he saw the light. The ocean breeze immediately touched his face, renewing his hope for finishing the journey, for reaching Britney. He refueled at the gas station: candy bars, sodas, chips. He hadn't eaten this much for days. Yes, his diet had gone to the dogs since Beto died. Just one more thing he didn't seem to care about anymore.

What would he tell Britney when he saw her? Hadn't they said everything that needed to be said? How could Miguel Ángel convince her to come back to him?

"You're crazy, man," a tiny voice whispered in Miguel Ángel's ear. He jerked around, confused. Nobody. Miguel Ángel could have sworn he'd heard Beto's voice.

"Man, those women are like the stars at night. They're to be admired, to be studied. But you don't marry a star, not if you're not one of them. And, my friend, you're not one of them."

Miguel Ángel shook his head. For a moment, he'd been transported to the moment when Beto gave him a scolding about Britney. Beto. How could he have been so wise and so stupid, Miguel Ángel wondered. He could see exactly what was what with him and Britney, but nothing about his own mistakes on his own path. Why is it so hard to look at reality, even if it is under our noses?

A calm started spreading in his chest as he entered Monterey along the recreation trail. It was all well-lit, and even at three a.m., there were still people jogging on it. White people are so funny, Beto would say. But it made Miguel Ángel feel safe, to have people around you trusting enough to be out in the streets this late—or early—at night. At the Alisal, Miguel Ángel never really thought about security, but as a young guy, he always knew he had to watch over his shoulder to see who was approaching.

Not here. He kept walking, stomping on eucalyptus leaves, careful not to step on dog poop—yeah, Gringos were not as clean as they pretended to be. In Monterey, he felt safe.

Maybe that's what he'd been looking for all along. To feel safe. That's why Beto had been carrying a gun, he told him many times. He needed a gun for protection. But if Miguel Ángel ended up making a life with Britney, away from the Alisal and closer to her family in Pebble Beach, he would not need that kind of protection.

A runner approaching him obviously slowed down his pace, moving away from Miguel Ángel to the farthest edge of the trail. He couldn't help but remember the suit-wearing lawyer type at the supermarket in Salinas, the countless other people who eyed him as if he were a leper at the shopping center and many other places where young Mexican men like him were not welcome or expected.

He picked up a furious march, past the Wharf and its touristy shops, past the fancy stores at Cannery Row and the aquarium. He no longer felt cold, tired or hungry, and the breeze on his face only served to remind him how much he loved the ocean. He'd made up his mind, and he would not stop until his decision was carried out. No more need for thinking, for tinkering with what needed to be done.

At Lover's Point, he walked down the stairs to reach the beach. This is where he needed to be, and finally he felt relieved. In spite of the darkness, and the fog, he could make out the silhouettes of several couples, people holding each other tight and whispering sweet words into each other's ears. Like he'd done so many times with Britney.

Despite the fog, Miguel Ángel could still make out the city lights on the other side of the bay, Monterey and Seaside for sure. Lights at night were always special, discreet witnesses to an impending adventure.

He climbed down the rocky shore and sat on a boulder, looked at the waves and let their rhythmic back-and-forth empty his head of all the crazy thoughts that haunted him. Right now he was going to end it all, put a stop to the madness that had taken over his life, his neighborhood.

Everyone who looked at him and didn't know him—the lawyer type, the runner on the trail—always assumed him to be the worst. A gangbanger. A thug. That's what everyone who did not know his neighborhood, the Alisal, always thought of its residents. They're animals. They kill each other. Don't go to that neighborhood, they'd tell one another. There's only killings over there.

It wasn't true, and Miguel Ángel knew it. There was room at the Alisal for hardworking people, immigrants like his mother, children of immigrants like him, to build bright futures and fill the place with art and beauty. It was a place of champions, like him.

We're not thugs, we're not animals. I'm an athlete, and I don't settle my scores with guns.

A long time went by, all the couples had disappeared. When he finally felt completely alone, sure that nobody was watching, Miguel Ángel pulled Beto's gun from behind his waist and threw it as far as he could into the waves.

CHAPTER 46

The Quonset hut had an air of familiarity and strangeness, like an old friend you reencounter after years have passed. Miguel Ángel had always stared at those soda can-like buildings and tried to decipher them, as if trying to read a book in a foreign language. Now he was walking into one that was still being painted by some of his boxing buddies. The old smell of grease, typical of a car shop, had not been completely covered by the new paint or the musk of dozens of athletes. The sounds, though, were definitely familiar: the *banda* music and gangster rap blaring from boom boxes, the bell, the tap-tap of fists pounding on leather. The faces he'd seen since he was a boy.

Coach saw him and nodded. Miguel Ángel nodded back, but didn't have enough energy yet to talk to him. Pain, he had discovered, was like a pair of tinted glasses: they changed everything around you. They made colors sharper, brought objects closer. Things you'd never notice before were now on your face all the time. Like Beto's yellow stress ball, Miguel Ángel now saw it everywhere he went. Pain changed everything, and there was nothing you could do to stop it.

It had been a few weeks since Beto had died. A month, maybe. Miguel Ángel couldn't remember anymore. The chaos, called his life, went into overdrive after that night. Mari Carmen came out of the hospital, but she couldn't go back to school just yet. His mother had to go to work, and there was nobody to stay home with his little sister, so Miguel Ángel took on the task. He was doing badly in school, anyway, so he just dropped out. Ana Estela was doing great, and Miguel Ángel didn't want her to quit—which is what their mother wanted. Money was so tight that he got a job at La Moderna grocery store. For all her yelling, his mother did not complain about the money, but Miguel Ángel could read her worries. She wasn't wearing her red hat anymore. There were more gray hairs on her head now.

A counselor in school told him to go back to training as soon as possible—as therapy. He needed the routine, the counselor said. But the images of Beto, of the night he died, were too embedded in his brain, too distracting. As soon as he started throwing jabs, Beto's bloody face returned.

"What's up, homes?" A boxer came over to shake with Miguel Ángel, waking him up from his daydream.

"Not much, man," Miguel Ángel said.

"You training today?"

"Nah, I'm gonna watch for a while."

"You still going out with that blonde chick?"

"Nah, that's over, man," Miguel Ángel said, turning away from the boxer. The guy got the message and left.

Britney was definitely history. She hadn't called him, and he didn't know how to reach her. Still, he'd freeze at times when the phone rang. He'd also sit by the phone for hours, hoping she would finally decide to reach out.

There were days when he didn't want to get up from bed, he hurt so much all over. Even his toes and hair follicles felt like they'd taken a beating. Only the cries of Mari Carmen wanting company dragged him out of himself.

"We could really use somebody like you, Miguel Ángel," big old Bruno Hernández said as he plopped down his humanity next to Miguel Ángel.

"What do you mean, man?" he said, looking at Bruno as if he had just landed from Mars. So Bruno got a desk at the Quanset hut too, Miguel Ángel thought.

"You know what I mean. I need counselors, role models. Young men like you to keep kids out of gangs," Bruno said, his arms doing half the talking.

"You're crazy, man. I don't think I can do that. How do you do it, anyway?"

"You go to schools and tell kids why they should stay out of gangs. How you got into boxing and didn't join one. How your friend got killed."

Miguel Ángel shook his head. Although he'd realized the gang was a monster, he wasn't sure he could convince anybody of its evils. He had grown up hearing from many how dangerous it was. He'd seen many of his friends join. He'd seen how hard it was to steer them away once they started in the life. And he couldn't even convince Beto to stay out. How could he convince others?

"I'll think about it, man," he told Bruno.

"You'd be great. I can feel it."

Miguel Ángel didn't respond. He just shook his head and turned away. At the entrance of the hut he saw Ita, smoking her cigarette and waving to him.

Before walking up to her, he glanced around the gym again. Coach was still wrapped up in some conversation with a fighter. The bell still rang every two minutes, the painters continued with their task, the *thunk-thunk* of gloves on bags still reached Miguel Ángel. It started to feel like home again.

"It's time, *m'ijo*," the old lady said, now standing next to him.

Miguel Ángel missed Ita's stories about the Mexican Revolution and her adventures roaming the country, and he enjoyed her company. After ignoring her advice so often, he now made sure to listen to her every time she spoke.

"Where have you been?" he asked.

"Oh, just running around," she said, pulling another cigarette from the purse she kept in her bosom.

"Are you ready?" Ita asked, her words chasing the column of smoke she had just let out.

"Yes, Ita. I'm ready."

He walked out of the gym, and the afternoon cold hit his face, the dewy air scratched his lungs. Winter was coming and the Alisal was getting ready for it. The men walked in bulky jackets, the women covered their faces with *rebozos,* but the harsh air didn't keep the street vendors inside. They still pushed their roasted corn and *paleta* carts, they still needed to make a living.

Today, he started running again, the first time in weeks. He began a soft trot that turned into a gallop a few blocks later. He ran past liquor stores and churches, beauty salons and saloons, mom and pop stores and big supermarkets. He passed mowed green lawns and parking lots. Past gigantic houses and strawberry fields.

When he got to the edge of the Gabilans, he found Ita sitting on the fence of the ranch he'd never dared cross. Until now.

"Ita, you think I'll see Beto if I go up the hill?"

"Nah, Beto won't be ready for a very long time. But it never hurts to try."

Miguel Ángel jumped the fence and ran up the hill, feeling the drying grass give under his weight. It was a steep climb, but he leaned forward and continued pushing upward as fast as he could. It was too late for the cows to be out, but some hawks and buzzards were still flying above in search of a meal.

At the top, he turned around to look at the city under the dying sun's rays. Not too far from here, Beto had been killed. Not too far either, his family lived. The Alisal was a place of beauty and pain, of love and sorrows. Miguel Ángel loved it just the same.

Acknowledgments

Writing can be a lonely endeavor, but throughout the process I've had the love of support of friends and family; without them, this novel would not be possible. There are too many to list, but they know who they are and I'm forever grateful for their presence in my life.

The following people read the novel at early stages and saw its promise: Katherine Ball, Valli and Reynaldo Barrioz, Juanita Contín, Frank Gómez, Leslie Escobar, Jasmine Morán, Mike Roddy and Yolanda Venegas. "Coach" gave me boxing lessons. Andrea Brown and her Big Sur Writers Conference was the push I needed to plunge into the literary world.

Writing groups are a great source of support, and I'm especially thankful to the Salinas group of Liz Picco and DS Kane, and the Lechuguenses group that includes Joe Livernois and Kathy McKenzie.

Andy Ross, Dr. Nicolás Kanellos, Dr. Gabriela Baeza Ventura, and all the folks at Arte Público Press are heaven-sent and are making this dream a reality.

There aren't sufficiently eloquent words to describe the incredible amount of support, help and encouragement I received from Julie Reynolds, girlfriend extraordinaire, member of Lechuguenses and the Salinas groups. I'm eternally in your debt.

Finally, Víctor Almazán gave me great feedback, encouraged me, cooked countless meals and made sure I had space for writing. His superb literary and musical tastes are a continuous source of inspiration. I love you, honey.